THE BASHKIR
EXTRACTION

ALLAN LEVERONE

1

"I am a foreigner, too."

Ryan Smith flinched at the sound of a woman's voice coming from just behind his right shoulder. It was a friendly voice, but he'd thought he was keeping a low profile, and he felt a slight spasm in his arms and lowering of his head in surprise. The reaction was minimal, probably invisible to the woman, but it caused a bit of his scotch and water to splash over the side of his glass and drip onto the table.

The bar wasn't crowded, and the fact that Ryan had become drunk enough to allow a stranger to approach unobserved was cause for concern.

But it's more than just cause for concern, isn't it? he thought. *Under the circumstances, it's potentially deadly.*

He decided this drink had better be his last. Four was plenty, anyway.

Ryan turned his head and focused his bleary gaze on a cute little blonde standing next to the table. She was dressed in skin-tight leather pants and a gauzy white button-down blouse that did little to hide the black lace bra underneath. She wavered slightly in her high heels, and Ryan guessed he was not the only one who had decided to blow off some steam with a few drinks tonight.

He cleared his throat and returned the girl's smile. She was undoubtedly a hooker, but Ryan didn't care. He'd spent the last six months operating under cover inside the Soviet Union, and during that time had seen many of his fellow CIA operatives murdered via the ghastly method of radiation poisoning, and he'd nearly reached the breaking point from stress and fear and even—oddly enough—boredom.

The running joke among longtime operatives was that under-cover work consisted of weeks of downtime followed by hours of sheer terror. He'd never really understood the point of the gag until recently. Now he understood.

In any event, Ryan had decided the time for female compan-ionship was long overdue, and if he had to pay for it, so what? It would probably be better if the cute little blonde were a pro, anyway. No invasive questions to sidestep, no personal entangle-ments to avoid, just a quick stress-relieving night together and they would both go their separate ways.

Or maybe she's just a friendly girl, just looking to pass the time. Way to get ahead of yourself, dummy, Ryan thought.

He realized he'd been staring at her for several seconds with a stupid smile plastered on his face, and if he didn't recover quickly even a hooker would be creeped out. He gestured at the empty seat on the other side of the table.

The cute blonde tottered gratefully to it and sat.

"Why would you think I'm a foreigner?" Ryan said. He was well aware that the moment he opened his mouth he would confirm the girl's statement—his Russian, though passable, would never be on par with a native's—but the first step toward a potential night of passion was conversation, and after four drinks, this was about the best he could manage.

The girl smiled. "It is obvious."

"How?"

She giggled and he said, "Okay, I'll admit it's obvious now, but you made your observation before ever I said a word. How did you know?"

"You are not drinking vodka. You are probably the only person in this bar whose glass is not filled with it." She shrugged. "It seemed clear to me."

Ryan chuckled. He felt like an idiot. Even after all this time inside the USSR, if a drunk working girl could identify him as an outsider so easily, he figured he must have gotten damned lucky not to find himself at the bottom of a shallow grave somewhere in the Russian countryside by now.

He nodded at her glass. "It looks like you're drinking vodka, and yet you said you're not a Russian, either."

She shrugged. "I like vodka."

"My name is Michael," he said, and extended his hand.

The cute little blonde reached across and shook it. "I am Hanna."

"Where are you from, and what brings you to Moscow, Hanna?"

"I am from Hungary originally. I came to Russia several years ago to work as a schoolteacher."

"I went to school, and none of my teachers ever looked like you," Ryan said with a boozy laugh.

"None of *my* teachers ever looked like me, either, and I hated them all. I wanted to be someone students could relate to."

"Lucky them."

"Thank you. What is your story, Michael?"

"It's not much of a story. I am originally from the German Democratic Republic. I am here working as a diplomatic liaison between our two countries on a temporary basis."

Hanna pursed her lips. They looked red and plump and extremely kissable. "Ooh," she said. "You are a very important man."

He laughed. "Not really. I'm just trying to survive in this world, like everyone else."

"That is an unusual choice of phrasing."

He smiled. "Blame it on four drinks."

They chatted and laughed and before he knew it, Ryan found himself ordering another round. He hadn't forgotten his earlier vow to stop at four, but this unexpected opportunity to interact normally—relatively speaking—with a pretty young woman was comforting. Whether he eventually ended up sharing Hanna's bed or not remained to be seen, but he wasn't quite ready for the night to end.

Before long those drinks were gone too, and Ryan was trying to decide how to approach the subject currently uppermost in his mind. Obviously, he couldn't bring Hanna back to a CIA safe house. He thought he had enough cash left after his night out for a moderately priced hotel room, but doubted he could cover the cost of lodging *and* a hooker's fee.

The problem was Ryan couldn't figure out how to determine whether he would actually have to pay Hanna to spend the night with him or not. She had made her interest in him quite clear; to the point Ryan felt he stood a good chance at getting her into bed. But she'd stuck to her story about being a teacher, so convincingly in fact that he damned near believed her.

She solved the thorny problem for him when she downed her drink and fixed him with a lustful gaze as she thumped the empty glass onto the table. "My apartment is just around the corner," she said. "I am not usually this forward, but it has been a long time since I met a man as…interesting as you, and I would hate to waste such a rare opportunity. Would you care to accompany me to my home for a nightcap?"

Ryan swallowed heavily, unable to resist. If this adorable girl really was a pro he would deal with the cash flow issue later.

Hanna mistook his hesitation for reluctance and smiled shyly. "I am sorry to be so clumsy," she said. "I am not in the habit of inviting handsome strangers to my apartment. 'Accompany me for a nightcap,'" she repeated, shaking her head and blushing. "That sounded so stupid. Forget I said anyth—"

"No," Ryan interrupted. "No, it wasn't stupid at all. I'm just having trouble believing my incredible luck. I would love to join you for a drink."

Her face brightened as she pushed to her feet and reached for his hand.

Ryan tossed enough money to cover the drinks and a decent tip onto the table and then shrugged into his coat, gloves and hat as Hanna did the same. They began threading their way through what had become a fairly large crowd, making slow but steady progress toward the front entrance.

They pushed through the door and into the frigid Moscow night. "I'm glad your apartment is close," Ryan said. "Otherwise I'm afraid our noses might freeze off. Among other things."

Hanna didn't answer, and he noticed she had removed her hand from his as they left the bar behind and turned down a side street.

He opened his mouth to ask where she lived and then froze as a small pistol appeared in the cute little blonde's suddenly ungloved hand. She placed the gun against the side of his head and he tried with little success not to panic.

"I take it this means we won't be having that drink," he said, wishing for a clear head more than he'd ever wished for anything in his life.

"I am sorry," she said. "You seem like a decent person, but a mission is a mission, as I am sure you well know."

"I don't understand," he said.

"Of course you do. I do not know your real name, but I know it is not Michael, and I know also that you are not a diplomatic liaison from the GDR."

He shook his head. "I really don't know what you're talking about. You're making a mistake. Let me go and—"

"That is enough." Suddenly the blonde didn't seem quite so little or cute anymore.

A pair of men dressed all in black materialized out of the Moscow night, one on each side of Ryan, and he realized he was in even more trouble than he'd thought.

And he wouldn't have thought that possible.

"Take my cash and my wallet," he said, only to be cut off by the blonde again. She was probably all of five feet two inches tall and one hundred ten pounds soaking wet, but she had no problem asserting herself, and neither of the men in black seemed inclined to interrupt.

"This is not a robbery," she said scornfully, "although before all is said and done, you will wish it had been."

"I already do," he said softly.

The not-so-cute and no-longer-so-little blonde nudged him with her gun and he reluctantly moved deeper into the murk of the alley.

"We have been watching you for some time. We know you are CIA, and we know you have been spying inside Russia. We know your disappearance will go unremarked-upon by your government, unless you turn up on the nightly news back in your country, standing trial for espionage."

"I still don't know what you're talking about."

"Of course you do."

Ryan closed his eyes and wished he were asleep in bed, suffering from a nightmare. "Is that the plan for me? A show trial, followed by a public execution?"

"I do not know," the blonde answered as Ryan reopened his eyes to discover the nightmare was real but the bed was not. "That is a decision to be made by others far above me in rank."

They continued walking and in seconds arrived at an automobile idling softly in the darkness at the end of the alley. Predictably, the car was black.

"Get in," the blonde said.

Ryan hesitated and the girl said, "You should know I have been instructed to shoot you should you resist. If you wish to have any chance of surviving beyond the next three or four seconds, you will climb into the back seat of the car. I will not tell you again."

Ryan cursed inwardly at his extreme foolishness, at the errors in judgment that would now cost him his life.

Then he sighed heavily and slid into the car.

2

January 29, 1988
8:10 a.m.
Washington, D.C.

Tracie Tanner wasn't quite sleeping when the knocks began sounding on her apartment door, but she couldn't claim to be fully awake, either.

She'd spent most of last night at Marshall Fulton's apartment, not sleeping any better there than she'd slept at home. First because they were busy conducting bedroom gymnastics, and afterward because Tracie couldn't manage to shake the depression that had dogged her since the conclusion of her last assignment in Moscow.

After falling into an uneasy slumber next to Marshall, she awoke around four a.m., instantly aware she would sleep no more in a strange bed, even as exhausted as she was. She kissed the man who had helped her deal with her rising crisis of confidence, careful not to wake him, then dressed quietly and slipped out of his apartment.

A few minutes later she was home. Without a clue what to do with herself at four-thirty in the morning, she slipped under the covers in her own bed and dozed fitfully for a couple more hours before stumbling into the kitchen at eight a.m. to make coffee.

She jumped, startled, at the three raps on the door, instantly filled with shame at her actions last night. *It's Marshall. He's angry that I left without saying goodbye, or even giving him the courtesy of a note. After all he did for me, he's mad and he's come over here to chew me out, and I deserve every last bit of his anger.*

But almost as soon as the thought flitted through her brain she dismissed it. Storming across town to confront Tracie was not Marshall's style. He was, quite simply, one of the kindest and most generous people she'd ever met, a man seemingly blessed with an almost mystical ability to see deep inside her soul.

Marshall would understand her leaving in the middle of the night.

It didn't justify her actions, he deserved better, but whoever was outside Tracie's door, it was almost certainly *not* Marshall Fulton. And eliminating Marshall as a possibility also pretty much eliminated any reasonable guesses as to who it could be.

Tracie rarely received guests, partly because she was rarely in D.C., more often traveling the world as CIA Director Aaron Stallings' personal black ops specialist. But even when she *was* home, she simply didn't mingle like the typical late-twenties single woman living in a large metropolitan city.

She didn't have friends, at least not in the conventional sense.

She rarely dated.

Didn't enjoy meeting new people.

Three more knocks came at the front door, insistent, crisp raps from determined knuckles that suggested almost a military precision.

Tracie sighed and took one more sip of her coffee. Then she moved to the door. Peered through the peephole and blinked in surprise.

She stepped back and pulled the door open and launched herself into the arms of the man standing on the other side. He held her and squeezed, lifting her small body off the ground and twirling her a full three hundred sixty degrees before setting her down again.

When he did, she smiled up at him and said, "What are you doing here, Dad?"

"A man can't pay his only child a visit?"

"Of course he can, but you're so busy and I'm hardly ever here, and I—" She stepped out of his embrace and gazed up at him suspiciously. "How *did* you know I would be here?"

"Jeez, you're not going to invite me in before giving me the third degree? Where does a guy have to go to get a cup of coffee in this neighborhood?"

"Come on in, Dad. I'd love to share a cup of coffee with you." She ushered him inside and closed the door and led him into the kitchen. Her tiny table offered only enough room for two diners, and her father eased into the space without the half-empty cup in front of it as Tracie busied herself selecting a clean mug and pouring his coffee.

She placed it on the table in front of him and stood, hands on her hips. "And don't think you were successful in distracting me from the fact you didn't answer my question. How did you know I'd be here? How did you know I'd even be in the country?"

He winked at her. "I work at the Pentagon, remember? I have my sources."

She slipped into her chair and sipped her own coffee before answering. "You'll forgive me if I tell you I'm still skeptical."

"You don't think a two-star general has sources?"

"That's not what I mean when I claim skepticism."

"Okay, then what?"

"I've been in and out of the country before, between missions—"

"And even during," he interrupted with a grin.

Tracie glared. "No comment. You know the CIA doesn't operate inside the borders of the United States."

"Noted. But I just wanted to reinforce my point about sources. I try to keep an eye on my little girl. To the extent possible, anyway."

"Dad, I'm twenty-eight. I'm hardly your little girl anymore."

"Sweetheart, you'll still be my little girl when you're fifty-eight, if I'm lucky enough to have a pulse by then. You'll be my little girl when you're eighty-eight. You'll always be my little girl. That will never change."

"You're sweet. And I appreciate the thought, especially today."

Her father gazed at her over the rim of his coffee mug. "Something you need to talk about?"

She shrugged. "I can't. At least, not with any degree of specificity."

"I can appreciate that. But it's obvious something's bothering you."

"Is that so?"

"Yes. You look like hell."

"Gee, Dad, thanks for the sensitivity. I feel a lot better now."

He grinned. "Happy to help."

"Back to my original point," Tracie said. "I'm skeptical that you showed up outside my front door completely at random, simply because you wanted to visit me, not that I don't appreciate the gesture."

This time her father laughed out loud. "I'd almost forgotten how relentless you can be when you set your sights on something."

"I don't know how you could forget. I learned it from you."

"Touché. But it just so happens you're right. This visit, as wonderful as it is to see you and as overdue as it may be, is not strictly social and it's not random."

"Okayyyy…"

"I received an interesting phone call late yesterday afternoon."

"Obviously I was the subject of your call."

"Correct," her father said, and took another sip of his coffee.

"Care to fill me in on who made this call?" Tracie said. "Or would you rather just sit there drinking my coffee and making cryptic comments?"

"That's a tough decision. You really are fun to tease. Always have been."

"Have I ever mentioned that part of my training at The Farm involved mastering multiple ways to kill another human being using only my bare hands?"

Her father laughed again and Tracie realized with some surprise that she was suddenly as happy as she could remember being in a very long time, even after all the turmoil of her Moscow assignment and her time with Marshall. She loved her mother very much, but had always been a Daddy's Girl. Some of her favorite memories from growing up were afternoons spent fishing with her dad, or tossing a baseball or football in the back yard, or going for long walks and talking about nothing and everything.

He cleared his throat and said, "The call came from your boss."

Tracie sat back. "Excuse me?" That was literally the last thing she'd expected him to say.

"I said your boss called me. You know, Aaron Stallings."

"Yeah, Dad, I know who my boss is. I just don't understand the connection. Why would a guy you've never met call you to talk about me?"

"Who says I've never met him?"

"So you know him?"

"I've worked at the Pentagon a long time, honey, and as you well know, Stallings has been in his position at the agency since… well…forever. So, yes, our paths have crossed on occasion."

Tracie was silent as she absorbed her father's words. It occurred to her with the suddenness of a lightning strike that she shouldn't be surprised by this revelation. But for some reason she'd never considered the possibility of her dad and Stallings having any kind of relationship, even a cursory one.

"You look like you've seen a ghost," her father said, amused.

"I guess I just never pictured Aaron Stallings talking to people like a regular person."

"You mean, rather than screaming and yelling and trying to intimidate them?"

"That's exactly what I mean."

"Well," he said. "Talking to Aaron is not *exactly* like talking to a normal human being, but he can't get away with abusing me like I know he abuses his employees."

"One of whom is me." She began to get a sense for where the conversation was going, and her anger began to rise.

"Yes. One of whom is you."

"So it's not enough that he treats me like dirt at work. Now he wants to involve my father in his manipulation?"

"Listen, honey. Stallings couldn't get into specifics, obviously, but he told me he knows he went too far with this last assignment. He wanted me to pass along his apologies and tell you he regrets not fully informing you about the full nature of that assignment."

Tracie recalled diving to the pavement of a shabby D.C. apartment complex in a desperate attempt to avoid a Soviet assassin's sniper fire and barked, "Oh, really? Is his phone broken? He didn't have the guts to talk to me himself, he had to get my own dad to do his dirty work?"

She flashed an angry look at her father, who returned her gaze calmly. "How long have you worked for Aaron Stallings?" he asked quietly.

"Since I got hired, obviously. So coming up on eight years. Although I spent most of that time working with a different handler."

"So you've known him personally for…"

"Almost a year," she said, still miffed.

"That's long enough to get a handle on the man's personality, yes?"

She snorted. "More than long enough."

"Okay. So, in all the time you've known Stallings, have you ever heard him apologize to anyone, for anything?"

She spit an angry laugh. "Never. I don't think he's capable of the introspection required."

"I'm not sure you're giving the man quite enough credit," he said quietly. "But that's neither here nor there. What matters is that you need to consider the significance of his actions."

"Meaning what?"

"Don't you think it means something that he would pick up the phone and call me, a man with whom he has only the most peripheral of relationships?"

"I suppose," she admitted grudgingly. "What's your point, exactly?"

"My point is he said you may have quit your job yesterday. He isn't quite sure. *Did* you quit your job yesterday, Tracie?"

"I'm not so sure, either." She mumbled her answer while staring into her now-mostly-empty coffee mug.

"The next question is obvious: how can you be unsure whether you quit a job or not? But since I watched you grow up, and got to see your fiery side firsthand for years, I'm not going to ask the obvious question. I can well imagine you getting angry and saying things that could be interpreted in a number of different ways."

"Can you please tell me what you're getting at, Dad?"

"I'm getting at this: if you *did* quit, he'd like you to reconsider."

"I don't know if I can do that."

"Because of the way he treated you."

"Yes. I'm used to him yelling and bullying. I can deal with that. He doesn't intimidate me at all. But he crossed a line with my last assignment." *So did I,* she wanted to add, *when I gunned down an unarmed old man,* but bit back the words.

She felt the intensity of her father's stare. After a moment he said, "Let me ask you a question. When you went to work at the CIA, did you do it because you were anxious to work for Aaron Stallings?"

Tracie laughed. "Of course not. I was only barely aware of who he was when I started at the agency."

"Then why let him affect you to such an extent that you're willing to give up the career to which you've dedicated your entire adult life? Why give him that much power over you?"

"You don't understand, Dad."

"Then educate me."

"Stallings intentionally put me in harm's way, without so much as the courtesy of a warning. Because of him, I could—and probably should—have been killed."

Her father sipped his coffee, clearly trying to decide how to respond. When he did, he surprised her. "I've never been prouder of you than I was the day you were hired to begin training as an operational asset for the Central Intelligence Agency."

"Thank you, Dad."

He continued as if she hadn't spoken. "I've also never been more terrified than I was that day, and than I've been every single day since. To know you're risking your life taking on the most dangerous assignments inside the most dangerous countries on earth, with little or no backup, is something no parent would ever want for his child. But do you know why I've never tried to talk you out of your decision?"

Tracie's father's eyes were moist as she looked into them. She shook her head.

"Because I know what it means to have a passion for serving your country. You chose to do it in a different way than me, but I understand."

"What are you getting at?"

"I'm getting at this: I would love nothing more than for you to decide you've had enough of getting shot at in foreign lands. But when I look into your eyes, I don't see a young woman who has had enough. I see someone who remains dedicated to her calling.

That being the case, I think it would be a mistake to give it all up in a fit of anger at your boss."

"But you don't know what Stallings did."

"I don't think you're being completely honest with yourself, sweetheart."

"Excuse me?"

"You heard me."

"I heard you, I just don't understand what the hell you mean."

"I don't think you're angry at Stallings for the reason you claim to be."

Tracie's temper flared. "I told you, you don't underst—"

"Let me finish. You say your boss sent you out on an assignment without adequate warning. Fair enough. But you've been the beneficiary of years of the finest training this country has to offer, training that has equipped you as well as is humanly possible to do your job. I refuse to believe for one second that you go out on any assignment without being fully prepared for whatever might happen. You didn't need a specific warning from Stallings any more than you've *ever* needed one."

It was Tracie's turn to sit back in her chair in rapt consideration. She admired her father more than anyone she'd ever met and put plenty of stock in his opinion on any subject. He was not a man to speak rashly or without due consideration.

He was making a lot of sense.

He was right.

"I think what you're really upset about," he continued, "is Stallings' manipulation. I think you're hurt by it and more than a little insulted that he would treat you in such a callous manner."

"You're damn right I am. There's no question about that."

"But here's the question you need to ask yourself, Trace. Do you really want to give up your career, and the thing that gets you out of bed every day, because your boss insulted you or treated you poorly? Particularly when you're well aware that's his nature. Aaron Stallings is a manipulative bastard. Everybody knows it, and it's that very personality trait that has made him so successful as head of the world's foremost intelligence-gathering organization."

Tracie lifted her coffee cup absently and brought it to her lips before realizing it was empty. She grinned and placed it on the kitchen table with a thud. "How did you get so smart, anyway?"

"Not smart," he said. "Just experienced. And more than anything I want what's best for my baby girl."

"I love you," she said.

"Likewise. And your sneaky, manipulative boss asked me to pass along a second message."

"There's more?"

"Yep. He'd like to see you in McLean tomorrow morning."

"How did he know you'd be able to…? Ah, never mind."

Her father laughed. "Now, what do I have to do to get more coffee?"

3

Dr. Vladimir Protasov squinted against the insufficient lighting as he prepared to crack the skull of his latest subject. Why the hell the KGB could not provide proper illumination inside his lab Vlad could not understand, but he had been in charge of this project for well over a year and had requisitioned lighting upgrades through official channels at least a half-dozen times.

Every one of his requests had gone unanswered.

He sighed softly. A prominent Russian parapsychologist and surgeon, Vlad had been recruited out of Novosibirsk University eighteen months ago, lured away from the comforts of academia by the promise of well-funded state sponsored research. He'd reluctantly accepted the KGB's job offer, not knowing what the consequences of turning it down might be but not wanting to find out, either.

He had left his family behind and been transported to this secret facility plunked down in the middle of the Ural Mountains, isolated and lonely. Opportunities to speak to his wife and children by telephone were rare, and even the tiny village located next to the base remained, for the most part, off limits.

Not that there was much to do in town, anyway.

He staved off the loneliness as best he could by throwing himself fully into the project for which he'd been recruited. Progress came incrementally when it came at all, but Vlad persisted. One of the benefits of working for the KGB was the opportunity to study the many classified scholarly texts and research papers he'd never seen while teaching at university. The research went back decades, some as far as the 1880s.

And if the grand breakthrough he longed for had thus far remained elusive, Vlad had played the academic game long enough to know it was best not to keep the home office apprised of every bump in the road. The less Lubyanka knew of his problems the better, so every status report emphasized only the positive.

Even when Vlad had to think long and hard to identify any progress at all, when test subject after test subject fell victim to the unsanitary conditions within the lab and died, or when Vlad's surgical technique proved too amateurish for the rigors of brain surgery and the subjects died, he still forced himself to remain relentlessly upbeat when communicating with his project supervisor, KGB Colonel Vasiliy Kopalev.

The job was difficult and often grim, but as long as he kept his mind occupied, Vlad was able to remain focused at work. It was a different story away from the lab, though, especially at night when he so often found himself tossing and turning in sweat-soaked sheets, unable to sleep.

During those times the ghosts of dead test subjects came to call.

Because many lives had been lost to the quest for progress.

Vlad understood the critical nature of his project in a theoretical sense, understood that human subject testing constituted a key element in completing the project successfully, understood even that lives would have to be sacrificed for him to stand any chance of bringing the project to fruition and getting the hell out of this dank, depressing prison.

He understood all of that, but understanding it didn't make keeping the ghosts away any easier.

Vlad blinked and shook his head and forced himself out of his cycle of self-recrimination. He returned his attention to the test subject currently lying stretched out atop a stainless steel surgical table. The subject was a man, and the man was immobilized thanks to dozens of straps securing his entire body to the table.

Still, the subject tracked Vlad's every movement with frightened eyes.

The man had found his way to the Ipatiev Research Facility, Vlad assumed, in much the same manner as the great majority of his test subjects: he'd been rounded up in one of the semi-regular sweeps of homeless vagrants conducted in Moscow, Stalingrad, Leningrad and other large Russian cities. This of course meant the man likely suffered from some form of mental illness as well as, in all probability, drug addiction or alcoholism. Or all of the above.

Researchers everywhere understood the correlation between the relative health of a scientific test subject and the accuracy of test results. It was a straight-line cause and effect relationship: the healthier the subject, the more reliable the results. Vladimir had emphasized that point repeatedly to Colonel Kopalev, imploring him for more suitable subjects, and yet the colonel continued to provide him with damaged ones like the man currently strapped to this table.

Vlad sighed and stroked the terrified man's arm distractedly. He twisted a thumbscrew opening the valve that controlled the intravenous flow of Thiamylal, noting with satisfaction the subject's almost immediate loss of consciousness.

Achieving the desired anesthetic state in his subjects had been an early stumbling block for Vlad. He'd come to Ipatiev with little experience in that area and had lost a number of subjects early on by overdosing them, killing them before ever getting them into surgery. But as an academician and a scientist, Vlad was well used to trial and error, and he could now reliably anesthetize a subject simply by gauging the man's body type and weight.

Vladimir's "research assistant" was a dour-looking man of perhaps forty, with thinning hair and a permanent five o'clock shadow. The man's name was Yuri, and he'd been stationed here at the lab since before Vlad's arrival. His lack of medical training was obvious, and something he made little effort to disguise.

Vlad was certain his assistant was a KGB plant whose main purpose was not to assist in the research at all, but rather to monitor Vlad and report back to Lubyanka on the state of the researcher.

And that was fine with Vlad, to a point. He believed progress was being made, despite the mounting death toll and the fact the project was a long, slow slog. Whether the KGB concurred with his assessment was anyone's guess, but either way he knew he must be very careful around Yuri, because the man potentially could make Vlad or break him in the eyes of Lubyanka.

In the meantime, Vlad was stuck with him, for better or for worse. He had taught Yuri enough over the course of his time at the lab to make the man at least marginally useful, and one of the tasks Yuri had learned was to prepare Vlad's subjects for testing.

It seemed Yuri had done his job in an adequate manner with the current test subject. The subject's arms and legs were secured to the table with sturdy leather straps. A thicker strap encircled the subject's waist over his medical gown, and a similar strap had been used to secure the subject's chest to the table, just under his armpits.

A combination leather/metal harness used screws and buckles to hold the subject's head in place, turned to the side in what had to be an uncomfortable position while the subject was conscious. But the goal of the project was knowledge that could be utilized by the KGB, not subject comfort, and in any event, the positioning was necessary to conduct the upcoming procedure.

A proper harness fit, however, would be critical for successful completion of surgery. Vlad took his time checking his "assistant's" work, as he always did, pulling and prodding at the buckles, attempting to slip his fingers between the restraint and the man's skull. Eventually he satisfied himself there would be no slippage.

He was ready to proceed.

Vlad felt the familiar flash of annoyance that he would be forced to perform the surgery alone, but Yuri had made it clear immediately upon Vlad's arrival at the lab that his assistance ended at the moment surgery began. Vlad had initially been dumbstruck—what was the point of having a helper who refused to help during the most critical stages of a project?—but Yuri had been adamant as to the limits of his job description, and no further assistants seemed to be forthcoming from KGB headquarters.

So Vlad did the only thing he could: he adapted.

He lifted the surgical drill and thumbed it on, muttering again at the inadequacy of the lighting. He leaned over the table and examined the subject's skull. The man's head had been shaved and Vlad himself had marked a small red "X" on the skin.

This was where he would bore the hole.

He tested the drill with a short squeeze of the trigger, and a high-pitched whine filled the lab and then faded away. Vlad nodded to himself and eased the surgical drill bit directly onto the mark he'd made on the side of the subject's head. Then he squeezed the trigger again and began punching a small hole through the unconscious man's skull.

Seconds later the sudden lack of resistance told Vlad he had broken through the cranium. He backed the drill out of the hole and placed it on the tray next to the surgical table. A small amount of blood trickled out of the hole and Vlad soaked it up with a wad of surgical gauze, then gazed at the tiny portion of brain now visible.

He turned to the surgical tray and picked up a pair of electrical wires. They were approximately ten centimeters in length and had been wound together into a single strand. One end of each wire consisted of a flat copper electrode, and at the other end was a small, spring-loaded alligator-jaw copper connector.

Vlad returned his attention to the test subject and began threading the wires through the hole with an instrument that resembled extra-long-nosed pliers. It was close work, and delicate, and Vlad took his time, carefully implanting the electrodes into the man's hypothalamus.

Sweat trickled out from under the high-intensity light secured to Vlad's forehead with straps. The straps holding the lamp in place reminded Vlad uncomfortably of the ones securing the subject's skull to the surgical table. He breathed deeply and wiped the sweat away as best he could, once again cursing Yuri's absence from the operating room.

When he felt satisfied he'd positioned the electrodes properly, Vlad withdrew the implantation instrument and placed it on the surgical tray next to the drill. He mopped up the blood that had accumulated around the incision, and then placed a thick square of gauze over the hole, leaving the wires trailing out from under the bandage toward the back of the man's head.

Next he began unbuckling the series of straps that had held the subject's skull motionless during surgery. He lifted them up and away until they lay flat on the table directly above the subject's head.

Finally he lifted a roll of surgical gauze and began wrapping it around the subject's skull, being careful to ensure a firm fit of the gauze pad to the surgical site while leaving the alligator-jaw connectors exposed for later use.

At last Vlad stepped away from the table. He removed the headlamp from his skull and wiped away the perspiration that had accumulated under the straps, feeling the familiar excitement begin to build. Perhaps this subject would yield the breakthrough that would eventually permit Vlad to report full success and project completion to Moscow.

He stepped to a small rotary telephone hanging on the wall next to a row of cabinets containing surgical supplies. Dialed "0" and waited for Yuri to pick up. Cursed under his breath when it seemed the call would go unanswered. *The man has little responsibility and even less to occupy his time, and still he cannot be ready when I need him?*

He was about to hang up, to slam the handset onto the cradle in disgust, when Yuri answered, his voice typically gruff. "What is it?" he said, his tone impatient, as if perhaps Vlad had interrupted him in the middle of an important business meeting.

Vladimir bit back his annoyance. He was an academic, a professional, and he would conduct himself in a dignified manner even if Yuri would not.

"Yes," Vlad said, doing his best to sound unperturbed. "The surgery is finished. Please come to the lab to clean and sterilize the equipment. I'll need you to maintain observation of the subject, and I wish to be notified immediately when he begins to regain consciousness. It should take less than an hour. When that happens, I want you to—"

It took a moment for Vlad to realize his "research assistant" had just hung up on him. He stood next to the desk, telephone clutched in his hand, staring at it in stunned surprise, eyes wide and veins throbbing in his temple.

This time he *did* slam the receiver onto the cradle, and with such force he was surprised somewhere in the back of his mind that he hadn't cracked the plastic.

He cursed under his breath and stalked out of the lab.

4

"I see you've decided to return, after all." Aaron Stallings looked up from the mountain of paperwork that seemed permanently fused to his desk. Although barely past seven-thirty in the morning, to Tracie it looked as though he'd been sitting in his chair for hours.

Hell, maybe he had.

"Was there really any doubt?" She tried to lace her comment with sarcasm, with no apparent success. The CIA director smiled widely, his fleshy jowls jiggling, and she shook her head in disgust. "Calling my *father* to get me to come back? Really? Is there no line you won't cross?"

"Come on, Tanner, have you learned nothing in your time at this agency? It's all about results. I will take any action necessary to generate the results I want, and you're so valuable precisely because you do the same. So if you think I should feel somehow ashamed that I asked a man you respect and admire to remind you what's important in this world, you're going to be sadly disappointed."

She sighed. "Obviously."

They stared at each other for a long moment, more being said in the silence than had thus far been spoken aloud.

Tracie shrugged. "Well, you wanted to see me. Here I am. Can we get on with it?"

"Sit down," he said.

She dropped into the chair centered in front of the mammoth desk in his home office, feeling like an errant schoolgirl sent to the principal's office. Stallings must have realized by now that his obvious attempt at using the chair placement for intimidation purposes wouldn't work on her, but he didn't seem inclined to stop trying.

It occurred to Tracie that this was the first time in as long as she could remember that she'd entered this room uninjured. *Unless you consider injuries to the spirit,* she thought glumly.

She shook herself inwardly. Set aside the fear festering in her soul that she was becoming an amoral killer, placing it into a secure niche deep inside her mind, locking it away and saving it for later contemplation.

It was important she not allow her boss to see any weakness, ever. The best way to accomplish that was to regain control of the moment. And she knew exactly how to do it.

"I appreciate your apology and your admission of wrongdoing in sending me out to face that Soviet sniper alone and without warning. I understand why you had to pass it along through an intermediary, and I'm sure you're happy to hear the apology is accepted."

Stallings' jaw dropped almost comically and his face colored, morphing from the pasty greyish-white of a decades-long bureaucrat to the shiny crimson of a man suffering a severe case of scarlet fever. The transformation took roughly half a second. "I most certainly did nothing of the—"

"Now that we've gotten the preliminaries out of the way," Tracie interrupted, "what did you want to see me about?"

"I…you…now listen here, Tanner, you can't just…" Then he stopped. He seemed to realize she was baiting him and he pushed himself back from his desk and clamped his jaws shut. To Tracie it looked exactly like documentary footage she had seen once of a shark chomping down on its latest meal.

She thought he was going to explode into a furious rant, as he'd done so often in the past. But to his credit, he took a moment to compose himself, sitting silently and locking eyes with Tracie as the blood slowly drained from his face.

He cleared his throat.

Sighed.

Coughed into his fist.

Said, "Do you feel better now, Tanner?"

"Immensely," she answered with a grin. "You have no idea how much I needed that."

"Well, don't get used to it. I don't tolerate insubordination. Under the circumstances I'm willing to overlook it. This time. But we need to get serious and focus on your next assignment, since I'm assuming from your presence here you've decided to remain in my employ."

"Fine. Let's get on with it."

"We've recently become aware of the existence of a secret Soviet military base located in the Ural Mountains."

"Recently become aware?"

"Yes. Intel generated from the two Russian operatives captured last May led us to—"

"Russian operatives? Last May?"

"That's right, Tanner. Try and keep up."

"Are you referring to the two KGB killers I served up on a silver platter, right before stopping the assassination of President Reagan and then being threatened with termination, a threat you later made good on?"

This time Stallings' face darkened. He leaned over his desk, elbows plopped on the surface, and said, "Don't push me, Tanner. The fact that you're sitting here means you still have a job. Don't force me to reconsider."

"Just trying to put your information into historical perspective. I think I understand it now. Please continue."

"Honest to God, Tanner, you're going to put me in the grave one of these days."

She sat primly, hands folded in her lap, a pleasant smile on her face. *You deserve every bit of aggravation I can give you and more,* she thought.

After a long pause, Stallings continued. "Anyway, under intense questioning, one of the operatives let slip the existence of a secret base nestled in the Ural Mountains. It's called the 'Ipatiev Research Facility,' and of its existence we'd previously known nothing."

"We were completely in the dark about its existence? Seems unlikely."

"That was what we thought at first. But—"

"But you immediately went to the second operative and verified the information."

Stallings' obvious annoyance at being interrupted seemed offset by his appreciation of her tactical awareness, and he nodded. "That's right. Apparently, construction of the base was begun, and mostly completed, during the 1970s, although expansion has occurred on a more or less regular basis in the intervening years."

Tracie cupped a hand under her chin. "I assume we've stepped up aerial surveillance in the Urals."

"Of course. We've flown hundreds of surveillance missions since the intel came to light, employing both the U-2 and the SR-71."

"But the fact that we're having this discussion means there's a problem."

"Yes. That's putting it mildly. All of those missions have accomplished next to nothing, besides verifying that there is, in fact, a facility inside the Bashkir Autonomous Soviet Socialist Republic that was previously unknown to us."

Tracie raised her eyebrows. "I've run missions in most of the Soviet republics at one time or another over the past seven years, but never there."

Stallings nodded. "And that makes sense. No intel we've ever developed has led us to believe anything of strategic significance was happening inside Bashkir."

"And hundreds of missions using the most sophisticated aerial surveillance aircraft ever developed have revealed nothing of value?"

He shook his head. "We believe the vast majority of the base has been constructed underground, that the Soviets have burrowed into the Urals like little Communist rabbits. Our theory is that they've developed a vast system of tunnels and subterranean work areas meaning, of course, that we can run surveillance from above for the rest of eternity and will never come any closer than we are right now to learning the significance of this base."

"And if the USSR has gone to such great lengths to keep the base a secret, there must be something important happening there."

"One would think."

Tracie felt a rising sense of anticipation. It was like a low-voltage electrical current thrumming through her body, just under the skin. She thought she knew the answer to her next question but she asked it anyway. "Where do I come in?"

"You're going to conduct surveillance on that base. You will extract its secrets. And then you'll going to come home and divulge them all."

5

January 30, 1988
1:15 p.m.
Ipatiev Military Research Facility
Mezhgorye, Bashkir Autonomous Soviet Socialist Republic

The test subject was sitting up in bed when Vladimir Protasov entered his room.

Each subject was accompanied upon his arrival at the facility by a file consisting of all known facts relating to the man that might bear relevance to the testing protocol. Given most subjects' status as homeless, addicted, mentally ill or some combination of all three, the sizes of their attendant files varied significantly, but in almost all cases the subject's name was known.

And in almost all cases Vlad was careful to ignore that information.

He had discovered shortly after his arrival at Ipatiev that knowing the test subject's name did nothing to contribute to the success of the project. All it accomplished was to make a good night's sleep even more difficult for Vlad when something inevitably went wrong and the subject died.

Obviously, however, conducting research would be impossible without somehow identifying the test subjects, so Vlad developed his own classification system. It was simple but workable, consisting of the month of the subject's arrival at the facility, followed by a number indicating the order of the subject's testing for that particular month.

This subject was thus known as January 3.

Vlad knew it was silly of him to waste time worrying about developing an identification system for the test subjects when it would be so much easier just to use their given names—particularly when there was so much of greater import to be concerned with—but the dead men haunted his sleep persistently enough when they were dehumanized prior to surgery. Knowing he'd ended the life of a "Sergei" or an "Ivan" or a "Georgi" would have been too much to bear, even if—as was the case—their deaths were justified in the name of scientific progress.

And it wasn't like the test subjects gave a damn how they were identified. They were far more concerned with issues like holes being drilled into their skulls to manipulate their brain tissue than what was written on the tag pinned to their hospital gowns.

January 3 watched Vlad dully from his hospital bed, tracking every movement with his eyes while trying to hold his head as motionless as possible. The reluctance to move made sense, given that less than twenty-four hours earlier a sharp instrument had bored through his skull and into his brain.

Vlad moved to the bed and examined the dressing on the subject's head. A small amount of blood had seeped into and through the gauze at the site of the incision, and Vlad made a mental note to change the bandage later. It was the sort of detail his assistant should handle, but Vlad wouldn't consider delegating that chore to Yuri as long as January 3 remained a viable test subject.

If and when that viability changed, so too would the amount of responsibility entrusted to Yuri.

Vlad stepped to the side of the bed and smiled at the subject. He hoped the gesture looked more sincere to January 3 than it felt to him.

"How are you feeling today?" He always started out this portion of the process with the same question and was inevitably surprised when the subject didn't respond, "Like a man with a hole in his head," or something similar. But so far none of them had.

This particular test subject didn't bother responding at all. He met Vlad's gaze, but with the hollowed-out look of an alcoholic being tossed in jail for public intoxication.

Vlad worked to control his frustration. January 3 had exhibited a similar malaise during Phase One of the process, and Vlad suspected strongly that the lack of cooperation was unrelated to the testing program but rather a reflection of the man's general ill health and long-term substance abuse.

Poor test subjects lead to poor test results.

Vlad shook his head and got to work.

* * *

In the corner of January 3's room was a wheeled table. Atop the table sat a strange-looking machine, perhaps three meters high, featuring meters and dials and warning lights mounted above a large pair of stereo speakers.

Vlad closed the door to the subject's room and then grasped the table by handles positioned on either side. He trundled it into position at the end of the subject's bed and then reached up and grasped a nylon cord hanging from the ceiling. He pulled on the cord like a man lowering a window shade and a white screen extended into place next to the strange-looking machine at the end of the bed.

He lifted a small remote control device that featured an electrical cord running from one end to an outlet in the wall. When he pressed a button on the remote, a video projector built into the wall next to the subject's bed flashed to life and the image of a rat appeared on the screen in front of January 3.

The man blinked in surprise, the first time he'd done anything but stare dully at Vlad since he walked into the room. Vlad supposed he should consider that a step in the right direction.

He smiled again at the man as he picked up a pair of electrical cables. The end of each cable disappeared into the back of the strange-looking machine, and each had been wound neatly and placed side by side on the table next to the remote. Vlad approached January 3's bed, the cables unwinding smoothly behind him, the subject becoming noticeably more agitated as concern clouded his already muddy expression.

This reaction—or something similar—was not unusual at this point in the process.

"We're going to do a little baseline testing," Vlad said pleasantly.

January 3 glanced suspiciously between Vlad's eyes and the cables and then back. He didn't seem particularly enthusiastic about doing baseline testing or anything else. It didn't matter.

"Now," Vlad continued as he reached for the two electrical wires he'd implanted in January 3's brain yesterday. They dangled next to the subject's left ear and Vlad doubted the man was even aware of their presence.

He deftly attached the copper connectors at the end of each cable to their corresponding electrical wires via the spring-loaded alligator clips and said, "Your job is going to be very simple, perhaps even enjoyable."

He stepped once more to the movable table he'd placed at the foot of the bed. The image of the rat continued to be displayed on the projector screen, and even though Vlad had seen it dozens of times while testing dozens of subjects exactly like this one, it always made him feel slightly uneasy. It was as if the damned thing was tracking his progress with its beady black eyes. Each time it happened he vowed to leave the projector off until he was ready to begin, and then each time he started working with a new test subject he forgot and flashed that damned rat up there too soon.

He was being ridiculous. *Concentrate on your work instead of your paranoia.*

Vlad lifted the final item from the table. It was a small remote controller, similar in size and design to a controller used in those damned video games that had been developed in the West over the last fifteen or so years and that everyone seemed to enjoy playing.

This controller had been simplified. Instead of knobs, joysticks and a series of buttons, this plastic device offered just two options. A button on the left was labeled I AGREE, in large block Cyrillic script, and another on the right had been labeled I DISAGREE.

An electrical cord ran from the back of the device to the same outlet in the wall into which Vlad's remote had been plugged. The cord was long, easily long enough to permit Vlad to hand it to the subject sitting up in bed, which he now did.

The man accepted it reluctantly, his look of suspicion turning quickly into one of concern and maybe even fear. Still, he had no real alternative but to take the device from Vlad, and so he did, holding it gingerly in two hands like perhaps it might be about to explode.

"A series of common animals, plants and other items will be projected onto the screen in front of you," Vlad said, still speaking conversationally. "Your job, as I said before, will be quite simple, and perhaps even fun."

The man didn't look any more convinced now than he had the first time.

Vlad continued. "As each item is displayed, I will announce to you the name or term by which that item is typically known. You will respond by pressing the button on the device you are holding that most closely corresponds with your feeling about the term I have used."

The man continued to sit silently, but he'd held Vlad's gaze the entire time and Vlad knew that along with suspicion and fear was comprehension. January 3 understood what was expected of him.

"For example," he said. "If I announced 'rat' when the animal on your screen was displayed, you would press the 'I AGREE' button. Please do so now."

The subject held Vlad's eyes for a moment and then looked down at his remote control device. He looked back up at Vlad before pursing his lips and pressing the button on the left side of the remote.

Vlad nodded approvingly. "Very good. If, on the other hand, I had said the word 'elephant' when the animal was displayed, you would of course press the button labeled 'I DISAGREE.' Please press the 'I DISAGREE' button now."

The man did as instructed and his entire body spasmed instantly as a low-grade electric shock was delivered to his system via one of the electrodes Vlad had implanted in his brain yesterday. His eyes blinked rapidly and his expression tightened and then slackened and he flashed an angry—and frightened—look at Vlad.

"As you can see," Vlad said, "it is to your benefit to pay close attention and to be as accurate as you can in your responses."

The subject's eyes narrowed and he stared at Vlad, still without speaking.

Vlad cleared his throat officiously. "Before we begin, do you have any questions?"

No answer. The subject still hadn't said a word since Vlad's appearance in his room or, as far as Vlad was aware, at any other time since his delivery to the camp by the KGB.

"Alright then. Let us begin."

6

January 30, 1988
8:30 a.m.
Washington, D.C.

Tracie departed D.C. in the CIA Gulfstream almost immediately following her briefing with Director Stallings. The haste with which she was being sent into the field again after her last mission was a clear indication of how seriously the agency was taking the intel regarding the discovery of a previously unknown Soviet military installation hidden deep in the Ural Mountains.

At the end of their conversation in Aaron Stallings' home office, the director had come as close as he ever would to offering her an apology. "I know your last assignment ended badly," he'd said, "and I know you were caught off-guard by the assassination of David Goodell. But this mission should be much different."

Tracie raised her eyebrows in surprise. "Really? How so?"

"I'm not asking you to infiltrate this secret Soviet base, like I did with Operation Phoenix last fall in West Germany. I'm not asking you to eliminate anyone, or engage the Soviets in any way. All I want is for you to find a safe mountain perch from which to observe the facility for a few days. By doing so, I'm hoping you can begin to get a feel for what the USSR might be trying to accomplish in such secrecy. Any information you can extract from a distance will be better than what we have now. But it's a low-profile mission, if there is such a thing in this business. You go, you take notes, you come home, you brief agency specialists."

"That's all?" Tracie said warily. Making life easy for her had never been high on Aaron Stallings' list of priorities.

"That's all. Nothing more. It should be a piece of cake for you."

Stallings' words of reassurance seemed at odds with his insistence that she leave immediately, but she'd received her assignment and would be expected to complete it. Everything else was extraneous. The discussion with her father had reenergized her, and while she continued to feel the black ache of horror and guilt over what she'd done in Moscow, she'd come to realize there was no going back. There was no changing her actions. Her only option was to keep putting one foot in front of the other.

So that was what she did. She returned to her apartment for her go-bag, and within fifteen minutes was picked up by an agency driver and shuttled to Washington National.

The G4 flight had been uneventful. Tracie was well familiar with transatlantic air travel, having made the trip to or from the U.S. and Europe/Asia many times over the course of her career, and in many different types of aircraft, including this same CIA jet last November.

Being the only passenger in the big Gulfstream was unsettling, despite the fact Tracie in general disliked crowds and enjoyed solitude. The last time she'd ridden in the plane, she had spent most of the trip studying intel and cramming for her assignment, but this flight was different. Her mission was necessarily open-ended, and since it involved reconnaissance of a Soviet base that was a complete mystery to the intelligence community, there was little intel to study.

After attempting unsuccessfully to relax, Tracie stood and wandered up to the flight deck. The same crew of two that had flown her on the last trip was back behind the controls, and the younger of the two pilots—the man she'd briefly spoken to her first time aboard the plane—turned around and smiled as she approached.

"You're not going to shoot me and toss me out of our airplane at thirty-five thousand feet, I hope," he said with an impish grin.

Tracie laughed. Those were the exact words he'd used two months ago when she'd responded angrily after being interrupted while studying her notes. "Nope, no shooting on the flight deck," she said. "I've been there, and the experience was a lot less enjoyable than you might imagine."

The young man raised his eyebrows in mild surprise. As a CIA pilot, he'd undoubtedly seen a lot and flown plenty of sketchy characters in this very airplane, but he didn't seem prepared for that response. To his credit, though, he kept his composure and maintained his professionalism.

"I'm glad you're still here to tell about it," he said, and then stuck out his hand. "I'm Jesse Belleau, and the man behind the controls, pretending to fly while we're actually on autopilot, is Captain Ed Byron."

Tracie shook Belleau's hand. When Ed Byron turned away from the controls and offered his hand, she shook that as well. "I'm sure you understand if I don't tell you my name," she said with a wink, and both men chuckled.

"What can we do for you?" Belleau asked. "Would you like a snack or something to drink? Pillow and a blanket?"

"No, nothing like that," Tracie answered. "I got bored sitting back there in that beautifully appointed cabin all by myself. I just decided to come and say hello. I hope I'm not disturbing you or interfering in any way."

"Of course not," the second-in-command answered. "You're welcome to stay up here as long as you'd like, although with a flight time of nearly nine hours, I'm afraid you'll get tired of our conversational skills almost as quickly as you got bored back in the cabin."

He leaned back and flipped down a small seat located just behind his own. "This torture device is our jump seat," he said. "Make yourself comfortable, if such a thing is even possible. This isn't leather-covered and padded like the seats you were just using."

She eased into the jump seat and buckled in. "You said we're looking at about nine hours flight time?"

"Actually a little more than that," Ed Byron said. "This beauty is sleek and fast, but doesn't quite have enough range to take us direct to southern Turkey from D.C. We'll have to make a quick pit stop in Italy for fuel, so that will add a little time."

"How much time?" Tracie asked. She'd flown through Rome before and recalled sitting through extensive departure delays at

Fiumicino Airport. Stallings had made quite clear the urgency of her assignment, and the notion of sitting for hours on a tarmac was not ideal.

Belleau grinned as if he'd read her mind. "Don't worry," he said, "we'll only be on the ground long enough to high-speed-taxi to the ramp, suck down some fuel, and then turn around and high-speed-taxi back to the runway for takeoff. We'll be on the ground no more than twenty minutes, I promise."

"How can you be so sure? What if there's a lot of traffic?"

"They'll make room for us."

"I don't follow."

"We're not going to land at a civilian airport. We'll be refueling at Aviano Air Base in northern Italy. They're pretty familiar with this particular airplane. We fly through there several times a year, and the controllers and ramp personnel are aware of our priority status. Trust me, we'll barely be stopped long enough for you to unbuckle your seat belt."

"It's nice to be the big fish," Tracie said with a smile. "I could get used to that."

"I don't know if we qualify as a big fish, exactly, but flying through military airfields with advance coordination sure makes for an easier—and faster—aviation experience," Byron said, giving her a thumbs-up.

"So," Tracie said, doing some math in her head. "Ten hours of flight time, give or take, and Incirlik Air Base is, I don't know, maybe five thousand miles from D.C?"

"It would actually be about fifty-six hundred fifty miles," Belleau said, "if you could go direct, Point A to Point B. We can't quite go direct, and we have to fly just slightly out of our way to stop at Aviano, but this Gulfstream will cruise at more than six hundred fifty miles per hour without breaking a sweat. We're actually doing better than that because we were advised this mission is of a critical nature."

Tracie gazed out the windscreen at the vast Atlantic Ocean, sparkling greenish-blue far below, stretching off in every direction as far as the eye could see. She thought about Stallings' reassurance that the assignment would be relatively easy. "Piece of cake," he'd said.

She measured that reassurance against her boss's history of duplicity and the young pilot's assertion that he'd been told the mission was of a critical nature. Something wasn't adding up.

7

January 31, 1988
3:15 a.m. local time
Incirlik Air Base, Turkey

The C-130 cargo plane rattled like an eggbeater as it taxied for departure at Incirlik Air Base in southern Turkey. After the silky smoothness and easy power of the Gulfstream, the C-130 felt like it was fighting for every inch of altitude, its four turboprop engines biting aggressively into the air. The big cargo plane banked north almost immediately after leaving the runway and leveled off far below the altitude the CIA G4 had used.

Time on the ground at Incirlik had been minimal, barely more than the fifteen minutes it had taken to refuel the Gulfstream at Aviano. Tracie climbed down from the comfortable business jet after thanking both members of the agency flight crew, walked across a concrete tarmac, and climbed into the C-130, known in military jargon as a "Hercules."

This time she didn't even bother trying to relax in the back of the airplane. For one thing there was no comfortable cabin in which *to* relax, and for another, she wanted information on this final leg of the flight that only the C-130 crew could provide.

The easy banter of the Gulfstream crew was replaced with a tense professionalism inside the Hercules. The crew was friendly enough, but all business, with a high level of military discipline mixed in.

Flying a precise route once the Hercules crossed the midpoint of the Black Sea would be critical to ensuring the Soviets not see them coming and shoot them out of the sky, so the pilot-in-command and navigator were understandably busy. Both men introduced themselves to Tracie politely but quickly and then returned their attention to their duties.

Then it was left to a young airman to fill Tracie in on the plan for depositing her safely on the ground in Bashkir. His name was Lieutenant Brian Schlichter, and he was earnest and quiet. He looked to Tracie like he should be on his way to a high school algebra class, not risking his life flying a CIA operative into the mountains of a Soviet satellite state.

"I'll be happy to answer any questions you might have, ma'am," Schlichter said. He kept his voice down in an obvious attempt to avoid distracting his fellow crewmembers.

"Thank you," Tracie said. "I guess the obvious question is why such a big airplane? Wouldn't it be a lot easier to smuggle someone into the Soviet Union in something a little…I don't know, faster and more maneuverable?"

Schlichter grinned. "Something like that beautiful G4 you came in on, you mean?"

"Well, maybe not that exact plane, but something similar, yes."

"Believe it or not," the lieutenant said, "this Hercules is perfectly suited to today's mission."

"How so?"

"For one thing, we were asked to bring along a piece of cargo that would have had a hard time fitting into a Gulfstream, or almost any other airplane for that matter."

"What cargo?"

"Look for yourself," Schlichter said, nodding toward the cargo hold, which stretched out behind the flight deck like a warehouse. "The order to include it came straight from the highest levels at the CIA."

Tracie craned her neck to see around a large aluminum tank bolted to the floor directly behind the seats. Behind the tank, in the rear of the aircraft's hold, a vehicle had been lashed securely. Small and compact, resembling a slightly scaled-down version of the Jeep Cherokee or Ford Bronco, Tracie recognized it immediately from her time working in the USSR. It was a Lada SUV.

Manufactured by the Soviet carmaker AutoVAZ, the Lada was one of the most popular automobile brands in Russia. With so much of the Soviet Union facing brutal winters year in and year out, many Ladas featured a four-wheel-drive option, and this one was no exception. It sat high off the ground for clearance and featured muscular-looking tires designed to offer superior traction in heavy snow.

"Where did that come from?" Tracie asked.

Lieutenant Schlichter raised his hands in a warding-off gesture and smiled. "I don't know, ma'am. A Turkish citizen delivered it to the front gate and the man disappeared before anyone could question him. But according to our commanding officer, the order to deliver the car—and you—to our landing zone came from a senior administration official. When you hear things like that, you keep your mouth shut and follow orders."

Tracie realized this young man was in the habit of keeping his mouth shut and following orders in *any* situation. He now reminded her less of a high school kid and more of what he actually was—a dedicated naval aviator.

"Very thoughtful of that person," Tracie said. *It had to have been Stallings.*

"Yes, ma'am. And if you're going to spend any amount of time—like more than five minutes—in the Ural Mountains, a four-wheel-drive vehicle like this one will be absolutely essential to your survival. The area is rugged and breathtakingly cold."

Tracie nodded. "What's the other reason, Lieutenant?"

"Excuse me?"

"When you answered my question about why this C-130 was the right plane to deliver me to the Urals, you said 'for one thing,' and then you showed me the truck you were carrying in the cargo bay. That implies there's a second reason."

He chuckled. "Well, yes, ma'am. This being an illicit mission into enemy territory, we can't just call up air traffic control and request permission to land. For obvious reasons, we can't go anywhere near an airport, not that there are any in the mountains where we're headed, anyway."

Tracie blinked in surprise. She hadn't even considered that

factor. "So…where *are* we going to land? This airplane is big. How will it even be possible to put it on the ground?"

"Yes, this is a big airplane, but big doesn't always translate into a requirement for a lengthy runway. The C-130 is no longer officially classified as a STOL airplane, but that's more for political and budgetary reasons than anything else. STOL is exactly what it is."

Tracie shook her head. "STOL? What does that mean?"

"I'm sorry, I should have explained. STOL stands for 'Short Takeoff and Landing.' Essentially it means that the aircraft requires significantly less runway than other airplanes of a similar size and performance."

"STOL." Tracie tried the word on for size. She liked it. The notion of an aircraft as large as this one using just a small portion of runway appealed to her. It meant…

"Wait a second." She scratched her head. "You just said we can't land at an airport, and that makes perfect sense. What difference does it make how much runway the C-130 uses if we're not landing at an airport?"

"This airplane doesn't need *any* runway."

"I don't understand."

"You probably didn't notice when you came aboard because it's the middle of the night and you're understandably more concerned about accomplishing your mission—whatever that might be—than about the configuration of your transport plane. But if you'd been looking at the landing gear as you approached, you would have seen something unexpected."

"And what would that be?"

"In addition to conventional landing gear, which we used on departure at Incirlik, this airplane is equipped with skis."

"Excuse me?"

"Yes, ma'am, you heard me right."

"Skis."

"Yes, ma'am."

"We're going to use skis to land on the side of a mountain."

"Not exactly," the lieutenant said, "but you're on the right track. We've studied surveillance images taken from SR-71 overflights to identify a large frozen lake located right in the middle of the area in which we were instructed to deliver you. We're going to use the skis to land on top of the frozen, snow-covered lake."

Tracie was stunned. No wonder the atmosphere inside the flight deck had been tense since her arrival.

She shook her head in wonder. "I've never heard of an airplane this size being equipped with skis."

"That's because it's extremely unusual," Schlichter said. "The concept of a C-130 on skis was developed back in the 1950s to assist in expeditions to Antarctica. A similarly outfitted airplane—this one—was delivered to our unit several years ago for use in exactly this type of situation."

Tracie glanced back at the large aluminum tank bolted to the floor of the Hercules directly behind the crew. "That's an auxiliary fuel tank, isn't it?"

Schlichter smiled in appreciation of her observational skills. "Yes it is, ma'am. Given our unit's location, this aircraft was customized to permit longer-range operations than would normally be possible with the typical C-130 fuel capacity."

"Without the tank, you would risk running our of fuel to deliver me to the landing zone."

"Yes, ma'am, that's correct."

"But with the auxiliary tank, that's not an issue."

"Uh…" Schlichter looked at his fellow crewmembers for help, but both men returned his gaze with blank expressions. It was obvious they were letting him know it would be his own responsibility to escape the corner into which he'd painted himself.

"It shouldn't be an issue," he finished weakly.

"Shouldn't be. What does that mean?"

"It means that given the winds aloft, the route we're forced to take to avoid Soviet radar systems, and the conditions we expect to encounter once we get into the mountains, we should have sufficient fuel to deliver you to the landing zone and return to Incirlik safely."

"*Should* have sufficient fuel? You don't know for sure?"

"We've never flown this type of mission before, ma'am, certainly not under combat-type conditions. Theoretically, we should be fine. It's just that we haven't stretched fuel capacity to the maximum before."

Tracie felt sick. These men were risking their lives to help the

CIA accomplish a mission. If they were to run into fuel problems it would obviously be on their way back to Turkey, long after they'd dropped her off. She closed her eyes.

Schlichter sensed her unease and repeated, "We should be fine, ma'am." Then he grinned and said, "But I'm sure you'll understand if we don't hang around sipping coffee and swapping war stories once we get on the ice at the landing zone. We're going to kick you out the door, drop the rear cargo hatch and roll out your car, and then be on our way."

At that moment the Hercules lurched as it began descending sharply. Tracie grabbed a handhold built into the airplane's fuselage and tried to remain calm as she flashed back to last May, and the uncontrolled descent of a B-52 into the woods outside Bangor, Maine.

"Don't worry, ma'am," Lieutenant Schlichter said. "This is just part of our flight plan."

"You guys have a lot to learn about passenger comfort," she joked, her heart pounding wildly in her chest.

He smiled and said, "Sorry about that. But we're at the point where we have to descend to the lowest possible safe altitude to avoid radar detection."

"What altitude would that be?"

"Less than fifty feet while we're over the Black Sea."

8

January 31, 1988
4:40 a.m.
Black Sea, west of Sochi, Russia, USSR

The C-130 hurtled over the Black Sea, which remained invisible in the early-morning darkness. She could sense the water's presence, though, lurking just beneath the aircraft like an angry monster waiting to rip the plane to shreds at the first opportunity.

"How do you know your position in relation to water you can't see?"

"You trust your instruments," Schlichter said. The tension, already apparent on the flight deck, ratcheted up even further at the beginning of the riskiest portion of the flight.

"We have onboard radar," the lieutenant assured Tracie. "We won't run into a ship, I promise."

She wanted to ask about the accuracy of the altimeter, the gauge that prevented them from descending too low and plowing into the water, but instead said, "What happens once we cross the Black Sea?" The question was meant more as a distraction to ease her nerves than out of an actual desire to hear the answer.

"We're going to cross into enemy territory just north of the Soviet Republic of Georgia, near the Lazarevskoye Microdistrict. This area was chosen carefully because as seaside real estate goes it's less populated than other portions of the coastline. We believe it offers the least overall chance of interception by the Russians."

"Sounds risky."

"Only if we've been detected as we crossed over the water. If we've flown low enough to avoid Soviet radar, by the time they see us approaching the shoreline they won't have time to scramble interceptors before we disappear again into the mountains."

"And if we weren't low enough to stay below the radar?"

"Then we'll be met by a very unfriendly welcoming committee."

In the distance ahead, Tracie could se what appeared to be a series of lights, dimly visible but rapidly brightening. Within seconds they began to resolve, and shortly after that, she recognized them for what they were: automobile headlights. They appeared almost level with the C-130's windscreen and were approaching at incredible speed.

"Holy shit!" she exclaimed as the pilot-in-command applied power and eased back on the yoke.

"Time to climb a little," Schlichter said. "The Black Sea is a popular Soviet vacation spot and as such, there's a coastal highway running through this area. That's what you see."

"And if the Soviets saw us coming, we'll find out about it any second now," she said.

"Yes ma'am."

The cars on the highway passed below the C-130, the plane missing them by what felt to Tracie like a matter of inches, although logic told her it had to be more than that. She pictured the surprised drivers getting a close-up view of a U.S. Air Force cargo plane rocketing just over their heads and disappearing toward the mountains to the northeast.

The pilot eased left and descended once again over a river, making slight course adjustments to follow the meandering water. Time slowed, turning tense seconds into minutes, and after what felt like a very long time they left the relatively densely populated Black Sea coastline behind. As they did so, the crew breathed a sigh of relief almost in unison.

Tracie thought she knew why. "If the Soviets were going to intercept us, they would have done so by now, wouldn't they?"

"Yes, ma'am, in all probability we would already have either been shot down or received a fighter escort to the nearest Soviet base. We should be okay."

"But we're northeastbound. I thought the Ural Mountains were a more northerly heading from Incirlik."

"I see you've done your research," Schlichter said. "And you're correct. But remember, we can't use the most direct routing because it's critical we avoid known Soviet radar installations. And taking advantage of the cover provided by the terrain in this area will allow us to do that. The plan actually is to continue more or less on this heading, overflying the northwestern portion of the Kazakh Soviet Republic, before finally turning to more of a northerly heading and making for Bashkir."

The terrain had already begun turning rugged, with signs of human habitation few and far between. The pilot flying this leg began climbing as he continued to follow the river, eventually leaving the waterway behind.

There was still no sign the Soviets had become aware of their presence.

*   *   *

January 31, 1988
8:40 a.m.
Ural Mountains, Bashkir Autonomous Soviet Socialist Republic

Daylight had begun to insinuate itself into the sky above the Ural Mountains of Bashkir as the flight crew initiated descent toward an impossibly small landing area. Actual sunrise wouldn't occur here for another thirty minutes or more, but the diffuse light was sufficient to finally reveal the snow-covered landmasses above and around which the C-130 had been flying for nearly the past four hours.

When Lieutenant Schlichter first pointed out the landing zone—the "LZ," as it was known in military aviation jargon—Tracie was unable to discern any area that appeared remotely large enough upon which to land an airplane this size.

Or any size.

She shook her head in confusion. "I'm sorry," she said. "I don't see what you're looking at."

The senior airman, who had flown the entire leg and who would trade places with Schlichter for the trip home, circled twice above the LZ before turning outbound to begin final descent. As the plane banked but before the area disappeared behind them, Schlichter pointed firmly out the side window and said, "Right there, ma'am. You see that area where there are no trees?"

"I see it," she said.

"You can't tell because of the heavy snow cover, but that's a frozen lake. It's why there aren't any trees. That's where we're going to put down."

Tracie was dumbfounded. "I don't mean to question your professional judgment, but your plan is to land this giant piece of metal on that little frozen patch down there?"

"That's the plan, ma'am. We're treating the lake as if it were a short runway, so right now Major Corrigan is turning to the arrival leg known as the downwind. We'll fly away from the LZ for a distance of about five miles, then we'll turn to what's called the base leg before turning again almost immediately onto the final approach course. By then the aircraft will be fully stabilized and slowed to our final approach speed."

She was still having trouble processing the notion that they would be attempting what seemed a suicidal maneuver.

"Okay," she replied, hating the obvious skepticism in her voice but unable to silence it. "So we're going to turn a five-mile final to a runway that's not really a runway, but rather a snow-covered lake. Then what?"

"Then we're going to clear the trees ringing the shoreline at the lowest possible altitude and drop right onto the surface of the lake."

"Just like that."

"Yes, ma'am, just like that."

"But the lake seems so…"

"Tiny?" Schlichter suggested helpfully.

"Yes, exactly. It seems far too small to land *any* airplane on, never mind something the size of this C-130."

"Remember, this is a STOL airplane. Yes it's big, but we can land it in a surprisingly short distance. Also, the flaps on this baby can lower to nearly ninety degrees, allowing a much steeper descent profile than the typical airplane."

"What does that mean?"

"Typical descent profile is three to three-and-a-half degrees when landing. With the C-130 we can descend at around seven degrees, even more steeply if necessary. This means clearing the tops of the trees and then dropping onto the lake is feasible for us, whereas it would be an impossibility for most other aircraft."

"If you say so," Tracie muttered. She realized her comment had gone unheard by Schlichter, who had turned his full attention to the flight deck's instrumentation. He wasn't flying the plane, but he was concentrating every bit as hard as if he had been.

The skies had lightened noticeably in just the short time she'd been discussing the specifics of the landing with Schlichter. Still, visibility was low in the shadowy half-light of a mountain winter morning. The plane turned from base leg to final, still descending, and Tracie had to strain mightily just to see the lake LZ from a distance of five miles.

The pilot had slowed the plane while descending until now, as the C-130 approached the snow-covered "runway," it felt to Tracie like they were almost hovering, moving toward the landing zone at barely more than a snail's pace.

She realized she was perfectly fine with the notion of delaying this seemingly insane maneuver, even if only by another minute or two. Adrenaline pounded through her system, causing her arms to shake as she gripped the handholds tightly.

She tightened the seat restraints one more notch and breathed deeply through her mouth in a failed attempt to calm herself. Her nerves were thrumming exactly as they did before engaging an enemy one-on-one, but this nervousness was much more difficult to deal with because she had absolutely no control over the outcome. Her status was reduced to that of helpless observer, forced to rely on the training and judgment of others, men she had known only for a few hours and who, upon mission completion, she would likely never see again.

She wasn't the only one feeling the pressure as the plane leveled off one final time, now practically skinning the treetops. The atmosphere on the flight deck was electric. All extraneous chatter had ceased, the only words spoken being those necessary for a safe landing. The flight engineer was reading off numbers at set intervals, and after a moment Tracie recognized them as altitudes above the surface of the ground expressed in feet.

Airspeed seemed to increase as their descent stopped, the trees sliding beneath the windscreen, massive and ancient and terrifying. Again Tracie flashed back to her last panic-filled seconds inside the cockpit of a B-52 making a desperate attempt at an emergency landing at Bangor International Airport last spring.

The stricken Major Tom Wilczynski had succumbed to his injuries in the last few seconds before touchdown. Tracie recalled grabbing for the yoke and missing as the plane descended into the forest. It was the last thing she remembered before regaining consciousness inside the vehicle of the man who'd pulled her from the burning wreckage.

This is different, she reminded herself. *These guys are professionals and they've practiced maneuvers exactly like this hundreds of times, probably thousands.*

The pilot called out a number she guessed was probably airspeed. The speed that had seemed so slow a moment ago now seemed much too fast, and the small snow-covered lake rushed toward them, filling the windscreen in a monochromatic white.

They cleared the last of the trees and Tracie's stomach dropped as the C-130 lurched downward. The nose of the plane pointed directly at the LZ and for a moment she feared they would prang into the frozen lake like a lawn dart.

Then the pilot raised the nose in a gentle flair and the rear skis touched down with a muffled thump that was noticeable, but only just, over the sound of the engines screaming in the high-altitude air. The nose lowered until the front skis impacted the surface as well, and then the plane was decelerating rapidly. Brakes would be useless during a landing on snow and ice, obviously, and Tracie realized the pilot was using reverse thrust on the four props to slow the aircraft.

The moment the front skis touched down, the props whipped up the powdery mountain snow. Near whiteout conditions instantly enveloped the plane, resembling the worst winter blizzards Tracie had ever seen growing up in the D.C. area. Visibility through the windscreen plummeted, dropping from poor to nearly nonexistent.

And she knew the trees at the far end of the lake were approaching.

The plane began to slide to the right, like a car in an uncontrolled skid. The pilot cursed softly and adjusted the power settings. Tracie assumed he was adding power to the engines on one side. Whatever he did seemed to work, as the aircraft straightened out again but continued to slide forward.

She was holding her breath but couldn't force air into her lungs as she peered through the windscreen. She was certain the last thing she would ever see would be the massive figures of the trees looming through the blowing snow, then impact and violence and darkness and death.

And then it was over.

The C-130 shuddered to a halt and the blowing snow began to settle. Visibility through the windscreen improved again, and as it did, Tracie saw that her concern about the trees lurking at the far end of the LZ had been justified. The shoreline stood no more than fifty feet from their position, marked by a slight incline and then the trees, omnipresent and lethal.

Tracie breathed deeply for what felt like the first time since they'd turned toward the LZ five miles ago.

Major Corrigan turned to face her and said, "I don't mean to rush to you, ma'am, but every drop of fuel is precious if we're going to make it back to Incirlik. We need to offload you and get back in the air absolutely as quickly as possible."

"Of course," Tracie said, and began unbuckling her safely harness.

As she did so, Corrigan flipped a switch and the C-130's rear hydraulic cargo door began lowering. Within seconds it had dropped to the snow, acting as a ramp off which the Lada SUV would drive.

Frigid mountain air raced into the cabin and for the second time in a matter of minutes, Tracie found it hard to take a breath. The first time was from tension, this time from the shock of exposure to the extreme cold. She shrugged into her parka and lifted her equipment bag onto her shoulder before following Lieutenant Schlichter to the cargo area.

"The keys are in the vehicle," he said, "and one of our people filled it with as much fuel as it would hold back at Incirlik before we loaded it aboard the plane. Obviously I don't know your assignment and I don't want to know. But we were told this LZ is no more than thirty miles from your mission location."

Tracie nodded and the man continued. "The long-range weather forecast is for a couple of days of high pressure and then gradually worsening weather conditions, with a storm system moving into the area in four to five days. We can't land here if the conditions are too poor, because we have no nav guidance, so we'll be back here February third at fourteen-thirty hours to extract you. It's the most time we can offer you given the incoming weather."

"Understood," Tracie said. That gave her four days to accomplish as much surveillance as possible.

"I want to stress," Schlichter said, "our fuel situation will be the same in four days as it is now. You've got to be here and ready to go when we land, because we can't afford to hang around. If you're late, you'll be standing on the lake alone because we'll have to turn around and take off for Turkey again immediately. Do you understand?"

"I do," she said. "And thank you. Your fuel situation is obviously a major concern. Are you guys going to be okay?"

"We'll be alright," Schlichter said. "But Major Corrigan's point about a quick turnaround is a good one. We can't return to Turkey via the same route we used to get here, because there's a good chance the Soviets would be waiting for us. The return route is somewhat longer, so even with our aux fuel tank we'll be cutting it close. We really need do to get airborne again ASAP, and that scenario will be equally critical when we return."

"Got it," Tracie said. She opened the Lada's driver side door and tossed her bag into the passenger seat, then looked back at Schlichter to see him removing a series of four heavy chains from the vehicle's frame. The chains had been pulled taut and attached to U-bolts embedded in the C-130's fuselage to keep the truck from shifting inside the cargo hold during the flight.

He completed his task in seconds and then approached her

quickly. He offered a salute and a smile and she stepped forward and surprised him with a quick hug. "Thanks for everything," she said. "And please pass along my appreciation to the rest of your crew. You guys are the best."

"You can thank them in person in four days when your mission's complete," he answered.

"I look forward to it," she said.

She released her hold on the lieutenant and slipped behind the wheel. The Lada's engine caught immediately as she turned the key, and she shifted into reverse and began backing down the cargo ramp, mindful of the crew's need to get in the air immediately.

The moment all four tires crunched into the snow and Tracie rolled away from the C-130, the cargo door began lifting back into position. She backed a safe distance away and then shifted into first gear, thankful for the four-wheel-drive transmission. Without it she doubted she would have gotten ten feet in the deep snow.

In the time it took to reach the shelter of the trees at the edge of the lake, the flight crew had turned the C-130 one hundred eighty degrees. Snow flew in a wind-whipped frenzy around the airplane and Tracie imagined the men inside straining to see anything at all through the windscreen. The plane began inching forward. In seconds it had reached takeoff speed and lifted into the air, seemingly on a collision course with the same trees they had barely cleared on arrival.

She realized she whispering, "Come on, come one, come on," as she watched, alone inside the Lada.

For a moment she was sure they weren't going to make it. Then the plane nosed more aggressively toward the sky. It leaped over the trees and vanished, still climbing steadily.

Tracie listened as the roar of the C-130's engines faded to a distant hum.

Then the sound disappeared entirely and she was alone.

9

The silence that descended on the isolated mountain lake following the departure of the C-130 was as all encompassing as anything Tracie had ever experienced. She'd undergone sensory-deprivation training during her time at The Farm, and the current lack of aural stimulation brought her right back to that experience, even now, nearly eight years later.

There were no birds chirping in the trees.

There was no airplane noise.

No faraway construction sounds.

No vehicles rolling past on a distant highway.

Nothing but the low hum of the Lada's engine, idling softly as Tracie sat on the snow-covered ice. She cranked up the heat and prayed it was operational.

*   *   *

Although nothing concrete was known about the secret Soviet installation, Stallings had provided what little intel he could prior to Tracie's departure for Incirlik. One of the items she'd been given was a vague set of directions to the base, known as Ipatiev.

The Air Force C-130 crew had transmitted a list of three potential landing zones to the CIA after studying the aerial photos provided by SR-71 surveillance. The LZs were numbered in order of preference from one to three, based on proximity to the Soviet base and estimated degree of difficulty in traveling to the installation.

If the flight crew had determined that their first landing option was not feasible—and there were an almost limitless number of reasons why a mountainous LZ could have been deemed unusable, from reduced visibility to low ceilings to obstruction clearance to aircraft performance—they would have proceeded to their second option and, if necessary, to their third.

The return flight in four days held the potential for being much more problematic. There would only be one useable LZ for the flight crew: this one. If conditions did not permit a C-130 landing here, traveling to a second or third landing zone would be pointless, because there would be no CIA operative there to pick up.

That was a worry for later.

For now, utilization of the first option meant Tracie would be afforded the easiest and most direct route to Mezhgorye, the small Bashkiri town located just outside the secret facility she would be surveilling. *Everything is relative, though,* she thought. *The definition of 'direct and easy' travel in the Ural Mountains probably bears little resemblance to the same definition almost anywhere else in the world.*

But first things always had to come first. Before worrying about getting to Mezhgorye she had to first find a way off the lake. Among the intel Stallings had provided for each potential landing zone was a crude map worked up by an agency analyst showing the approximate location of the nearest road and its orientation to that particular LZ.

In this case, Tracie estimated that if she were able to exit the lake on a north-northwesterly bearing she should cross the road to Mezhgorye in less than a quarter mile. But a quarter mile of driving through these harsh conditions would not be easy, and Tracie was anxious to get started.

She shifted into first gear and crept along the lakeshore, peering into the forest as she drove. Official sunrise would occur within the next few minutes, but the sky was overcast, thick with clouds, and the trees and mountainous terrain cast everything in a shadowy cloak. It seemed clear the twilight-like conditions would remain until the sun had climbed high into the sky, and maybe even well past that time.

Tracie compensated for the lack of daylight by zigzagging as she drove, angling the Lada toward the forest to illuminate the trees with her headlights, then turning away, driving farther onto the surface of the lake to allow herself to angle back toward the shoreline again.

The trees were dense and thick, packed closely together, and before she had traveled a hundred yards she began to fear she would be unable to find sufficient clearance for the vehicle to exit the ice anywhere. The occasional gaps between trees that were large enough to steer the SUV through were filled with smaller trees and scrub brush, and she suspected that were she to try to ram through the brush, her wheels would be lifted off the ground and traction would disappear.

And then she would be stranded.

The LZ was located close enough to Mezhgorye that hiking into town would present little challenge under normal circumstances. Tracie estimated the distance from LZ to mountain village as barely farther than a typical training run, something she could complete in just a few hours.

But these were not normal circumstances. The bitterly cold January morning temperatures at five thousand feet of elevation on a Soviet mountain would require specialized equipment were she to attempt a hike of more than a few hundred yards, equipment she did not have. Her go bag contained heavily insulated clothing designed to protect against sub-zero temperatures while conducting surveillance, but nothing that would permit traveling long distances on foot under these conditions.

So she continued driving, scrutinizing the shoreline, covering as much ground as possible before turning back toward the middle of the lake and starting again. The wind whistled through the trees, swirling onto the open expanse of lake and kicking up snow eddies, occasionally gusting strongly enough to replicate the near-whiteout conditions experienced by the C-130 flight crew during landing.

Tracie's spirits began to sink. The trees were everywhere, crowding the shoreline, hanging over the lake, bunched together like bristles on a giant's hairbrush. *Dammit. Might be time for Plan B. If only I had a Pla—"*

There.

A small gap in the thick timbers.

Maybe.

She couldn't quite tell if what she thought she could see was an optical illusion. It was an area slightly outside the yellow semicircle cast by her headlights, but it offered the first tantalizing hint of a possible start toward Mezhgorye since the C-130 had disappeared toward Incirlik.

She adjusted her driving path slightly to the right and accelerated, feeling a rising sense of excitement as she closed in on the shoreline. There was definitely an opening in the trees. And what was more, the opening didn't appear to be natural. It looked man-made, like it had been hacked out of the forest at some point in the not-too-distant past.

She slowed again as she neared the opening, approaching it head-on and breaking into a relieved smile. What had at first appeared in the distance to be a small gap in the trees continued as far into the woods as she could see. The path was straight, more or less, and wide enough—barely—to permit passage of the Lada.

It was definitely man-made, a trail or primitive roadway that nearby residents must have cleared at some point to allow them access to the lake for fishing or swimming or boating.

Or whatever.

Tracie didn't care why the trees had been taken down and the area cleared. If it was man-made then it stood to reason the rough trail led to an actual road. This region was so remote, so isolated, that Tracie guessed that road would in all probability be the one leading to Mezhgorye.

And if it weren't, she would worry about that when the time came.

She aimed the SUV into the opening in the trees and hit the gas. The truck clawed its way up the embankment and plunged into the relative darkness of the forest, bouncing and lurching. The cover of snow made the trail appear relatively flat, but in reality it was anything but. It became clear within fifty feet that there had been no grading involved when this track or pathway had been constructed.

Branches scraped the side of the truck, gouging the paint job and slapping at the windows, and she kept going. Tracie ran over something hidden under the snow without a clue it was there, slamming up and over what she guessed was a downed tree, fortunately a small one, and she kept going.

Her fear was that if she stopped the vehicle she would lose traction and become stranded, even with the heavy-duty off-road tires on the Lada. She was committed to her current course of action and come hell or high water would ride it out to its end.

The track's width varied, at times becoming so narrow she thought she might have to reverse course and look for another avenue away from the lake. Then it would widen out again and she would continue on. What had originally appeared to be a straight-line trail hacked out of the forest was actually, Tracie realized, a gradual curve to the left.

To the north-northwest.

The direction of the road to Mezhgorye.

She slipped into a trench and the rear of the vehicle whipped to the right, impacting a tree trunk before being jolted back onto the trail. The crunch of crumpling metal told her she'd damaged the rear fender, offering a stark reminder of her isolation, as if she needed one.

She continued another fifty feet, weighing her options, and then reluctantly eased to a stop. Her intention had been to continue moving forward until either reaching the end of the trail or getting stuck, but the situation changed with the literal fender-bender.

Checking the damage to the Lada now became a top priority. She wanted to be sure a sharp piece of sheet metal wasn't even now wearing through the right rear tire. If it was, she would need to find something to use as a hammer to pound the dent out enough to provide tire clearance. Suffering a flat out here could be a death sentence.

The engine idled softly, sending white plumes of exhaust floating into the frigid morning air. Tracie opened the driver's door and the chill struck her like a baseball bat to the side of the head. The SUV's interior had already warmed enough that the difference in temperature between inside and outside was jarring.

She shivered reflexively and stepped into the snow, sinking almost up to her knees, suddenly grateful for the bitterly cold temperatures. The average for the Urals in early February was minus-four degrees Fahrenheit, and of course temps plunged much lower than that at night and during cold snaps.

But what made for a danger to the human body was a benefit for travel, because even though the snow was relatively deep, it was also light and fluffy. The Lada was able to brush it aside as it moved forward, like a boat cresting the waves while moving through water.

Tracie slogged to the rear of the vehicle. The metal was creased and damaged, but it appeared as though there was still sufficient clearance for the tire to rotate unimpeded. As long as she avoided hitting a second tree she thought she should be fine.

She sighed and scolded herself for allowing her concentration to slip. All it had taken was a half-second's inattention to put herself in a potentially lethal bind.

She retraced her steps to the driver's seat and climbed back behind the wheel. *Here goes nothing,* she thought, slipping the transmission into first gear and easing down on the gas. The truck bucked and slipped and began to slide sideways, exactly as had happened when it struck the tree. This time, Tracie eased off the gas until the tires caught.

She swung the steering wheel right and added power and the truck straightened out on the rough track, then the vehicle again began fighting its way forward. Several hundred feet later the murkiness began to lighten and Tracie's initial thought was that the sun had finally risen high enough in the sky to begin penetrating the thick forest canopy.

But then she realized there was an even better explanation for the sudden increase in visibility: the road was dead ahead. She pumped her fist and pressed a little harder on the accelerator and fought her way through the remaining stretch of forest. She would never know who had cleared the trail from the roadway to the isolated lake, or why they had done so, but she thanked the anonymous Bashkirans all the same.

Seconds later she burst from the trail onto the road and cut the wheel hard to the right. Then she eased to a stop. The road was deserted and barely wider than the cow path she'd just left, but it was paved and relatively clear of snow, and Tracie felt sure it was the one that would lead to Mezhgorye.

She breathed a sigh of relief and continued on.

10

January 31, 1988
9:15 a.m.
Ipatiev Military Research Facility
Mezhgorye, Bashkir

Vladimir Protasov rapped on the closed door with his knuckles and then entered January 3's room without waiting for a response. None was necessary, as the knock was strictly a courtesy.

Vladimir was a civilized person, and as such would conduct himself in a civilized manner. But at this point there was no question—if there ever *had* been a question—about the balance of power between a man shackled to a hospital bed with electrical wires poking out of his head, and another man who was free to come and go as he wished, particularly when the second man was performing experiments on the first.

It was not the test subject's place to prevent Vlad's entrance.

It was not the test subject's place to determine his fate.

It was the test subject's place only to participate in the experimentation process as required.

Vlad stepped into the room and smiled at January 3. "How are we feeling today?"

He expected no answer and received none. The subject gazed up at him in the strange manner Vlad had now come to expect: eyes tracking Vlad's progress around the room while his head remained virtually motionless on his pillow.

Vlad had initially assumed the man's cranial stillness was to minimize pain from the brain surgery, but he had begun to suspect that was not the case. The subject had given up. He knew he would never leave this facility alive, and his depression was so complete he could not be bothered to expend even the minimal energy required to lift his head from his pillow.

No matter. Thus far he had participated fully—if begrudgingly—in the testing protocol, and Vlad was beginning to see signs of light at the end of a very long tunnel. These signs led him to believe he was on the right path, that he could eventually present positive findings to his masters at Lubyanka and be telling the truth, rather than participating in a sham.

This success would take place only after what he knew would be extensive further testing, Vlad refused to kid himself about *that.* He would still be stuck in this drab concrete Soviet military base for a very long time, no matter the results of today's experimentation, or tomorrow's, or next week's or next month's. But he would not deny himself the luxury of optimism; he *could not* deny himself that luxury.

Because the plain fact of the matter was that Vladimir Protosov was every bit as much a prisoner as was January 3. His accommodations were better, there was no question about that. His apartment in Mezhgorye was quite comfortable, and anything he requested—within reason—would be supplied in less than two weeks by the KGB, no small accomplishment given Ipatiev's extreme isolation.

But it was all for show.

Vlad was not stupid; on the contrary, he was highly educated, extremely intelligent, and perceptive to the point of cunning. And the situation was so simple that even the clearly mentally challenged January 3 would have no problem recognizing it: should Vlad decide to leave he would be prevented from doing so.

Therefore he was a prisoner. His cell contained no bars other than the well-stocked, handcrafted oak one in his living room, where he drank every night after work and listened to his beloved Russian opera singers on the stereo: Feodor Chaliapin, and Lev Sibiriakov, and Vladimir Kastorsky.

And as far as prison bars were concerned, what would be the

point of installing any? The Ipatiev Research Facility was located hundreds of kilometers from anywhere, thousands maybe, constructed in an isolated corner of the Ural Mountains, cold and forbidding and inhospitable. Confining Vladimir to a jail cell would be utterly unnecessary when, should he attempt to leave Mezhgorye by automobile, he would run out of fuel long before ever making it to the next town. He would then freeze to death, and he knew it.

And the KGB knew he knew it.

So he soldiered on. At least the work that had drawn him here was fascinating.

*   *   *

Vlad busied himself preparing the testing equipment, doing his best to ignore the unsettled feeling he was getting from January 3's complete silence and total lack of movement. It was that damned stillness that bothered him the most. January 3 had barely moved a muscle since Vlad's entry into the room.

He rolled the wheeled cart to its familiar spot at the end of the subject's bed as he'd done so many times before. He lowered the video screen and turned on the projector. He connected the cables to the electrical wires protruding out of the small burr hole in January 3's skull.

Then he handed the plastic remote to the subject and reminded the man of his obligation in this experiment.

"As I'm sure you recall from yesterday," he said—although he was not at all sure the man remembered, given the extent of his mental deterioration—"images of animals and other familiar objects will be flashed onto the screen in front of you. As each photograph appears, I will announce the name by which the animal or object is commonly known. You will then press either the "I Agree" or the "I Disagree" button on your remote control device. Sometimes the name I announce will be correct, and sometimes it will not. Your only requirement is to differentiate between the two."

Vlad held the subject's gaze and gave him the opportunity to respond, despite feeling certain he would not.

He did not.

Vlad cleared his throat. "Very well," he said, ignoring the awkwardness. "Let us proceed."

* * *

The roots of Russian interest in mind control predated the existence of the Soviet Union, extending all the way back to the 1870s. Almost immediately after the 1917 revolution that deposed the Tsarist autocracy and installed the rule of the proletariat, the government that would eventually grow into the Union of Soviet Socialist Republics expanded such research, funding secret projects designed to utilize mind control methods to expand the influence of the Soviet state.

Modern Soviet research into the subject was known as "Psychotronics," and among other things focused on utilizing covert means to manipulate the thoughts, desires and actions of human beings, either against their will or without their knowledge. Some methods of manipulation were simple, such as shaping subjects' mental state through involuntary ingestion of drugs and/or alcohol, or through the use of torture or physical force and intimidation.

To Vladimir Protasov, methods such as these were simplistic. Barbaric, even, suited more to sixteenth century castle dungeons than to modern scientific endeavor. Vladimir, and others like him, believed the future of psychotronic research lay in the realm of electrical stimulation of the brain.

Extensive research had demonstrated conclusively that human brain function was accomplished through electrical impulses passed between receptors located in the brain tissue. By introducing low-frequency radio waves or electrical currents into certain sections of the brain, Vlad—among others—believed it would be possible to influence human behavior by manipulating the portions of the brain that controlled such behavior.

The difficulty lay in isolating the proper regions of the brain in which to apply electrical stimulation, and then in determining the intensity of the stimulation required to achieve the desired results.

It was a challenging and fascinating subject, and one to which Vlad had devoted his entire adult life. Until being recruited by the KGB last year, his research had been largely theoretical, but his visibility within the Russian scientific community had risen over the decades until it eventually brought him to the attention of Lubyanka.

He'd been unable to decline the offer when approached by KGB representatives, not that it would have mattered if he had. They wanted him to run the project, so he would run the project, period. His enthusiasm for the research had made threats against him or his family unnecessary, but he had known all along the illusion of choice was exactly that—an illusion.

But aside from missing his family, and the knowledge that he was stuck in the Urals for as long as it took to complete his project—minus the two weeks a year he was permitted to return home for vacation—Vladimir figured he had little reason to complain. He was performing critical research in the area of his passion, and would be world-renowned upon the successful completion of his project.

And it *would* be successful.

*   *   *

Vlad realized he'd been daydreaming and he straightened his shoulders, annoyed he'd allowed his attention to wander in front of a test subject. He offered another insincere clinical smile and repeated, "Let us proceed, shall we?"

He thumbed the button on his remote control to display the first slide, watching January 3 carefully to ensure the man focused his attention on the rat filling the screen. Then he adjusted the knob controlling the intensity of the electrical charge being delivered to the subject's brain and pressed a button while announcing, "This is an eagle."

After a moment's hesitation, January 3 thumbed the "I Disagree" button.

Vlad pursed his lips and nodded and made a notation on his pad regarding the intensity of the charge and the subject's response.

Then he adjusted the intensity further and changed the picture on the screen. A snake was now displayed. "This is a snake," Vlad said, and waited for the subject to respond.

11

January 31, 1988
9:55 a.m.
Ipatiev Military Research Facility
Mezhgorye, Bashkir

Typically, the sessions lasted no longer than thirty minutes. Vlad had discovered early on in his research that longer-term stimulation of the brain tissue resulted in extreme exhaustion for the subjects, which in turn led to wildly fluctuating results.

Today, however, he had decided to lengthen the testing period a bit. Progress required sacrifice, and if the price of that progress was a longer nap for January 3 upon completion of the session, well, so be it. The man's entire existence inside this facility was spent on his back, anyway. It wasn't like he would be expected to leap out of bed and perform tiring manual labor, either before *or* after testing.

Vlad punched his controller and a horse flashed up on the screen at the foot of January 3's bed. "This is a cow," he said.

The subject hesitated. He seemed confused, agitated. He dropped the remote control into his lap and raised his hand to his head as if to brush his hair out of his eyes before apparently remembering his skull had been shaved. He clasped his hands together and squeezed them tightly. He separated them and ran them along his blanket-covered thighs.

Then he picked up his remote and very slowly pressed the "I Disagree" button.

A flash of impatience and frustration exploded through Vlad like a lightning bolt. This was not the result he wanted to see. He'd been gradually increasing the level of electrical stimulation to the subject's brain while repeating the obviously false assertion that the animal standing in the middle of a sun-splashed field in the photograph was a cow and not a horse.

The electrical stimulation was not painful to January 3, Vlad was certain of it. The point of feeding the current to this particular portion of the brain was to increase the subject's suggestibility, and to a certain degree, January 3's hesitation was an indication it was working.

But why would the damned subject not respond fully to the treatment? Why could Vlad not find the sweet spot, the perfect level of electrical brain stimulation that would result in total suggestibility? He was close to doing so, he could feel it, and yet he could not quite get over some invisible final hurdle.

And the level of electricity coursing through January 3's brain was becoming dangerously high. Vlad knew there was a finite limit to the brain's ability to tolerate such stimulation, and he knew also that he was approaching that limit.

Quickly.

He eased the dial on the box that resembled an electrical transformer to the right ever so slightly and repeated his statement, forcing a calmness into his voice he most certainly did not feel.

"This is a cow."

Again January 3 fidgeted. Again he dropped the remote into his lap in order to free his hands to make nervous, fluttery gestures. Vlad got the distinct, unsettling impression the subject was unaware he was doing so.

Finally the man picked up his remote and again, moving ever so slowly, either out of confusion or reluctance, pressed, "I Disagree."

Vlad pursed his lips and huffed.

Reached down to the electrical box and cranked the dial further to the right.

Said, "This is a cow," his voice firm and tight and filled with conviction.

January 3 dropped his remote for a third time. He looked from the movie screen to Vlad and back to the screen where the horse continued to stand proudly against a backdrop of rolling hills and blue skies, a few puffy white clouds punctuating the beauty of the scene.

"This is a cow," Vlad repeated, willing January 3 to give him the result he craved. Vlad's fingers twitched impatiently, and then he reached down to the box one last time and increased the level of electrical stimulation again.

The subject's eyes widened. His hands clamped into fists and pounded the bed next to his legs as his mouth snapped closed with an audible *clack*. His head began to shake violently, and then the shaking rolled through his body like a storm cresting the peaks of the Urals. In seconds he was convulsing helplessly. His eyes rolled back in his head, displaying only the whites.

Vlad cursed and slapped his hands together angrily. He flipped the power switch, instantly cutting the flow of electricity to January 3's brain as the subject continued his violent thrashing, muscles contracting and straining against the leather straps securing his arms and legs.

January 3's hands flailed. They could move just inches but the backs of them smashed over and over into the stainless steel bars on either side of the hospital bed, bruising and perhaps even breaking some of the small bones inside.

Cutting the electrical current to the subject's brain seemed to have done nothing to slow the convulsions, and Vlad sighed. He'd seen this result before. January 3 would survive—probably—but his usefulness as a test subject was finished. His brain had been fried, quite literally, and whatever progress Vlad had made would be lost forever.

Vlad would now be forced to start over. Brain surgery to implant the electrodes, then a brief recovery period for the subject followed by the early stages of testing.

Again.

This was the scientific method, the incremental nature of progress. Trial and error was the cornerstone of advancement, the building block for which there was no substitute, and Vlad understood that no matter how discouraging this moment was—and it *was* discouraging, extremely so—*progress had been made.*

Progress would continue to be made.

He turned toward the door, doing his best to ignore the snapping of the leather straps, and the clanking of the bars as January 3's hands smashed into them, and the animal gasping and grunting of the subject as his body continued to convulse.

Vlad stalked out of the room, pulling the door firmly closed behind him and hurrying toward his office, making haste as much to escape the infernal noise coming from January 3's room as to settle in at his desk to transcribe session notes. But the notes must be transcribed, and the sooner the better, while everything was fresh in his mind.

After that, Vlad had a telephone call to make.

12

January 31, 1988
10:40 a.m.
Ipatiev Military Research Facility
Mezhgorye, Bashkir

Vladimir Protasov had assumed that by the time he finished transcribing session notes from this morning's debacle with January 3, the sense of firm determination he felt regarding his upcoming telephone call would have waned. After all, he'd made similar calls in the past year, several of them in fact, all to no avail, and his personality tended toward reasoned caution rather than fiery conflict.

But he was surprised to discover that was not the case. He finished handwriting his notes and then slid the notebook into his top desk drawer, more convinced than ever that the damaged mental state of his subjects was negatively affecting his project.

Every last one of the men who'd been delivered to his lab suffered from mental illness, alcoholism or drug abuse, most a clear combination of the three. Virtually all were homeless and shiftless and suffering from malnutrition. They were untrusting and untrustworthy, the very definition of the dregs of society, and Vlad found the notion that he was expected to glean reliable test results from subjects as damaged as these to be offensive in the extreme.

He'd had enough. He was well into his second year sacrificing precious time with his family and a cushy career in academia, where he was lauded for his achievements and held up as a model scientist, for a life of asceticism and failure in the Ural Mountains.

He deserved better, and he was damned well going to insist on it.

He picked up the office phone and dialed the number for his KGB contact, a man named Kopalev. A series of clicks and beeps and other noises Vlad had never heard a telephone line make before his arrival at this remote facility ensued, and he waited patiently for the call to go through.

Vlad had been born in Moscow and spent his entire life living and working inside the Soviet Union, and while he didn't think he'd ever been the subject of intense KGB scrutiny prior to his acceptance of the head research position on this project, he'd always known the possibility existed. He was certain he was being closely monitored now, and he amused himself while waiting for the call to be answered by trying to guess how many people, and in how many different locations, might be listening in at this very moment.

He settled on four, give or take.

Eventually an aide to Kopalev answered the line, and Vlad was forced to endure another wait while his request for a telephone audience with the Great Man was considered.

Kopalev was a colonel in the Red Army, but of much greater importance to Vlad was his position as Vlad's direct supervisor on this project. It meant Colonel Kopalev was KGB, which meant he was as dangerous as an avalanche in a mountain pass, which meant he must be treated with the softest of kid gloves.

Vlad was beyond caring about any of that. *He* would be judged on the success or failure of this project, and in ways that were extremely uncomfortable to consider, should his psychotronic research be deemed a failure. The KGB was not known for their forgiving attitude.

This, of course, meant it was imperative the project succeed, which meant Vlad might occasionally be forced to take actions he would, in other circumstances, go to great lengths to avoid.

Actions like making this telephone call, and pushing men who in most cases were better off not being pushed.

The line was finally picked up and a gruff voice said, "Good morning, Dr. Protasov. I assume you are calling to report significant progress on your project?"

So much for small talk, Vlad thought. "Good morning, Colonel. The project is proceeding more or less as expected, yes."

"'More or less as expected' does not sound very much like 'significant progress' to me, Doctor, although I would be the first to admit my background is not in the sciences. Perhaps 'more or less as expected' is worthy of the heartiest congratulations. Perhaps even a celebration is warranted by your joyful announcement of 'more or less as expected.'"

He was being made fun of. When he answered, his tone was less cordial than it probably should have been. "The scientific process is rarely a straight-line graph, Colonel."

A note of annoyance crept into Kopalev's voice. "As I said, I am not a scientist. I am merely a patriot, working to advance the cause of the people in any way I can. Please explain."

Vlad reminded himself to tread carefully. "Certainly, Colonel. I merely meant that while the general trend of progress on this project is upward, there are of course always setbacks. It is to be expected in the course of any scientific endeavor."

"Setbacks."

"Yes, sir. But as I said, the general trend is upward."

"Are you calling today to report some sort of setback, Doctor?"

"Not exactly."

"It seems up is down in the scientific world, because that sounds a lot like a yes."

"Sir, I understand I have made this request in the past, but I really must reinforce it once again: it is critical we do our testing on the highest quality subjects available. When we work with subjects possessing diminished mental capacity, we run the risk of generating inaccurate results. These results may vary wildly from what we would learn from testing on superior subjects. The results could be so inaccurate even as to cause a project to stall entirely."

"I see. Is this your way of telling me, Doctor Protasov, that you are not making the general upward trend of progress as you claimed just moments ago?" Kopalev's annoyed tone had changed to one of suspicion, and Vlad swallowed heavily. This was not going the way he had hoped.

He forced a professional blandness into his voice that projected a sense of calm he did not feel. "Oh, no, Colonel, not at all. We *are* making progress here. Why, just today, I discovered—"

"Doctor Protasov, I am a busy man. I do not wish to know the specifics of your research, nor would I even understand such specifics, in all likelihood. And if I decide I would like to learn those specifics, I can read them in your weekly status reports. Unless, of course, you are not including all relevant information in those reports."

"No sir. I mean, yes sir. I mean, of course I am including everything in my status reports. They are as accurate and complete as they can possibly be." Vlad tried to inject a note of righteous anger into his voice but realized he came off sounding exactly the way he felt—terrified.

"Then there is no need to discuss specifics over the telephone. Please, Doctor, let us skip this tiresome dance and get to the point. Why are you calling me?"

"I am calling to reiterate my request for more suitable test subjects. The homeless men and addicts you have been sending me are simply not equipped, physically or mentally, to endure the rigors of the testing process. Their diminished capacity makes acquiring scientifically significant results from brain tissue manipulation extremely difficult to achieve."

"What would you have me do, Doctor? Enter the homes and businesses of Moscow residents at random and remove the strongest and healthiest of them, shipping them into the mountains for you to drill into their skulls?"

"Well, no sir, but I—"

"Perhaps we could start with *your* family, Doctor. Would that make you happy? You have a son who is a young adult, do you not? Maybe he would make a suitable test subject for you. Maybe we could even use your wife. I understand that to this point we have limited our testing to males, but perhaps the project would receive a boost from testing on women."

"No, Colonel, you misunderstand me. I did not mean to suggest you raid people's homes and remove them forcibly to take part in an experimental procedure."

"I think what you're saying," Kopalev growled, his voice low and soft and dangerous, "is you want to be sure *your* family is left alone."

"Well of course, sir. My family, along with others that—"

"I understand your point perfectly, Doctor Protasov. And I have good news for you."

Vlad had risen in panic at the suggestion that they begin harvesting members of his own family for testing. Now he slumped back into his desk chair. He closed his eyes and ran a hand shakily over his forehead. His heart was beating wildly and adrenaline flooded his system and he almost forgot his boss was awaiting a response.

"Good news?"

"That's right, Doctor. In fact, given the nature of this telephone call, I believe you will find it wonderful news indeed."

Vlad realized the man was toying with him, teasing him like a sadistic cat might tease a mouse whose legs he'd broken and who he'd decided to torture for awhile before finishing him off.

He realized it but didn't have the stomach to challenge the KGB man.

He supposed that was the point.

"What is the good news, Colonel?" He was now unable to disguise the shakiness in his voice.

"We have a subject en route to your laboratory that quite nicely fits the qualifications you seek. He is young and strong, intelligent and quick-witted. He will make a fine addition to the project."

Vlad's ears perked up despite his terror. "That *is* outstanding news, sir, thank you. Where did the subject come from? Where did you get him?"

"That is irrelevant to this telephone call, is it not?"

"Well, yes sir, I suppose. But the more information we have on our test subjects, they more successful I expect testing to be."

"This subject will be accompanied by a packet outlining all we know about him, exactly as your other subjects have been."

"Very good, sir. Thank you."

"You're welcome Doctor. Contrary to what you seem to believe, I have the greatest interest in seeing your project succeed. It is my goal to assist you in any way possible."

"I appreciate that, Colonel Kopalev. And may I say, I think it's clear that—"

"Oh, and Doctor?" Kopalev ignored Vlad, interrupting as though he'd not even spoken.

Vlad swallowed his anger, understanding instinctively that he'd just dodged a very large bullet and it would be unwise to tempt fate a second time. "Yes, Colonel?"

"Given what you told me about the importance of mental capacity, and given that I am providing you with a highly qualified subject with which to work…"

Vlad swallowed heavily. He thought he knew where this was going, and would have given almost anything not to answer. But it was obvious Kopalev was awaiting a response, and Vlad knew he had no choice but to offer one.

"Yes, sir?"

"From my perspective, this project seems to be floundering a bit. Lubyanka has invested significantly, in terms of both time and money, in your research and we have thus far received nothing of value in return."

"But sir, I—"

"Perhaps what you require to be successful is the proper motivation."

Oh, no. Vlad had thought he knew where Kopalev was going but he'd been wrong. Very wrong. "Oh, no sir, believe me, I am properl—"

"Perhaps giving you so much freedom to run the project in your own way was a mistake. Perhaps you require a more hands-on approach. Do you believe that to be the case, Doctor?"

"No, sir, I am quite confident I can—"

"I thought so. I do appreciate your willingness to take such an honest, unvarnished look at yourself and your shortcomings, Doctor."

"But Colonel, I—"

"Let me review my schedule and see when I can make it out there. Please hold."

"What? Make it out here? Sir, you misunderstand, you do not need to—"

The line went dead and Vlad sat frozen in his chair, horrified at the sudden turn the conversation had taken. Colonel Kopalev was a powerful man, Vlad knew that much just based on things he'd heard and read in reports since beginning this project. Vlad's assistant Yuri was a rock, a stone-faced sociopath as far as Vlad was concerned, and fear radiated out of the man like a black cloud at the mere mention of Kopalev's name.

And now the KGB man was planning a trip here? To "motivate" Vlad? A chill ran down his spine and he realized he needed the toilet. Badly. Maybe he could—

The line clicked loudly and then Kopalev was back. "Are you still there, Doctor?"

Deep breath. Show no fear. "Yes, Colonel, I am still here, but believe me, you do not need to—"

"I have good news, would you like to hear it?"

"Uh…of course."

"I have managed to move some things around on my schedule and have freed up a few days to visit with you. I look forward to seeing the progress you have made with my own two eyes, and to helping motivate you to achieve the greatest possible success."

"Uh…"

"Is that not wonderful news, Doctor?"

"Yes. Of course. Wonderful."

"My aides will coordinate the specifics of my arrival in the Urals with your base commander, but you can expect to see me very soon. I am truly looking forward to speaking in person. Face to face. Man to man. The personal touch is far preferable to a telephone conversation, don't you agree, Doctor Protasov?"

Vlad could barely breathe. Could barely think. He had never wanted anything more in his life than he wanted to hang up the phone right now.

"Doctor? Are you still with me?"

"Yes. Yes, of course. I am here. I look forward to seeing you."

"Good. It is settled. I will be there as soon as possible. In the meantime…"

"Yes?"

"In the meantime, given your complaints regarding the quality of test subjects I have provided, and given the fact that—"

"I was not complaining, sir. I was—"

"And given the fact that I am providing you with a highly qualified test subject who will arrive shortly at your facility, I fully expect that when we meet in person, you will have even better, more positive results to share with me."

"Uh…of course. So do I."

"I fully expect that, Doctor. Am I making myself clear?"

"Yes, Colonel. Crystal clear. However, I think it is important to remember—"

The line went dead.

Kopalev had hung up on him.

Vlad returned the telephone to its cradle and lowered his head to his hands. Making this telephone call might well have been the worst mistake he had ever made.

He sat at his desk for a long time contemplating that possibility.

Eventually he rose and got back to work. What choice did he have?

13

February 1, 1988
8:35 a.m.
The mountains outside Mezhgorye, Bashkir

After breaking through the tree line yesterday, Tracie had emerged on a lonely road. She wasted no time aiming north and hitting the gas, convinced she would come across a sign sooner rather than later confirming her belief that she was on the correct route to Mezhgorye.

And she was right. Within a mile—during which time she saw exactly zero vehicles on the road and no signs of habitation anywhere along the route—she was rewarded with a road sign indicating Mezhgorye was thirty kilometers ahead.

She smiled and drove twenty of those thirty kilometers before pulling to the side of the deserted road and leaving the truck idling. Mezhgorye was a small village, and more importantly it was located just outside a secret Soviet military facility that had been hidden from U.S. surveillance for who knew how many years. The arrival of a young civilian woman traveling alone would likely not go unnoticed.

The truck was small and cramped, but she would make do. Its interior was warm, which by default made it much more desirable for what she had in mind than the brutal cold outside. She reached into her go bag and rummaged around until finding a CIA-provided Red Army uniform. Then she changed quickly, donning the uniform and packing away the clothing she'd worn on her transatlantic flight.

The extreme isolation of Mezhgorye and its proximity to the Soviet base meant there was virtually no chance a stranger would enter the town without having some form of business at the base. The safest bet would be to hide in plain sight.

A Russian Army officer—even a female officer, a relative rarity in Soviet society—would engender respect among most citizens, or at least minimize the likelihood of too many people asking intrusive questions. The Soviet society was a closed one, its people paranoid in many ways and anxious to avoid the attention of their government. After more than seventy years of Communist rule, Soviet citizens knew the best course of action in almost every situation was to see nothing, ask no questions, and mind their own business.

Tracie changed in five minutes and then continued on, arriving twenty minutes after that in a small village, picturesque by Soviet standards, seemingly plunked down in this location on the side of the Ural Mountains for no particular reason. The boring, utilitarian square cement cube, so typical of Soviet-era construction, was nowhere to be found. Instead, the village resembled a community in the Swiss Alps, with beautiful A-frame wood structures built to withstand year after year of heavy snowfall.

Tracie drove immediately to what was clearly a family-run inn located on the outskirts of town. She parked the Lada in a small lot containing only one other vehicle and then marched inside with all the confidence befitting an officer of the Soviet Army.

The office was cramped and old, a relic of a bygone era, the 1950s or maybe even earlier. Perhaps predictably, scenic photographs of snow-covered mountain vistas covered the walls, and from a hidden radio came the sound of scratchy big-band music from an American artist Tracie recognized but couldn't quite identify. Glenn Miller, maybe.

An older woman was busying herself behind a counter the size of the bar in Marshall Fulton's living room when she entered. A bell jangled above the door, announcing the arrival of a guest on the off chance the innkeeper might not have noticed the blast of freezing cold air.

The woman completed whatever task she'd been occupied with and then raised her eyes to welcome her guest. They widened when she took in the Red Army uniform, but she covered her surprise well and said, "Welcome to Mezhgorye," in halting Russian.

Tracie breathed a sigh of relief. Between her CIA training, her background in linguistics, and her extensive experience the past seven-plus years working in and around the Soviet Union, Tracie was passably familiar with all Russian dialects and nearly fluent in the most common ones. But the co-official languages in this region were Russian and Bashkir.

She felt certain that "co-official" could only mean one thing: the Soviets had installed Cyrillic as an official language after occupying their satellite nation, but in reality the natives all spoke the language of their heritage, which was Bashkir, a Turkic language and one with which Tracie was unfamiliar.

Russian was clearly a second language for the innkeeper, one she had probably adopted late in life and with reluctance, but had done so out of necessity when the Soviets constructed the military base down the road. She had seen Tracie's uniform and made the obvious assumption it inspired.

Tracie smiled tightly in an attempt to project an air of efficiency. She marched to the desk and said, "Good morning. I will require a room for a few days."

"Of course," the woman said. She lifted a guest register and dropped it onto the surface before spinning it around to face Tracie. "And how long will you be with us?"

Tracie scrawled *Lieutenant Olga Koruskaya* as illegibly as possible into the book and said, "It all depends how long it takes to perform my audit." She felt confident the old woman would not question what exactly Tracie might be auditing. She would assume it was related to the base and treat the subject as one of those things best left alone.

Her assumption was proven accurate when the woman offered a bland smile. Her disinterest could not have been plainer.

Tracie said, "If it is acceptable, I will pay in advance for a five day stay. If I leave Mezhgorye sooner, I assume you will have no problem refunding?"

"Of course," the woman repeated. She seemed comfortable in

her ability to say the phrase in Russian, using it as a go-to filler in the conversation.

Tracie paid her in Russian Rubles. The innkeeper swept the money into an ancient cash drawer and then glanced at the guest register before closing it and whisking it away. She offered no comment at the name Tracie had written, nor did she request any form of identification, likely assuming the odds of anyone appearing in this remote village in a Red Army uniform who was not who she claimed to be were practically nil.

Tracie thanked the woman and received directions to her room. She took her key and her bag and disappeared into a small but surprisingly comfortable bedchamber for several hours of much-needed sleep.

By the time she awoke, darkness had fallen. She dressed quickly and found a quiet restaurant, then spent the next few hours familiarizing herself as much as possible with Mezhgorye. While doing so, she worked her way slowly north in the Lada, eventually leaving the village behind and continuing up the mountain.

She was careful to avoid any roads that would take her too close to the Soviet base, which loomed to the west like a cancer. There would be guard posts and patrols and Red Army sentries with automatic weapons, and drawing attention to herself was the last thing she wanted to do.

Her mission was to observe, not to engage.

The base's isolated location had served to keep it hidden from prying American eyes for years, so obviously placing it deep in the Ural Mountains had worked to the Soviets' advantage. But with the inadvertent admission of its existence by two captured KGB assassins, Tracie felt she could use the seclusion to her own advantage, which was why she found herself creeping up the side of a mountain hours after sunset inside a Soviet-made SUV.

Finding the proper perch from which to conduct her surveillance was a job best suited to daylight, but time was at a premium and Tracie wanted to be in position at first light. So the prep work would have to be done in the dark. Not an ideal situation, but she'd dealt with worse.

And as it turned out, finding the right spot took less time than she'd expected. The road north out of Mezhgorye was poorly maintained and even less traveled than the one she'd come into town on. The area was barren and unpopulated. She pulled the Lada off the road behind a screen of trees—the muscular tires and four-wheel-drive transmission was coming in even handier than she'd expected—and within an hour of hiking had settled on a surveillance location.

Then she'd gone back to town and slept.

This morning she sat just inside the tree line along a ridge overlooking the Soviet facility. Dressed in camouflage all-weather gear and carrying food and water, Tracie hunkered down just as the sky was beginning to lighten, prepared to spend a full day unlocking the secrets of the base that had been unknown to the United States until just weeks ago.

14

January 31, 1988
Time unknown
Location unknown

Ryan Smith had been trying to convince himself that he could deal with his new reality. He'd been working on exactly that from the moment he was forced into the back seat of a car outside a Moscow tavern.

He should have known better than to leave the bar with a pretty young woman who'd approached him out of the blue and begun chatting him up, should have assumed the worst in that situation rather than the best. Hell, he should never have *been* in that situation in the first place. He knew as much.

But living and working under deep cover inside enemy territory was a lonely business. The fear of slipping up was constant, of accidentally blurting out a phrase in English, or of saying the wrong thing to the wrong person and being uncovered as an American spy.

All he'd wanted was a little companionship, a few drinks with people his own age and a couple of hours away from the stifling responsibility of being the eyes and ears of the United States intelligence community in the home of the most dangerous adversary the nation had seen since the end of World War II.

What he'd gotten instead was his own worst nightmare.

Ryan had known capture by the Soviets was a possibility, had accepted that risk as the price of making a difference in the world. And he'd tried to prepare as best he could for that prospect before ever getting into the field. In fact, a fairly significant portion of his initial training two years ago had focused on what to expect from the enemy should be ever fall into their hands.

It was training all operational assets received, and Ryan had passed his with flying colors. But his method of dealing with the possibility of KGB capture had been to approach it as a theoretical situation, a game to be beaten, a puzzle to be solved.

Now that the theoretical situation had become hard reality, he realized he was nowhere near as prepared for it as he'd thought. He tried to present a stoic front to his captors, but fear was now his constant companion. The shaking hands, the queasiness in the pit of his stomach, the nearly crippling panic attacks, the sweat soaking into his shirt, it was all of that and more.

He would never again see his parents. Never tell his mom he loved her.

He would never again play softball on a Friday night and then grab a few beers with his buddies.

He would never settle down and get married, never have children.

He was destined to die alone and unacknowledged deep inside the USSR, just another nameless and faceless enemy of the Soviet State.

He closed his eyes and breathed deeply, choking back the bile that had begun to rise in his throat, forcing a calmness into his expression that he did not feel. The last five days had been a whirlwind of near-constant travel, of shouted accusations and endless interrogations, of good cop/bad cop questioning and ongoing threats of public execution.

Ryan thought he had acquitted himself well thus far. He'd given the Soviets nothing, insisting even in the face of hard evidence to the contrary that he was simply a young man traveling the world, that he'd sneaked into Russia on a whim and out of a misguided sense of adventure, nothing else.

The story was preposterous, of course. The KGB had him dead to rights. They couldn't prove their charges beyond a shadow of a doubt, but what the hell difference did that make? It was their country and their system, and they could do whatever they wanted to him, whenever they wanted to do it.

So far, that had meant moving him around.

A lot.

He'd been blindfolded and driven to a location in Moscow for his initial questioning, of that he was certain. The car ride hadn't lasted long enough to take him anywhere else.

He'd been tired and scared and a little drunk, and he'd known the Soviets would want to take advantage of his shock and confusion. There had been bright lights and angry interrogators and promises to shoot him in the head and dump his body in a trash-littered parking lot if he didn't admit to being an American spy.

He'd admitted nothing.

By the time the initial questioning ended, Ryan was more than frightened and exhausted; he was hung over as well. The Russians moved him immediately and he dozed in the cargo box of a truck, hands cuffed behind his back, body bouncing and flopping as the drivers seemed to take the bumpiest roads they could find, and at the highest speeds manageable.

Two of the longest days of Ryan Smith's life followed. He was kept constantly on the move. He slept when he could, denied accusations of espionage over and over. They were made by different people and in different places, but they were all essentially the same: that Ryan Smith was an enemy of Mother Russia and would be dealt with accordingly.

He denied them all, exactly as he'd been taught to do. But he knew he couldn't hold out forever. He wasn't close to breaking yet, but he would get there eventually, everyone did, and his worst fear was that the Russians would force him into a televised admission of espionage, an admission that would be broadcast around the world and that his horrified parents would see on the nightly news.

And then the Soviets would execute him.

After the second day of travel and questioning, the situation changed. It wasn't a dramatic change, but to Ryan, who had become hyper-aware of every element of his captivity, it was noteworthy. The travel continued but the questioning stopped, more or less.

He began to suspect the Russians had arrived at a decision about what to do with him, which opened up a whole new range of terrifying possibilities. Things had definitely shifted in terms of the KGB's actions. Instead of carting him from one location to the next, chaining him to a series of tables and marching interrogator after interrogator out to take their shots at breaking him, his captors loaded him into a truck—they always moved him in the back of a covered cargo truck, although why they would do that instead of using a car Ryan had no idea—and moved him again.

This time, though, instead of a one or two or three hour trip between KGB stations, they drove at least six hours, taking a short break after that time to refuel and allow Ryan to stretch his legs, and to take a leak. The six-hour driving time was a guess, since they'd confiscated Ryan's watch. It may have been longer.

The point, though, was that this trip felt different, like perhaps he was now headed to some final, more permanent destination, and that destination was nowhere close by.

Ryan received what he took to be confirmation of his theory when he was tossed once again into the truck immediately following his bathroom break, and the vehicle hit the road for another marathon driving session.

The condition of the thoroughfares was passable in and around major cities such as Moscow, but Russia was vast, and great swaths of its infrastructure were crumbling from neglect. Most of the roads the truck was now traveling were bumpy and curvy, poorly engineered to begin with and then haphazardly maintained.

Ryan's hands remained cuffed behind his back, and a length of thick chain kept his ankles shackled to an iron strut bolted into the truck bed. With no seat belts and only a rough bench on which to sit, he was at the mercy of the winding roads and sadistic driver, being tossed side-to-side, the risk of a broken neck a constant.

Eventually he decided to forego the bench entirely. Instead of sitting on it he crouched on the floor below it, jamming his feet against the strut and pushing himself against the back wall of the cab. In this way he was able to minimize the likelihood of cracking his skull open by being thrown across the cargo hold.

But it was a tiring way to sit, and a dangerous way to travel, which he supposed was the point.

And he was bitterly cold. Perhaps that was the reason the KGB was using a truck to transport him when a car would have served the purpose just fine. The rear cargo area was unheated, and February in Russia featured temperatures that could take a man's breath away, and not in a good way.

Again, that was probably the point.

The Russian day was overcast, grey and dank. The thick canvas covering the cargo bed included a flap at the rear, approximating a door, through which Ryan was loaded and unloaded. His captors had left the flap unhooked and as it blew in the breeze, he could see darkness was falling quickly in the Russian countryside.

Temperatures would soon plummet, and as cold as it had been riding in the back of the truck during the day, Ryan knew his situation was about to get much more dire.

He wondered if the plan was to drive through the night.

He wondered if he would still be alive by morning if that *was* the plan.

The truck began to slow and Ryan felt a flash of hope. It was probably irrational, and he *knew* it was probably irrational but he didn't care. Maybe the day's misery was about to end. Maybe he could get at least a few hours of warmth and sleep.

The vehicle turned off the main road—if the pothole-strewn cow path they'd been traveling for the past several hours could even be called a road—and the driver slowed further, eventually screeching to a stop. The crunch of boots on frozen ground signaled the approach of someone on the driver's side, and then muffled voices floated through the canvas.

After a moment the driver shifted into gear and the truck lurched forward. The canvas flapped open and Ryan caught a glimpse of an armed sentry reentering a small guard shack. They'd driven onto a military installation.

The truck slowed again and then ground to a halt, and Ryan's previous optimism vanished in an instant. He'd known it was unfounded but hadn't been able to stop himself from getting his hopes up. The smell of diesel fuel assaulted his senses, almost eye-wateringly strong, and he knew they weren't stopping for the night.

They were barely stopping at all.

They were refueling again for the third time and would be continuing on. The two men in the front of the truck were obviously trading off driving, probably dozing inside the cab between stints at the wheel. It had become clear they were going to continue virtually non-stop until arriving wherever the hell the KGB had decided to transport their newfound prize. It was probably uncomfortable duty for the drivers but it was almost unbearable for Ryan.

The driver's door creaked open and then slammed shut, and a moment later one of the Russians appeared at the rear flap. He unlocked the chain binding Ryan's ankles to the iron U-bolt and then gruffly signaled him to exit the truck.

Ryan slid along the floor and then dropped to the ground, shivering uncontrollably. The driver escorted him to a restroom while the driver's partner fueled the truck.

A sense of hopelessness threatened to overwhelm Ryan as he relieved himself in the tiny bathroom that was barely more than an outhouse. A portable heater struggled to warm the shack but mostly failed.

He looked desperately for a way out, but the bathroom had only one entrance, and a Russian soldier armed with a Makarov semi-auto pistol was standing on the other side of it.

And even if Ryan could somehow manage to escape, what would be the point? His handcuffs had been removed to allow him to pee, but the heavy length of chain remained shackled to his ankles, and this installation was located deep in the Russian wilderness. He was poorly dressed for the weather conditions and would likely not survive the night in the brutal cold even if he could somehow get the drop on his captor and make his way off the base.

Trying to hide on the base would be pointless.

Thoughts of escape were pointless.

Everything is pointless, Ryan thought miserably.

He zipped up and exited the bathroom, stopping for just a moment to remove the hopelessness from his features and replace it with bland nonchalance. He would not give the Soviets the satisfaction of knowing they'd broken him this quickly and easily. He thought about his father, who had served in the infantry during World War Two and who was one of the toughest men Ryan had ever known. He focused on Dad and on making him proud, even though the reality was his father would never learn Ryan's fate.

He clamped his jaw tightly shut and exited the bathroom. The soldier escorted him back to the truck and secured the chain.

The escort disappeared without a word. A moment later he reappeared holding a blanket to his chest. "You are not supposed to have this," he said in Russian, "but what my superiors do not know will not hurt them, eh?"

Ryan focused on the blanket with the single-minded intensity of a starving man admiring a steak dinner. When the guard tossed it to him and then returned to the truck's cab, Ryan felt a rush of gratitude unlike anything he'd ever experienced. He'd heard of the Stockholm syndrome but had never understood how a captive could feel anything but a burning hatred toward the people who had taken him.

Now he understood.

He wrapped himself in the blanket and felt marginally warmer, although he continued to shiver violently.

The truck's diesel engine coughed to life, and moments later they were back on the road, churning through the gathering night toward an unknown destination.

15

February 1, 1988
2:15 p.m.
The mountains outside Mezhgorye, Bashkir

Tracie had arrived at her surveillance location just as the first hints of light were brightening the skies behind the mountains to the east. Daybreak was an extended affair, as the sun seemed to climb only with extreme reluctance. Eventually it cast sufficient light for her to see through her binocs and she got down to business.

Her initial impression as she scanned the facility was that the place didn't seem big enough. It appeared somehow incomplete. A large sign erected out by the road read

IPATIEV RESEARCH FACILITY
NO PUBLIC ACCESS
ARMED GUARDS – KEEP OUT!

The words were posted in Cyrillic block letters large enough for her to see clearly through her binoculars, even from this distance, and while no mention was made about the facility being under military control, none was necessary. The guard towers looming over the property and the twin rows of barbed wire fencing were enough to pass that message loud and clear.

Clusters of barracks dotted the landscape, built in the traditional Soviet style: long, low and drab. But the thing that struck Tracie most forcefully as she watched the workers pouring out of the housing complex to begin the day was that there were far too many of them than would be required to staff the facility based on the number of other structures dotting the landscape inside the security fence. There just weren't that many buildings.

Something was off with this place, and the most likely explanation was that Aaron Stallings' theory was correct: any significant work being done here was taking place underground. So how the hell was she supposed to learn any of its secrets through a pair of binoculars from a half-mile away?

Tracie shelved that concern for the moment and examined the remainder of the facility. It was an odd feeling knowing she was the first American ever to lay eyes on it.

The base had been hacked out of the heavy mountain wilderness surrounding Mezhgorye. Viewed from a distance, it resembled a small bald spot made all the more noticeable by the long hair on the remainder of an aging hippie's head. The buildings had been constructed relatively recently but were not brand-new. The signs of weathering from the vicious mountain winters were plain, and the intel extracted from the pair of Soviet assassins back at Langley—that the base had undergone initial construction in the 1970s—seemed accurate for the condition of the structures.

A pair of chain-link fences encircled the installation. Gauging the height of the fences was difficult from a distance, but Tracie estimated each at better than ten feet. Both were topped with rolls of razor wire.

The area between the pair of fences was literally a dead zone: a fifty-foot-wide no-man's land, similar to what she had encountered last month entering the closed Russian city of Kremlyov. She knew that buried beneath the barren ground separating the fences would be a series of sensors designed to detect the vibration produced by footfalls. The sensors would alert sentries to the approach of any unexpected visitors.

Not that it would even be possible for anyone to slip through or scale the outer set of fencing undetected. A series of guard towers, large and high and intimidating, had been constructed at regular intervals surrounding the camp. The towers were positioned just inside the inner ring of fencing and from Tracie's position it seemed clear that every square foot of space inside the facility was within view of at least one guard tower. In most cases two or more towers offered coverage from multiple perspectives.

The setup was similar to what would be seen at a maximum-security prison, and the feeling of strangeness Tracie had experienced earlier returned. There was clearly more to this place than met the eye. What could be going on inside this facility that would justify such stringent security measures? The above ground portion of the base looked like nothing more imposing than a drab, dreary Russian office complex.

Tracie nibbled protein bars and sipped water she'd stored inside a small cooler—not to keep it cold but rather to prevent it from freezing solid in the near-zero-degree Fahrenheit temperatures—as she observed the activities of the camp.

Most of the workers leaving the housing complex had moved to one of three separate structures dotting the base, buildings that appeared as bland and anonymous as the rest. They resembled warehouses in the shape of oversized Quonset huts, rusting metallic buildings with curved roofs and few windows.

The workers entered the buildings, clustering around the narrow doorways and then funneling inside. The three Quonset hut-like buildings drew most of Tracie's attention for two reasons: first, they were the locations into which the majority of the workers disappeared, and second, virtually all the other structures inside the facility were readily identifiable.

There was a mess hall located a short distance from the housing units. A PX, or Post Exchange, basically a small store at which the base's residents could shop, had been constructed directly across a quadrangle from the dining hall, both buildings nestled amidst the residence units. A recreation center had been constructed next to a small movie theatre.

Occupying a separate area of the base but within walking distance of the residence units was what Tracie took to be the administrative complex. This would be where the Soviet base commander and his staff would operate. It was also easily identifiable because virtually everyone entering those buildings wore Red Army uniforms of various ranks, while the people who trekked the longer distance to the big Quonset-type structures appeared to be dressed mostly in civilian clothing beneath their heavy winter coats.

The number of people entering the administrative zone equated roughly to what Tracie guessed would be required to ensure the continuing operation of a base consisting of the number of workers she had observed. But assuming those workers were civilians, what would they be doing on a secure military base constructed in the middle of nowhere?

They had to be researchers. Scientists of some sort. And given the proper support, she supposed scientific research could be conducted anywhere. But wouldn't it be prohibitively expensive to ship that support via a small rural road to the middle of the Ural Mountains as opposed to, say, utilizing a research facility in Moscow or Leningrad or Stalingrad?

She shook her head and set down her binoculars. Removed her gloves to unwrap a protein bar and then quickly slipped her hands back inside them as she munched on her snack, lost in thought. This first day of surveillance seemed to be raising more questions than it answered. She pictured Aaron Stallings thrumming his fingers on his desk impatiently and she smiled.

The day had warmed nicely—relatively speaking—with the bright sun beating down on the six thousand foot elevation, raising the temperature almost to fifteen degrees Fahrenheit. But it wasn't even midafternoon yet and the sun had already started its long slide toward the horizon. Soon darkness would fall, arriving with shocking swiftness compared to the lengthy struggle it had taken the sun to rise in the morning.

And once that happened, the temperatures would plummet. Even dressed as she was in highly insulated survival gear, Tracie knew she would become extremely uncomfortable should she remain exposed to the elements. She decided she would do some nighttime surveillance within twenty-four to forty-eight hours if daytime work revealed as little in terms of generating useful intel as today's had.

But it would not take place tonight.

She swallowed the last of her protein bar and sighed softly. She had well under a week in the Urals to gather intel before meeting her extraction team in the C-130, and nearly two full days had already slipped away. She wasn't the slightest bit closer to completing her mission than she had been when she stepped out of the airplane and onto the frozen surface of the lake yesterday. That kind of performance wasn't going to cut it.

The mountain shadows were lengthening as she lifted the binocs to her eyes and resumed surveillance. Instantly she perked up, grateful she'd chosen this moment to return her attention to the base.

Because a truck was approaching the front gate.

This was noteworthy. In nearly eight hours spent camped on the side of a mountain peering down at the secret Soviet installation, not a single vehicle had entered or departed. Not one. Cars had driven around inside the base, and a few had passed the facility on their way into or out of Mezhgorye, but the facility had maintained an unbroken isolation from the village.

Until now.

Tracie watched with interest as the cargo truck turned off the main road and crept along the paved drive leading to a sophisticated-looking guard shack placed at the front gate. The vehicle was slightly larger than a full-sized American pickup truck. The interior of the cargo bed was invisible, concealed by a dirty canvas covering, so there was no way to know what might be inside.

A sentry stepped out of the guardhouse as the truck eased to a stop. The driver rolled down his window and handed a clipboard to the soldier, who glanced at it for approximately three-tenths of a second and then returned it. He made a comment to the driver and both men shared a laugh.

The sentry started walking back toward the guardhouse but then he stopped and asked the driver a question. The driver answered and the guard nodded his head and then walked to the rear of the truck. He lifted the canvas flap and peered inside, standing motionless for maybe thirty seconds as he gazed at...something. Tracie couldn't imagine what might be inside that cargo bed that was so fascinating.

Eventually the man dropped the flap and marched to the guardhouse.

A moment later the first gate began to trundle open. The truck rolled slowly through and stopped again in front of the inner entrance. The first gate closed fully before the second began to open. Finally the truck accelerated onto the base and turned toward the administrative zone.

It pulled into a space directly outside what Tracie had come to believe was the main admin building. Both cab doors opened and a soldier stepped down out of each at the same time three men dressed in Red Army uniforms exited the building.

One was a major and Tracie suspected she was looking at the base commander. The other two approached the now-stationary vehicle with sidearms drawn, further piquing Tracie's interest. What the hell could the truck be carrying that would require an officer's appearance, along with a pair of armed escorts?

The base representatives spoke to the two men who had gotten out of the truck and then all five men moved to the rear of the cargo bed. The soldier who'd exited the truck's passenger side opened the canvas flap and tied it back, then pulled a key ring out of his pocket and searched through it for a moment. When he found what he was looking for, he disappeared through the flap and climbed into the back of the truck.

He returned a moment later and when he did, Tracie's eyes widened in shock. She felt her jaw drop. She pulled the binoculars away from her face and blinked, then replaced them and once again looked down on the secret military installation.

She couldn't believe her eyes.

Being led out of the cargo bed in chains was the CIA operative who'd helped her escape Russia not two weeks ago inside a hidden compartment built into a truck remarkably similar to the one she was looking at right now.

This was impossible, but the evidence was right there in front of her.

The man being delivered to the secret facility was Ryan Smith.

16

Ryan stumbled out the rear of the truck. Literally. Were it not for one of the guards grabbing him by the elbow, he would have fallen on his face when his feet hit the ground.

With the exception of the rare stops for fuel and to piss, the truck had driven through the evening and well into the next day. Even huddled inside the blanket it was the longest night of his life. Ryan had no way of knowing the temperature, but he shivered incessantly and his toes felt like small blocks of wood inside his socks. He imagined if he took off his shoes and struck his feet with something hard the toes would shear off and scatter around the cargo bed like so many marbles.

After daybreak, the outside temperatures had gradually moderated with the rising of the sun. Ryan discovered that the sheet of canvas covering the truck bed captured the sunlight and helped trap some small amount of warmth inside, but his core body temperature was by then so low he continued to shiver, his teeth rattling inside his skull. It got to the point he wondered whether the men sitting in the warmth of the cab could hear it.

Between the chill permeating his body and the constant bouncing of the truck over the subpar Soviet roads he could not sleep, and the exhaustion settled over him like a blanket much thicker than the one he'd been provided.

He was miserable.

And this was only the beginning of his suffering; the end was not in sight. In fact, there would be no end. This was now his existence. He belonged to the KGB. He was at the mercy of an organization that *had* no mercy, and his destiny would be determined entirely by his ruthless overlords.

The hours passed slowly, particularly during the interminable night. But even after daybreak, Ryan discovered it had become impossible to gauge the passage of time. He occupied himself for a little while trying to determine where the KGB might be taking him and for what purpose, but dwelling on those subjects chilled him even worse than did the temperature.

One thing he knew was that he was being taken farther and farther off the beaten path. They were moving steadily east, he could gauge their direction by the positioning of the sun, but that in itself didn't tell him much. The Soviet Union was vast, much of it mountainous and unexplored, even in the late-twentieth century, and knowing the direction of travel was not much more helpful than knowing he should never have set foot inside that damned Moscow tavern four nights ago.

Or was it three? Five? He couldn't quite recall.

The canvas-covered opening in the rear of the cargo bed continued to flap in the breeze, and it had offered him enough of a view to know that the truck was nowhere near a city. It was nowhere near anything. The terrain was bumpy and hilly, and Ryan came to realize they seemed to be following a gradual upward incline. Over time the incline became more noticeable.

Where the hell are they taking me?

He'd fallen into a partial slumber—feet jammed against the iron strut, back pushed up against the rear of the cab, head slumped painfully on his shoulders—when his rolling prison began the now-familiar process of slowing to turn off the road. The air brakes squealed and the driver ground the gears and Ryan's skull slammed painfully against the sheet metal.

He blinked fully awake and shook his head to try to clear away the confusion. His immediate assumption was that it was once again time to refuel the truck. His captors had given him a snack during the last pit stop, but it hadn't been nearly enough, and Ryan's stomach growled and cramped. He realized he couldn't remember the last time he'd eaten an actual meal and not just whatever scraps the Soviets tossed his way.

He forced his thoughts from his gnawing hunger and it occurred to him that it was too soon to be refueling. Exhaustion and fear had undoubtedly dulled his perceptions, but he was certain they'd gotten gas no more than three hours ago. That amounted to less than half the time between the previous stops, and the Soviets had shown no inclination to pull off the road any more often than they absolutely had to.

Something else was happening.

Another stop at a guard shack, and then the truck entered a military installation, exactly as it had done several times over the course of Ryan's captivity. But this time when they squealed to a stop inside the base, there was diesel fuel stench. No unscrewing of a gas cap. No liquid being pumped into the truck's tank.

Nothing at all happened for at least a minute, and then the flap was pulled aside and the man who'd supplied Ryan with the blanket last night entered the cargo bed. He unlocked Ryan's chain and helped him out of the truck, keeping him upright when Ryan stumbled. The brightness of the sun was jarring after the muted light inside the truck bed, and he blinked hard and squinted.

"Take the prisoner to my office," a man in a Red Army major's uniform said, before turning and walking briskly up a set of stairs and then disappearing into a building.

Ryan found himself being pulled along behind the officer, flanked on either side by the men who'd driven him here. A pair of Russian soldiers with their handguns drawn followed behind, apparently concerned Ryan might overpower his captors and make a break for freedom, all while dizzy from hunger and lack of sleep, shivering uncontrollably, and without a clue where the hell he might go even if he *could* escape.

The reality, at least for the moment, was that Ryan was so relieved to be out of that damned truck, and so happy to be going inside a building that was presumably warm and comfortable, that he wasn't about to cause anyone any trouble. He was perfectly happy to follow the commander into his office, where he would undoubtedly be interrogated. Again.

Once inside the building he moved past a young woman seated at a desk, clearly some sort of secretary or administrative assistant. She stared at him with wide, wary eyes, and it occurred to Ryan she was probably seeing an Evil American in the flesh for the first time in her life.

Then he was whisked past the woman and seconds later found himself inside an office that looked more comfortable than anyplace he'd been since he was captured. Hell, it looked nicer than anyplace he'd been since he left the States.

The men escorting him seemed to have no idea what to do next. They stopped just inside the office doorway, so of course Ryan stopped as well, and everyone waited as the major moved to his desk and sat.

A second man had been awaiting their arrival inside the office, and he was seated next to the major's desk, looking almost as uncomfortable as Ryan felt. Unlike the officer, he was dressed in civilian clothes beneath a white lab coat.

The major crossed his hands on his desk and met Ryan's gaze. His eyes were cold and hard. He said, "You look uncomfortable, my friend," although there was nothing friendly about his tone.

Ryan didn't see any point in agreeing, but he wasn't about to argue, either, so he kept his mouth shut and waited to see what would happen next. An empty chair had been placed in front of the desk facing the major and the man in the lab coat, and while Ryan would have bet his life's savings the chair was meant for him, he knew better than to sit in it—or even to take one step in its direction—without being instructed to.

The major seemed mildly disappointed not to have received an answer. He shifted his gaze to Ryan's escorts and said, "Remove his coat and shackles."

The men hesitated. Clearly they had been instructed to maintain the highest level of security where their prisoner was concerned, and the notion of taking the handcuffs and chains off him seemed counterintuitive.

"Do it," the officer said. His annoyance at not being obeyed immediately was plain. "This man is no longer your responsibility.

My secretary is completing the transfer of control paperwork even as we speak, so you need not concern yourselves any further about liability.

"Besides," he continued, his gaze drilling a hole into Ryan. "The prisoner is not stupid. He knows there is a base full of armed soldiers who would love nothing more to put a bullet in the head of an American spy, and that even if our new friend the American spy were to escape, there is absolutely nowhere for him to go. He would be dead from exposure to the elements before he made it fifty kilometers. Isn't that right, my new friend?"

Ryan clamped his mouth shut and did his best to maintain a stoic demeanor, but the major was right. There would be no point in resisting these men and no point in attempting escape, at least for now.

His Russian escorts moved quickly after the curt words from the commander. Thirty seconds later the shackles had disappeared, as had his coat, and the Russian escorts vanished into the outer office as well. Ryan rubbed his sore wrists and waited.

"Now," the major said. "Please take a seat." He waved in the direction of the empty chair, and Ryan moved to it and sat, grateful to be off his feet now that the steadying hand of the escort was no longer on his elbow.

"Let me introduce you to your new reality," the major said, nodding in the direction of the man seated next to him. "This is Doctor Vladimir Protasov, and as you will soon discover, you are about to become closer to Doctor Protasov than you could possibly imagine."

Ryan looked from the major to the doctor and back again. He kept his expression impassive, but he didn't like the direction this conversation had taken, and the familiar feeling of dread was again worming through his intestines.

"Good afternoon," the doctor said, speaking for the first time. "I must say it is a pleasure to make your acquaintance, and I mean that more sincerely than you know. I don't suppose you would care to introduce yourself."

Ryan wanted to laugh at the notion that he would tell these people anything. He wanted to, but he couldn't quite manage it, thanks to the fear. The best he could hope for was to maintain a grim silence.

"No matter," the doctor said. "Allow me to break the ice by speaking for a little while. Believe me," he said with a cold smile, "we have much to discuss."

17

February 1, 1988
4:25 p.m.
The mountains outside Mezhgorye, Bashkir

"How long has it been since Ryan Smith checked in with his handler?"

Tracie hadn't planned on speaking with Aaron Stallings until returning to D.C. This was strictly a surveillance mission, relatively low-risk as these things went, and there had been no reason to expect she would have to communicate with the man who'd personified the term "plausible deniability" during his more than four decades working for—and then heading up—the CIA.

But she'd brought her secure satellite phone to the USSR anyway, sacrificing other items inside her go-bag to leave room for the heavy, boxy communications device. Long experience had taught her that things *always* went sideways, and no matter how simple or straightforward a mission might seem inside a briefing room, once in the field things inevitably changed, and rarely for the better. Retaining the ability to contact the only person in the world who could offer assistance was far more valuable an asset than anything else she might have stuffed inside the bag.

Stallings hesitated, surprised at the question. "Who?"

"I know him as Ryan Smith, so that's certainly not his real name."

"Could you be more specific?"

"He's the operative who drove me into Kremlyov last month in the modified Soviet truck with the false bottom, and who helped me escape the country after I completed my mission."

"Since we've lost so many operatives inside the USSR recently, I know who you're referring to, although I don't know his real name off the top of my head. I'll have to contact his handler to get that information, and I'm extremely busy. I have no intention of taking those steps unless there's a damned good reason to do so."

Stallings had made no effort to conceal his testiness, so Tracie made no effort to conceal hers. "How about if I told you I just saw him being driven onto the secret base you have me monitoring? How about if I told you the Soviets pulled him out of the back of a truck at gunpoint and in chains, and marched him into what I believe to be the base commander's office? Would that constitute a good reason?"

The CIA director ignored the rhetorical questions, but when he answered, his voice was measured. "Are you sure it's the same guy? You only worked with him on one mission."

"It was only one mission but we spent several hours riding in the cab of a truck together, and after that he helped me plan an ambush that took out a KGB operative. That ambush allowed me to capture the scumbag who poisoned half a dozen good men. In all, I must have worked at close quarters with him for eight hours or more. It's the same guy. I'm one hundred percent certain."

Stallings grunted. Tracie pictured him squinting at his desk in concentration, face red and angry, as if the notion of another American operative falling into the KGB's hands was a personal affront. In some ways, she supposed it was.

"I'll call Smith's handler, but if you're as certain as you claim to be, it's—"

"I am," she interrupted.

"Then my call becomes moot. We know the Soviets have him. His real name becomes irrelevant at this point."

"Okay."

"The question is what are they doing with him, and why has he been transported to a secret installation in the mountains? Why not show him off to the world? Why not conduct a public trial on state-run television and use him to embarrass the United States?"

Tracie knew he was thinking out loud. Those questions were above her pay grade, and while that wouldn't have stopped her from offering an opinion in answer to any or all of them, the fact was she *had* no opinion. Without a better handle on what the hell the USSR was working on inside the strange camp built into the side of a mountain, she couldn't even hazard a guess regarding Smith's fate.

And ultimately, it didn't matter anyway. Whatever the purpose in trucking a captured CIA clandestine operative to the base, she knew it wouldn't be good. Ryan Smith was facing a grim fate, and Tracie already knew what she had to do.

"I'm going to go in there and get him," she said.

"No you're not."

"Excuse me?"

"You heard me." Stallings's voice was crisp and decisive. "Your mission has not changed. You are to monitor the installation and gather as much intel as you can before flying back to the states to brief our people."

"Sir, with all due respect, you know as well as I do that seeing Smith paraded in front of the television cameras while the Russians conduct a mock trial is the *best* possible outcome he can expect. You know as well as I do that once the trial is over—and it's not like there's any doubt about what the outcome would be—our man will be marched into a public square somewhere in Moscow and hanged. Or shot."

"Tanner, I'm telling you—"

"And, again, that's the best-case scenario. The much more likely occurrence is that the short trip from the back of a cargo truck into the base commander's office at gunpoint is the last time we'll ever see Smith, dead or alive. He'll disappear. He'll never be seen again. His family will never know what happened to him."

"Now you listen to me, Tanner. Assuming the man you saw even *is* the operative you know as Ryan Smith, you're—"

"It's him," she said obstinately.

"Fine. It's him. That changes nothing. You're a thousand miles from anyone who could help you, and even those people aren't coming to Bashkir to extract you for days. Entering a Red Army installation with no backup and no plan, after one day's surveillance, would be suicide."

"But sir, I can't just—"

"And what would the end result be?" Tracie couldn't help but note the tone of satisfaction in Stallings's voice after cutting her off mid-sentence, as she had done to him twice already. "I'll tell you what: we would lose not just one more operative inside a country where we desperately need eyes and ears, we would lose two. That is *not* what I consider to be an acceptable risk."

"I can't just let them take him. It was sheer random luck I was here to see them unload that poor man from a truck, surrounded by four soldiers pointing guns at him like he's the most valuable prize in the world. We can't squander what will be our only opportunity to get him back."

"You have your orders, Tanner, and—"

"I'm sorry sir, you're fading in and out. There must be some sort of interference. Sunspots maybe, I don't know, but your last few transmissions have come through almost completely garbled. I'm pretty sure you approved my mission inside the base, though, that was what it sounded like. Thank you, sir. I'll be back at Langley with Smith soon."

"Don't you even think about—" Stallings was shouting now, and if Tracie hadn't already been turning down the volume knob, she thought she would have been forced to do so just to keep the sound of her boss's rage from echoing down the mountainside and into the Soviet base far below.

She broke the connection on the sat phone and then lowered its antenna and returned it to its carrying case.

Despite the gravity of the situation—and calling it "grave" was an understatement—she couldn't help but smile at the reaction she'd provoked. Aaron Stallings had tried his best to bully and intimidate her since the first time they met. He must have learned by now that it wouldn't work, that she would be unfazed by threats and shouting and belligerence, but it hadn't stopped him from trying, and any day she could turn his bellicosity against him and get under his skin she considered to be a good day.

Even if, like today, the reality was anything but.

By now the sun had long-since slipped below the crests of the

Urals. The darkness was nearly complete and the temperature was falling rapidly. Even dressed head to toe in survival gear Tracie was rapidly transitioning from mildly uncomfortable to freezing cold.

Her plan had been to conclude the day's surveillance at least an hour ago, but the unexpected sight of Ryan Smith had thrown a monkey wrench into the works.

She recalled the help he'd given her just last month. His unassuming manner and his easy smile and his willingness to do anything necessary to ensure her mission's success. He was probably close to her own age, but he'd only been in the field a few months and she'd viewed him almost as a little brother. She'd offered advice about operating in hostile environments that had been gratefully received, even if—obviously, given his situation— poorly implemented.

Then she thought about Aaron Stallings's insistence that she stick to the original mission.

Maybe Stallings was right. Maybe attempting to rescue Smith was the wrong move. Hell, *probably* it was the wrong move.

She didn't care. She couldn't leave a man to the kind of fate facing Ryan Smith if there was any chance she could take action to change that fate, even if she had no idea yet what that action might be.

She got her things together and began hiking through the woods to the Lada SUV, only now realizing she'd begun to shake violently.

Much more so than the temperature would warrant.

18

February 1, 1988
Time unknown
Base Commander's office, unknown Soviet military installation

"We have much to discuss," the man said, his lips fixed in a mirth-less smile. The Russian major had introduced him as a doctor, and the title mystified Ryan almost as much as it frightened him.

Why a doctor? Ryan doubted very much that the Soviets were so concerned about his health they'd brought in a medical pro-fessional to give their new prisoner a physical. That left only one real possibility he could come up with, and it was one that made his stomach turn and sweat break out on his forehead, despite the chill still permeating his bones from his time in the back of the cargo truck.

Torture.

This man in the white smock was a KGB doctor, and he was here to introduce Ryan Smith to previously unimagined levels of pain.

Ryan swallowed heavily and pressed his lips together. He would stand strong as long as he could. If the Soviets truly wanted to break him, to learn details of the missions he'd run inside their borders, and to learn the names of other operatives still operating in country, he knew they would do so eventually.

But he vowed to make it absolutely as difficult as possible before they ever got one word out of him.

The doctor—he'd been introduced as Vladimir Protasov, as if Ryan might care about his name— and the Red Army major stared at him without speaking. Ryan felt like a bug being examined under a magnifying glass by a couple of curious twelve-year-old boys.

But Protasov hadn't yet asked a question, so Ryan felt no answer was necessary. He didn't know what was coming next, but he guessed it would be a lot more unpleasant than the current situation, and he had no interest in speeding the process along.

The silence dragged out. Ryan's heart was racing as adrenaline pounded through his system, but he thought he was—so far, at least—doing a pretty good job of maintaining an impassive expression. Without a watch it was impossible to tell for sure, but Ryan guessed ninety seconds or more dragged by without anyone speaking or even moving.

Eventually it occurred to the two men sitting across the desk that their prisoner would not be pressured to fill the screaming silence in the room, and Doctor Protasov tried again. "I am sure you are wondering where you are and why we have brought you here."

Another declarative statement requiring no response. Again Ryan remained silent. Whatever Protasov's specialty, it was clear he wasn't a professional interrogator.

The familiar awkward silence dropped over the room. Ryan felt like a man who'd been stranded in a broken elevator with a couple of strangers.

The silence was much shorter this time.

Protasov frowned and said, "Your reticence is understandable but I assure you it changes nothing. We know you are an American CIA operative, and we know that you have been working inside the Soviet Union toward the destruction of our country."

Ryan cleared his throat and attempted to maintain his mask of calm.

"But that is only part of the reason you are here," Protasov said. "You see, my work here has been hampered by the poor quality of my test subjects. Men afflicted with mental illness or long-term addiction to drugs or alcohol suffer changes in brain chemistry. This makes successful manipulation of the brain tissue through electrical stimulation extremely difficult, if not impossible, to achieve."

Protasov paused and met Ryan's eyes. Ryan was proud he held the man's gaze steadily despite the terror coursing through his system.

The doctor continued. "I have been insisting to my superiors for quite some time that I require higher quality test subjects if I am to continue making progress in my research."

He smiled. "This is where you come in, my American spy friend. A man such as yourself, able to work inside a foreign country, gathering military and civilian intelligence and passing it along to the enemies of that country, is clearly blessed with intelligence of his own, not to mention a quick wit, and, it goes without saying, bravery.

"Of course," he added with an acid smile, "the fact that you are sitting here with us today tells me you may not be *quite* as intelligent and quick-witted as you thought you were, but you've undoubtedly reached the same conclusion on your own by now, so there is no need to cover *that* ground, don't you agree?"

Ryan thought the pounding of his heart inside his chest must be visible to these men by now. It felt as though it might just explode and blast through his ribs like a small nuclear device.

He remained silent.

"But that is neither here nor there," Protasov continued. "My point remains unchanged. You possess a level of intelligence and high-capacity brain functionality that far surpasses that of any previous test subject. This is why I am so pleased to make your acquaintance."

The Russian major had remained silent while Doctor Protasov spoke, but it was obvious he'd seen enough of Protasov's timid soft shoe routine and decided to take control of the meeting.

"You have heard from Doctor Protasov," the major said. "You will soon become intimately familiar with the good doctor and his work. However, I have a few words to say as well. As an American CIA operative, I am sure you—"

"I don't know what you're talking about," Ryan said. His voice was strong and his tone decisive. He didn't know how he was managing it, but he was proud of himself. "CIA? That's ridiculous."

"Please," the major said with a dismissive wave of his hand. "Do not waste my time and insult my intelligence. We have been watching you long enough to know exactly *what* you are, if not who you are. We have people searching your apartment even now. No matter how careful you may have been, I feel confident we will find additional evidence of your treachery against the Soviet Union. Feel free to argue my point, if you believe you can."

"I don't know what you're talking about," Ryan repeated.

"Let us not get bogged down with peripheral issues. As I was saying before your pathetic attempt at denial, we know you work for the CIA. As such, I am sure you can understand how valuable it will be to the cause of the Soviet Union when you appear on television in defense of not just our government, but indeed our entire way of life. You will become world-famous, my friend."

Ryan knew he had to respond. "I understand that if you torture a human being long enough, you can get that person to admit to anything. And if I understand that, the rest of the world will understand it as well."

"I quite agree," the major said. "Which is exactly why you've been selected to participate in Doctor Protasov's research."

"Why continue referring to him as a doctor?" Ryan said. "If he's a torture specialist, just call him that."

"I most certainly *am* a doctor," Protasov blurted, his eyes flashing. "A research professional, not that I have to explain myself to the likes of *you.*"

The major continued as if Protasov had not even spoken. "Tell me what you know about psychotronics," he said, folding his hands together on his desk like a university professor awaiting an answer from a student who'd been caught daydreaming.

Ryan blinked in surprise. He wasn't sure what he'd expected to come out of his interrogator's mouth, but that wasn't it. He shrugged in honest confusion.

"Never heard of it," he acknowledged.

"I am no research scientist," the major said with a smile that was every bit as cold as the one Protasov had offered earlier. "I am just a career military man working in service to his country. So I am afraid I cannot offer a textbook definition like Doctor Protasov can. But I feel it is important you hear this from me."

The nausea in Ryan's belly began ramping up. Despite the cordiality of the major's words, his tone was harsh and his voice cutting. Ryan felt certain what came next would not be something he wanted to hear.

He was right. The base commander said, "You heard Doctor Protasov speak of his work in manipulating brain chemistry. That is one small part of the psychotronics program, a program that has been ongoing among scientists working in concert with the KGB for decades. Psychotronics, in its most general form, can be understood as mind control. It is the process of achieving desired results from a subject, or group of subjects, via external manipulation. The subject, of course, is typically unaware of any such manipulation."

"Psychological torture might work eventually," Ryan said, "but it's going to take a long goddamned time before I bend to your will."

"Did I say anything about utilizing psychological methods with you? I believe Doctor Protasov mentioned once already that his area of expertise is in electrical stimulation of brain tissue. There is nothing 'psychological' about it."

Ryan stared at the man in mute horror.

"Oh, yes," the major continued, clearly pleased he'd finally cracked Ryan's stoic shell. "Perhaps you would like details?"

Ryan tried to hold the major's gaze.

"I will take that as a yes. You see, the doctor will shave your head. He will drill through your skullcap and into the brain tissue. He will insert an electrical lead through the hole and using electrical impulses, will alter the very makeup of your brain."

The commander smiled widely. "If the procedure is successful, inside of forty-eight to seventy-two hours, you will be saying whatever we tell you to say, willingly and enthusiastically. And you will be saying it to the entire world.

"And if he is not successful, well, let us just say you will be disposed of in the same manner as Doctor Protasov's previous failed attempts. You will disappear, and I assure you, your body will never be found."

19

February 2, 1988
7:50 a.m.
The mountains outside Mezhgorye, Bashkir

When she'd begun surveillance yesterday, Tracie had paid little attention to the administrative area inside the mysterious Soviet facility.

She had been far more interested in the razor wire fencing encircling the base, the positioning and sightlines of the guard towers and sentry stations, and the potential uses for the warehouse-like structures into which the base personnel filed first thing in the morning, only to reappear at the end of the day.

The administrative zone and its personnel had been an afterthought, the cadre of secretaries and assistants, all of them young women, who pushed pencils, filed forms, and answered telephones. They'd meant little to Tracie. Secretaries were secretaries, whether in the Soviet Union, the United States, or Timbuktu, the same in every culture: overworked, underappreciated, invisible.

But they were no longer invisible to Tracie.

They were suddenly of the utmost importance.

Because they were the one group of workers staffing the facility—besides senior personnel—who lived off base.

They were obviously locals, young women from Mezhgorye who had been hired by the Red Army following construction of the facility. The Soviets had apparently decided it was pointless to

113

uproot administrative personnel from Moscow or Leningrad or Stalingrad and ship them out to the middle of nowhere to do a job any moderately intelligent woman could handle.

For the women who'd been hired, it had probably been the Bashkiri version of hitting the lottery. In a sleepy little village perched halfway up a remote mountain, virtually cut off from the outside world, job prospects must previously have hovered somewhere between minimal and nonexistent.

But the half-dozen or so secretaries and administrative assistants employed on the base were the exception. Steady employment, relatively high pay in comparison to the work they would otherwise be doing as waitresses or housekeepers, not to mention the prestige of going to work every day for the glorious Red Army, would instantly have raised their standard of living a notch above everyone else of their age and station in life.

Tracie had spent most of last night working on two tasks: warming up after spending the day hunkered down in the snow and wind of the Ural Mountains, and considering the problem of how the hell she was going to stand any chance of infiltrating a fortified military base all by herself without being captured or filled full of Russian bullets.

And she had come to the conclusion that the secretaries were the key.

She kicked herself for not paying closer attention yesterday morning when the young women had been reporting for work. The fact that she'd considered them irrelevant to her assignment at the time didn't matter—she should have spent just as much brainpower and mental energy analyzing them as she had every other aspect of the camp.

Today she would rectify that oversight.

She'd made sure to get up plenty early. Ate a hot breakfast and stuffed all her survival clothing into her bag, then tossed it into the front seat of the Lada before motoring through town and back up the mountain to her surveillance location. She hadn't dared risk bringing the wrong kind of attention to herself by leaving Mezhgorye while dressed in her all-weather gear, so she'd been forced once again to change clothes inside the SUV upon reaching her destination.

But she did so without interruption—the odds of another vehicle passing by on what amounted to a little-used mountain lane were practically nil—and by seven-thirty a.m. was back in her little surveillance nook. Yesterday the administrative personnel had begun arriving for work just before eight, and she assumed today would be no different.

She was right. The first secretary turned onto the base's long access road a little after seven forty-five, and the other five followed shortly after in a steady stream of ancient Ladas, Volgas and one hideous orange Moskvitch sedan that had to be older than Tracie.

By eight o'clock all six of the women had parked in what was apparently their designated lot and entered the administration building. The arrival protocol Tracie thought she had observed yesterday, when she had only been half paying attention, was repeated with each secretary's arrival.

Two of the women carpooled to work and arrived together, so there were only five vehicles to observe rather than six. But the guards handled every arrival in exactly the same manner: the secretary rolled up to the sentry's shack, and then slowed and waved what looked like an ID badge at the building. Before she had even come to a stop, the gate was opening in anticipation of her arrival, and each time the secretary motored through the front gate and onto the base undisturbed.

In not one instance did the sentry step out of the guard shack.

In not one instance did the secretary roll down her window.

In not one instance was the badge inspected by a sentry.

Tracie tracked the last arrival until the woman disappeared inside the administration building, then sat back and considered what she had just observed.

The sentries' laxness was not particularly surprising, she decided. For all its impressive security measures—the dual, presumably electrified razor-wire fences, the multiple guard towers, the patrolling sentries with automatic rifles slung over their shoulders—this facility was isolated almost beyond imagination.

It had clearly been here for years and yet had never been detected by the United States, even through the most sophisticated airborne surveillance measures available. The only community for hundreds of miles in any direction was Mezhgorye, and the KGB had undoubtedly vetted its citizens rigorously during construction of the base.

That corners were being cut and security measures ignored was human nature. There was little reason for the Soviets to feel any sense of concern regarding security. Each secretary had obviously been issued an identification card or badge of some sort, and the official entry protocol was probably a visual inspection of the ID by the gate guard.

Over the years, and day after endless day of boring routine, the sentries had gradually become less observant of security protocol, the current slipshod operation being the inevitable end result. The sentry's nose was probably buried in a book—based on the extremely limited flow of vehicular traffic entering and leaving the base, manning the guard shack had to be one mind-numbingly tedious detail—and he probably had little desire to step outside the heated shack and into the brutally cold morning mountain temperatures.

Tracie smiled and nodded to herself. There still were some details to work out, but she'd already decided the Soviets' substandard security measures would be her ticket onto the base.

She lifted the binoculars to her eyes and resumed watch.

* * *

February 2, 1988
10:10 a.m.

Tracie had by now accepted as a certainty that anything of interest happening on the secret base was happening underground. It would explain everything:

The fact that there were far more workers stationed at the facility than capacity to accommodate those workers inside the limited number of structures above ground.

The fact that the personnel stationed on the base swarmed out of the residence buildings first thing in the morning and then, with rare exceptions, disappeared from view until late afternoon or evening.

The fact that the buildings into which the workers disappeared each morning were so bland and unidentifiable. There was nothing to indicate their possible uses, because they *had* no use, other than to act as subway stations of a sort, departure points for the personnel in their descent via elevator or stairs to various areas of responsibility.

It made perfect sense from the perspective of the Soviet Union. If you were going to construct a secret facility deep inside a remote mountain chain, why not take the extra step of tunneling into the side of the mountain? Doing so would provide increased security and render the base nearly invisible from the prying eyes of your enemy.

It would have been an expensive and time-consuming project, but with the Soviet economy and policies geared toward the military, and the Russians' obsession with secrecy, the expenditures of time and resources probably seemed not just reasonable, but desirable.

And the notion of constructing a military facility underground, of tunneling into a mountainside, was far from unprecedented. The United States had done exactly that with the Cheyenne Mountain Complex in Colorado Springs, building the facility over the course of half a decade back in the early 1960s.

Tracie had never been to Cheyenne Mountain, but she knew the base was fortified to withstand a nuclear attack. She wondered if this facility was constructed to similar standards.

She supposed she would soon find out.

* * *

February 2, 1988
4:55 p.m.

The surveillance dragged. Few vehicles entered or departed the base. During the hours between early morning and late afternoon, when most of the non-administrative personnel were under-ground—assuming Tracie's theory was correct—the place became a virtual ghost town.

Still, she remained attentive, determined not to miss anything of significance. In reality, though, she was just passing the time. Waiting for the five o'clock administrative quitting time.

When it finally arrived, she sat a little higher in the snow, boredom gone, completely focused on the administration building from which the secretaries were beginning to emerge. Tracie would have only thirty seconds or so during which she could observe all six women before they reached their cars, so intense focus would be necessary if she were to select the right woman and give her plan the best chance of succeeding.

She eliminated two of the secretaries from consideration the moment they exited the building. They were both overweight, noticeably so, with body types utterly unlike Tracie's.

Another woman was eliminated next, due to her height. Tracie guessed if they stood side-by-side, the secretary would tower over her by a good eight inches or more.

That left three possibilities, and Tracie zeroed in on them one-by-one, spending several seconds on a quick examination of each before moving to the next. None were exactly what she was looking for, as was to be expected.

But one of the young women looked as though her height was probably within an inch or so of Tracie's, and her weight within maybe eight to ten pounds. Her mousy brown hair didn't come close to matching Tracie's flame red, but that difference was a minor one and could be easily mitigated.

Tracie made her decision. She abandoned her long-distance examination of the other five women and trained her binocs solely on the one she had selected. The woman looked a few years younger than Tracie, maybe twenty-two, and she climbed into a little yellow Volga sedan that had probably rolled off the assembly line sometime around Tracie's eighth birthday.

The five cars carrying the six women started up at roughly the same time, and they motored toward the front gate in a slow-mov-ing conga line. Greyish-white exhaust trailed the vehicles, swirling into the sky and disappearing. The sun had set almost an hour ago, and the cars exited the parking lot's ring of dirty light, their headlights illuminating the darkness of the access road with varying degrees of success.

Less than a minute later the convoy reached the guard shack. In what was obviously a nightly ritual, the guard opened the gate as the vehicles approached, and all five cars passed through while barely slowing. They continued along the access road and then turned right as one and accelerated toward town.

The perch Tracie had chosen from which to conduct her surveillance was located high above not just the base, but Mezhgorye as well. Her aerie offered a decent view of perhaps seventy-five percent of the village, and she hoped the woman she'd selected—and continued to track with the glasses—made her home somewhere inside that portion of town.

If not, she would be forced to tail her quarry tomorrow night as she left the facility. It would cost an entire day, and that was time Tracie could ill afford to lose.

The cars reached the village and split up, each turning toward their own homes. Tracie caught herself mumbling, "Come on, come on," willing the woman she'd selected to stay within her line of sight.

She did.

The Volga sedan motored through town and then wound its way into—and through—a residential area before easing to a stop outside a large, blocky wood-frame structure.

Tracie zoomed in on the scene as best she could. She wished she had higher-power glasses. From this distance she stood no chance of reading street addresses—if there were even road signs or building numbers, which she doubted—so she would have to commit the general location of the home to memory and then retrace the route as best she could once she'd descended the mountain.

The secretary climbed out of her car and hurried to the building's entrance, her breath condensing and drifting away in the illumination of a single security lamp. She yanked open the exterior door and was gone.

Tracie lifted the glasses and studied the structure. It was two stories, built in a rectangular configuration, basic and austere.

Clearly an apartment building. Judging by its size, Tracie guessed it contained six separate residences, three small apartments on each level.

There was obviously no way of knowing which apartment belonged to the secretary, or even on which floor she lived, but that problem Tracie could work around. Of much greater importance was the question of whether the woman lived alone or shared the apartment with a roommate, or perhaps even a husband.

That was unknowable as well.

Tracie would have to do what she always did: prepare as thoroughly as possible and then improvise when things went wrong.

She watched the building a little longer, not sure what she was looking for. No one came or went. She took some extra time and committed the driving route to memory, then packed her equipment and returned to the Lada, chewing on her bottom lip, lost in thought.

20

Ryan had no idea what time it was when Doctor Protasov entered his room. Might have been afternoon of the day he'd been brought here, might have been the next morning. Might have been neither. Someone had administered a sedative the moment they plunked him into this hospital bed, and there was no way of knowing how long he'd been unconscious.

Or whether he'd been fully unconscious at all. On the few occasions he felt himself drifting off, his mind had immediately wandered to the terrifying conversation earlier in the day with the Russian base commander and the doctor who'd spoken of experimenting on him using techniques straight out of a Grade B horror movie.

Drilling through his skull and into his brain.

Inserting wires and using electrical currents to manipulate his thoughts and actions.

Making him compliant and suggestible, a pawn the Soviets would then use to conduct political propaganda, assuming he survived the procedure.

Could they really do that?

Either way, how the hell was he supposed to sleep after hearing it?

So maybe he'd just lain in bed in a semi-conscious daze, nightmare scenarios flashing over and over through his head like a movie running on a continuous loop.

One wrist had been cuffed to a heavy metal railing bolted to the side of Ryan's bed. The railing looked similar to what might be found on an American hospital bed, except it was much heavier and seemed affixed permanently to the bed frame. It didn't appear to be removable or adjustable in any way. This meant his range of motion was severely limited. He could lie on his back or on his right side.

More or less.

And every time he turned, the rattle of handcuff on iron was like a goddamned alarm clock clanging away.

Time had dragged. It might have been three hours or three days. After being chained to the bed by an unsmiling Russian man who'd wrinkled his nose in distaste at the prospect of dealing with Ryan, he'd been left by himself for what felt like a very long time, during which it was all he could do to avoid a panicked meltdown.

He'd never felt so alone, so isolated, in his life.

Or so afraid.

He was lying on his back with his eyes closed in a futile effort to stop his mind from spinning when the door opened and the Russian doctor entered. The room was completely windowless, so without his watch Ryan had no idea whether it was day or night.

Ryan's eyes flew open and he came instantly alert.

Protasov was toting a small leather satchel. It looked like something an American doctor might have carried back in the days when medical professionals still made house calls.

Ryan tracked the man's progress as he crossed the room, doing his best to remain calm, or, lacking that, at least to project an air of serene defiance. The effort was wasted, however, as Protasov had yet to even acknowledge Ryan's presence in the room.

A small table on wheels sat in the corner, and the Russian moved to it and rolled it to the foot of Ryan's bed. He placed his bag on the bed next to Ryan's feet and unzipped it, then began removing items and placing them on the table. His back was turned to Ryan and his body mostly blocked Ryan's view, so it was impossible to see what sorts of medical instruments he might be unpacking.

Ryan assumed this was done intentionally, to force his racing imagination to fill in the blanks produced by the lack of visual information.

It worked like a charm.

Ryan could feel his pulse skyrocket and he began to sweat as badly as he'd done yesterday—or whenever it had been—in the base commander's office. Maybe worse.

Finally Doctor Protasov turned and faced Ryan. A patently insincere smile flitted across his face and then vanished.

He said, "I trust you are comfortable in your new home?"

When Ryan didn't answer he continued, "These are not the finest accommodations, I know, but very soon you will not care. Very soon you will discover your opinion as to the quality of your surroundings—or your opinion on any subject, for that matter—will be whatever I want it to be. Whatever I dictate to you."

Ryan stared at the man, forcing himself not to react. It took a supreme act of will.

Protasov didn't seem to notice. He smiled for half a second and said, "Your situation will be very freeing in many ways, I believe."

"If you're so sure about that, how about we trade places," Ryan said. He'd sworn he would not respond to his captors, no matter what was said or done to him. Sworn he would remain stoic and impassive to the best of his abilities for as long as possible. But the man's comment was so infuriating he just couldn't help himself.

Another smile crossed the doctor's face this time, but it disappeared just as quickly as had the previous one. "I think we will leave things the way they are for the time being."

He lifted something from the wheeled table and moved next to Ryan. The object was trailing an electrical cord and after a moment of confusion, everything snapped into place and Ryan understood.

Of course.

It was an electric razor.

Protasov was going to shave his head as the first step toward taking the Russian equivalent of a goddamn Black and Decker and drilling a goddamn hole into the side of his goddamn head.

For a moment, sheer unreasoning panic caused Ryan to forget every word of Russian he'd learned and he lay in his bed, head shaking vigorously.

Then he regained at least a bit of composure and he said, "Forget it. You're not touching me with that thing. It's not happening. No way."

Protasov waited patiently until he stopped talking. When the Russian spoke, it was with an exaggerated calm. "We can do this the easy way or we can do it the hard way. It makes no difference to me. You can lie still while I prepare you for surgery, or I can have you restrained, with your head placed into an uncomfortable metal and leather harness. Or I can simply sedate you. I have a multitude of options at my disposal."

"Don't do this," Ryan said. He knew the words were pointless before they ever left his mouth but he blurted them out anyway.

"You need not be afraid," Protasov said. "The procedure is relatively painless."

"Says who? The other victims? The ones you've buried in shallow graves?"

Again Protasov ignored him. He reached down and plugged the razor into an electrical outlet in the wall next to the bed.

"Last chance," the doctor said. "Are you going to cooperate, or must I call my assistant?"

"Shouldn't your assistant be doing this, anyway? Taking care of your light work?" Ryan Smith couldn't have cared less about the division of labor inside this insane asylum, but if he could get the doctor talking maybe he could slow the inevitable, and even a momentary delay would be preferable to the alternative.

Protasov met his eyes and Ryan knew instantly he understood what Ryan was attempting to do. Still, he answered the question. "Quite honestly, I do not trust the man. He was provided to me by the KGB, more to keep an eye on me and my work than to 'assist,' I am certain."

"That's reassuring," Ryan mumbled.

"Exactly," the doctor agreed amiably. "And you are far too valuable to me to risk the kind of damage Yuri could do out of inexperience or lack of attention to detail. So I intend to handle every aspect of this project personally where you are concerned."

"I'm honored," Ryan said drily, trying to quell the panic that threatened to overwhelm him.

"Back to my original question," Protasov said. "Are you going to keep still?"

Ryan sucked in a shuddering breath and blew it out forcefully. "I'm going to look ridiculous as a bald guy."

No response. Apparently the causal conversation was over.

"Fine," Ryan finally said. "Do what you have to do, it's not like I can stop you."

Protasov flicked a switch and the razor began buzzing, the noise harsh and loud. To Ryan it was the sound of utter hopelessness.

21

Date unknown
Time unknown
Unidentified Soviet military installation

This time when Doctor Protasov entered his room, Ryan was dozing fitfully. It was an uneasy sleep, and his eyes flew open and he was instantly awake and alert—or as alert as someone can be who'd been drugged within the last twenty-four hours—at the rattle of the doorknob and the flapping of the man's lab coat upon his entry.

"How are we doing today?" Protasov said brightly.

A little too brightly, Ryan thought. *He's like a kid on Christmas morning looking forward to playing with his new toy.*

"We'd be doing a lot better if we were uncuffed and allowed to leave this house of horrors," Ryan snapped. "I don't appreciate being held illegally and without cause."

"Oh, please," Protasov said. "You might just as well drop the 'poor, innocent me' act. You're not going anywhere, at least not until this process has been successfully completed. And as far as your claim that you are being held illegally is concerned, we both know that is preposterous."

"Is that so?"

"Of course that is so. You are an unsanctioned agent of espionage, operating inside the Soviet Union for the express purpose of undermining the stability of our government and our very way of life."

"That's ridiculous," Ryan scoffed as the creeping sensation of terror inside him began ratcheting up again.

"It is not ridiculous, it is true. And as an enemy of the Soviet State I am certain you fully understand you are subject to whatever form of punishment my government sees fit to apply to your situation."

"I don't thi—"

"And as an enemy of the Soviet State," Protasov continued, steamrolling right over Ryan's attempted objection, "I am certain you fully understand that no one is coming to save you. No one from your country will even acknowledge your existence inside Russia, much less admit you have gone missing. We can treat you in any manner we see fit and there is not a single thing you, or anyone else, will do about it."

Ryan clamped his mouth shut and glared at the doctor, attempting to maintain a brave front, but it wasn't easy. Everything Protasov had just said was true, right down to the fact that he was helpless in the face of their twisted intentions.

"However," Protasov said, "you should be thanking me instead of lying in that bed spouting self-righteous nonsense."

"How in the hell do you figure that? I'm chained to a bed, head shaved, with the knowledge you're going to drill an extra hole into my skull, and *I* should be thanking *you*?"

"Yes, because, you see, once we've finished here and you've had time to complete your recovery, you will leave the facility and begin your new life."

"Wonderful," Ryan muttered.

"Oh, it will be. It will be a life where you are free to extol the virtues of the Soviet system to all who will listen throughout the world."

"Free to extol the virtues of the Soviet system."

"That is correct. "

"By my way of thinking, the words 'free' and 'Soviet system' really don't fit."

Again Protasov ignored him. "And as a former American spy, your words will be given a weight and significance far beyond those that might have been uttered by almost anyone else. It will be an honor for you, really. One you do not deserve."

"You're going to brainwash me into becoming a mind-numbed robot parroting the words of some Communist propagandist, and I'm supposed to consider that an 'honor?' I guess the Russian definition of that word is a little different than my own."

Another smile from the doctor. Each one struck Ryan as a little creepier than the last. "You will come around to our way of thinking, do not worry."

"Can't wait," Ryan said drily, his stomach heaving. He swallowed back the bile trying to force its way up his windpipe.

"In the meantime," the doctor said, his previous odd giddiness returning, "let us begin. You cannot move on to your new life if we do not first take the necessary steps."

"Don't do this. Don't drill into my head and start playing games with my brain. That's inhumane. It's indecent. It goes against every treaty signed by every civilized nation regarding the treatment of prisoners of war."

"Our nations are not at war, my friend."

"Of course they are. You know, I know it, and everybody on the planet knows it. So if I am, as you claim, an agent of the United States, that by definition makes me a prisoner of war, and you are honor-bound to treat me as such."

"Honor-bound," Protasov repeated. The words rolled off his tongue reluctantly, as if he'd never heard them before. He stood for a moment and then shook his head. "There is no such thing as honor in this world. Certainly not in the modern world, and probably not in the past, either."

"I'm sorry you think that."

"It is a fact. For example, you speak of honor like it is a one-way street. Like it applies only to the Soviet Union. But if you truly valued honor, you would acknowledge your role in attempting to destabilize the government of nations that are not your own, sovereign nations inside which you do not belong. And yet you lie there making denial after denial when we both know the truth. Where is the 'honor' in that?"

Ryan shook his head. "There's no point having a political or sociological debate. It's obvious neither one of us is going to change the mind of the other."

This time, Protasov's smile was so wide his lips seemed to stretch out until Ryan thought they might curve around the sides of his head. "That is where you are wrong, my misguided American friend. I *will* change your mind, and very, very soon."

22

February 3, 1988
7:25 a.m.
Mezhgorye, Bashkir
Narodnaya Revolyutsiya Apartment Complex

Tracie sat in an isolated portion of the apartment parking lot, waiting for her target to exit the building. She'd been here for almost an hour, sipping tea in the darkness, eyes riveted to the front door.

She assumed the young woman would leave for work sometime around seven-thirty, based on her previous two days' surveillance and the distance from the apartment to the base, but wasn't willing to risk missing the woman in the event her guess was wrong. So she rose at five a.m., packed her supplies and then ate a quick breakfast of protein bars and black tea.

She left the inn long before anyone else was up and about, and that was fine with her. The less she was observed, the better.

After completing surveillance last night, she'd driven immediately through town in an attempt to duplicate the secretary's drive and locate her home. Fortunately for Tracie the village was small and the route fairly direct, and she managed well, making just one wrong turn toward the end of the route.

A quarter-mile backtrack corrected her error, and five minutes later the Lada SUV chugged into the correct lot. Tracie spotted the woman's hideous yellow Volga and smiled.

She'd then driven straight to her boarding house, timing the trip.

Fifteen minutes, door to door.

Preparations complete, or at least as complete as possible given the fact she was making her plan up on the fly, Tracie had tumbled into bed and slept without dreaming.

This morning she slipped into the lot just after six and parked in a spot offering an unobstructed view of the apartment building's front entrance. Then she waited, her adrenaline slowly building until now, just after seven-thirty, her nerves were thrumming, her senses hyper-aware, as was always the case while operational.

Across the parking lot the front door opened and Tracie sat up straight. She reached for the Lada's handle and prepared to step out of the vehicle.

False alarm. She slumped back down in the seat in disappointment.

The departing resident was a different person, a young man who descended the three steps to the lot and hurried to his car. He started it up and drove away, white exhaust trailing the vehicle.

And then she was there. Tracie fixed her eyes on the front of the apartment just as the door swung open again and the secretary from last night stepped out.

Tracie grabbed the door handle and cursed under her breath as a second woman exited the building at the same time. She could take both if necessary but preferred to avoid needless complications, and involving a second innocent person in what she had in mind would define the term "complication."

She sat in the front seat, prepared to spring out of the car, watching and waiting for the right moment. The two women moved down the steps, chatting easily, and when they split up at the front of the lot, Tracie made her move.

She climbed out of her vehicle, backpack slung over one shoulder, and was halfway across the lot before either woman noticed her. The target's companion had parked closer to the building than the target, so the companion slipped into her car and pulled the door closed while the target continued toward her Volga.

Tracie stepped behind the target as the woman's companion backed out of her spot, smiling widely for the benefit of the other driver.

"Excuse me," she said, speaking while still a good ten feet away from the target. The last thing she wanted was to startle the woman and have her scream for help.

The target turned in surprise. "Yes?"

The target's companion stopped backing up and shifted into first gear, but then she sat for a moment, the car idling as she watched closely through the side window. She had obviously seen Tracie and wanted to be sure her friend was in no danger before driving away and leaving her alone.

Tracie smiled in the woman's direction and offered a friendly wave. *Nothing to see here, just a silly ditzy woman.*

"I'm sorry to bother you," Tracie said, "but I've forgotten my key and locked myself out of the building."

"This building?"

"Yes."

"I…I don't recognize you."

"Ah. I am Marina." Tracie moved to the woman and stuck her hand out hesitantly. "I just moved into the empty unit, and this is my first day of working my new job and I'm locked out and now I'm going to be late, and…this day is just a disaster already and it has only just begun!"

The target took her hand as an amused smile played across her face.

The target's companion watched the exchange from the inside of her car and took the target's apparent lack of concern as her cue to drive away. She waggled her fingers and then accelerated out of the lot.

And it was just Tracie and the target.

For now.

Tracie turned toward the building. "I don't want to make you late for work, but if you wouldn't mind unlocking the door…" She began walking hurriedly across the lot, knowing the target would follow.

She did, saying, "I didn't even realize there was an empty unit in the building. Which apartment are you in?"

"The one that just became available. You know, the one on the first floor."

They reached the door as the woman wrinkled her forehead

in confusion. "There isn't any empty unit on the first floor. I live in the middle one and I saw the tenants on either side of me just yesterday. Are you sure…"

By this time, Tracie had slipped the gun from her shoulder holster. She placed it gently against the woman's ribs and said, "I'm not going to hurt you unless you scream."

The target's jaw dropped open. She looked too surprised to scream, too surprised even to be afraid. Yet. She said, "I do not understand."

"Unlock the front door," Tracie said, "and take me to your apartment."

"I do not have anything worth stealing."

"I'm not here to steal your things."

"Then what do you—"

"Just do as I ask," Tracie snapped. Another resident could exit the building at any moment. If that happened, things could get complicated in a hurry. She needed to get to the relative safety of the woman's apartment.

And time was ticking away. For her plan to stand any chance of succeeding, Tracie needed to be out of here within ten minutes.

"But—"

"Move." Tracie shoved the weapon hard into the woman's side, and she reluctantly stepped across the threshold. Tracie followed, using her body to shield the gun from the sight of any unseen observers as much as possible.

The foyer was as drab and utilitarian as the apartment's exterior. Faded grey indoor-outdoor carpeting covered the hallway floors, worn almost completely through in high-traffic areas.

A door swung open at the far end of the first floor hallway. A beefy older woman lumbered through it and turned toward them and Tracie whispered, "Do not draw any unwanted attention to us or you die. Do you understand?"

The secretary nodded.

"Now, lead the way to your apartment."

They began moving slowly along the hallway. Halfway between the closed doors of the first and second apartments, they passed the older woman walking the other way.

"Olga," the woman said, "I thought I heard you leave already."

"I…" The secretary hesitated. Tracie cleared her throat and then the woman continued. "I forgot something inside."

"I see." The woman paused thoughtfully and then continued toward the front door. "Well, have a nice day. I'm sure I'll see you soon."

"Yes. Of course. Soon."

The heavy-set woman hit the front door and exited the building and Tracie breathed a sigh of relief. The secretary moved to the closed door of the middle apartment and slipped her key into the lock with one shaking hand.

She opened the door and they entered the apartment and the frightened woman immediately began begging for her life. "Please do not kill me. Take anything you want but please do not—"

"I told you already," Tracie said, "I'm not here to rob you and I'm not going to kill you. I won't even hurt you as long as you do exactly as you're told." She prayed no one else had chosen that moment to step into the hallway where they could hear the woman's pleas before the door had closed fully.

"Then what do you want?"

"I need to be you."

"Excuse me?"

"Don't worry," Tracie reassured the shaken young woman. "It will only be for a little while. Then you can be you again."

23

February 3, 1988
7:35 a.m.
Mezhgorye, Bashkir

"I do not understand." The look on the young woman's face was one of utter confusion. She backed away from Tracie and banged into a small living room table. She didn't seem to notice.

"I'm going to secure you inside your apartment. I will borrow your car and your identity, both of which I will return to you later today." She didn't bother adding *assuming I survive.*

"I do not understand," she repeated.

"You don't have to," Tracie said. She dropped her backpack onto the floor and unzipped it while keeping her Beretta trained on the target. She found her roll of duct tape and removed it from the bag.

"Where is your husband?" she said.

"Who?"

"Your husband. I assume he's still sleeping?"

"I am not married," the secretary said.

"Your roommate, then. Where is she?"

"There is no roommate. I live alone."

"Good," Tracie said. "Take a seat."

"I do not understand."

"Remember a moment ago, when I said I wouldn't hurt you as long as you do exactly as you're told?"

135

The woman nodded mutely, eyes wide and face pale.

"Right now you are not doing as you're told. Sit down or I *will* hurt you."

The woman shrugged out of her winter coat and dropped it where she stood. Then she edged sideways away from Tracie as if afraid to turn her back on her, as if by watching her she might somehow be able to change her fate if Tracie decided to pull the trigger.

She moved into the kitchen in three steps—the apartment was tiny—and pulled on one of the chairs placed face-in at her dinner table. She turned it around and sat.

"Good job. See? We're getting along just fine," Tracie said, and the secretary didn't respond. She licked her lips nervously and waited.

"Now, hand me your ID, please." A Red Army-issued identification card hung on a lanyard around the woman's neck. It was roughly the size of an American credit card and featured a headshot photo of the secretary as well as a series of indecipherable letters and numbers.

"You want…this?" She reached up and touched the card. She had been confused before, but now seemed nonplussed at the notion that the petite criminal holding a gun on her might want to gain access to a restricted area protected by trained soldiers armed with automatic weapons.

I don't blame you, Tracie thought. *In fact, I share your skepticism. This really doesn't seem like the smartest plan I've ever dreamed up.*

But she didn't say that. She just nodded and said, "Yes, I want that."

The secretary lifted the lanyard over her head and handed the ID to Tracie, who placed it around her neck, wearing it exactly as the woman had.

Then she said, "Now I'll need your keys."

This time the woman complied immediately. She'd been unlocking her car when Tracie appeared in the parking lot, and she still held a small fob featuring four keys in her right hand. She reached out and passed them over.

Tracie took them and then began opening kitchen drawers. On

the third try she found what she was looking for and removed a small dishtowel.

"I'm sorry to do this to you," she said, "but I can't have you screaming and drawing attention to yourself. So open up."

"I will not scream, I promise you, I will sit quietly and—"

"Open your mouth," Tracie said firmly, and the woman's eyes widened exactly as they had when she first got a look at Tracie's Beretta. She stopped speaking and obeyed.

Tracie stuffed the towel into the woman's open mouth and then secured the gag with duct tape. She wound it horizontally over her mouth and around the back of her head, and then vertically, winding it under her jaw and then over the top of her head. By the time she finished, the only portion of the woman's face left exposed was her nose and eyes.

Tracie finished by securing the secretary's wrists and elbows to the chair and then her ankles and knees.

Then she glanced at her watch. Seven forty. She could make it but she had to move *now*.

She straightened and faced the secretary, now bound and gagged and helpless. "You're going to have a long and uncomfortable day, but you'll be fine. Someone will come for you when I've finished doing what I need to do."

The woman looked unconvinced. She returned Tracie's gaze with pleading eyes, and Tracie felt a rush of shame at what she was putting an innocent woman through.

Then she thought about Ryan Smith, and how exhausted and helpless he'd looked being marched out of the back of a Soviet Army truck, facing who knew what sorts of horrors inside that military base, alone and possibly injured, and her shame vanished, replaced by a steely determination.

Without another word she spun on her heel. She picked up the woman's coat on the way out of her apartment and slipped into it. Then she double-timed out of the apartment building.

* * *

Tracie hurried out the exterior door and down the steps. She wanted to sprint but knew that doing so would only raise the suspicions of anyone who might happen to glance out an apartment window.

So she walked. Quickly. As she did so, she glanced at the army-issued ID card hanging on the lanyard around her neck. The woman whose identity she'd just stolen was named Olga Trentiova. She wondered if she would live long enough to return Olga's things to her.

She moved directly to the secretary's car and then past it, to the snow piled up at the edge of the parking lot. She picked up piles of it, fluffy and light in the bitterly cold temperatures, and hurriedly smeared it around the window on the driver's side door. Instantly her bare fingers turned red and numb.

Ignoring her freezing hands, Tracie opened the door and repeated the process on the inside of the window. She packed the snow as tightly as possible, stifling a grin even through her buzzing nerves and pounding adrenaline as she pictured someone watching her, trying to figure out what in the hell the crazy young woman was doing to her car.

She caked on the snow and then shook her hands. Clapped them together in a mostly fruitless attempt to stimulate blood flow. Took another look at her watch.

Seven-forty-five.

She was out of time.

She leapt into the driver's seat and pulled the door closed. Some of the snow she'd just packed onto the interior and exterior of the window fell away, but more than half remained in place. Hopefully it would be enough. If nothing else it should frost the window.

The car started on the first try—*thank God for small favors*— and Tracie raced out of the lot, fishtailing around the corners. She slid to a stop at the road, then pointed the car in the direction of the base and jammed the accelerator to the floor.

24

February 3, 1988
7:58 a.m.
Ipatiev Military Research Facility

Two cars were pulling up to the guard shack as Tracie approached the access road. She recognized them from yesterday as vehicles belonging to the secretaries. Her goal had been to arrive at the installation after the rest of the secretarial staff for the obvious reason that if any of the women were watching when she exited Olga Trentiova's car her cover would be blown immediately.

There was no way for Tracie to know whether any of the other women were still behind her and had yet to arrive, but she doubted it. The time was 7:58, and to a young woman living in a village the size of Mezhgorye, working inside the research facility would likely represent the best career option she would ever have. Tracie was willing to bet that barring an unexpected issue like a flat tire or other car trouble, none of the secretaries would risk losing her job because of a late arrival.

In fact, she was betting her life on it.

She slowed the car to give the women ahead of her plenty of time to park and enter the administration building. Arriving after eight o'clock would be a mistake in that it would make her stand out in the guards' minds, but she was close enough to "on time" that it would hopefully not raise their suspicions.

She blew out a nervous breath and turned onto the access road.

Walking the tightrope of timing was stressful as hell. It had been a long day already and it was only eight a.m.

It was about to get a lot longer.

Halfway between the street and the guard shack Tracie glanced to the left and nodded grimly. Her goal in packing the snow against the driver's side window had been to make it as difficult as possible for the soldier manning the security building to get a clear look inside the vehicle as she passed, and she believed she had accomplished that goal.

A bit of snow remained on the inside of the window and she brushed it away. Between the condensation on the interior of the glass and the splotches of snow left on the exterior, Tracie guessed it would be nearly impossible for the guard to see that the woman inside the Volga was not Olga Trentiova.

Unless, of course, he stopped her and forced her to roll down the window.

She approached the gate, moving slowly. Lifted Trentiova's ID and displayed it, picture side out, against the window. She'd covered her flame-red hair with a kerchief this morning, and given the similarity in body type between her and Olga, Tracie figured there should be no reason for suspicion on the guard's part.

Still, she would be completely exposed should the sentry stop her. She'd placed her Beretta 92SB on the seat under her right thigh, and she fingered it nervously with her right hand while holding the ID card against the window with her left, still rolling slowly and almost abeam the shack.

She'd almost come to a complete stop now, nowhere to go, and she made a gesture of impatience with her hands. *Come on, dammit, raise the gate. I'm late for work.*

Just as she resigned herself to a messy scene—she could get the drop on the gate guard easily enough, but undoubtedly some of the men in the guard towers were watching, and with scopes and high-powered rifles they would fill the Volga full of holes long before Tracie ever got close to the end of the access road—the wheeled gate began trundling open.

She breathed a sigh of relief but wondered whether the guard's hesitation in opening it had been due to suspicion or if he simply hadn't been paying attention. If it was the former, she could be in big trouble because someone would be watching closely when she exited the car.

There was no way to know the answer to that question, and it was moot anyway, because the gate had now opened widely enough to allow access.

Tracie hit the gas and chugged into the facility. With the exception of Ryan Smith, who had arrived yesterday in chains, she would be the first American—in all probability the first non-Soviet, period—ever to set foot inside this base.

It was not a comforting thought. She was going to attempt the rescue of an American prisoner with no backup, no prior knowledge of the facility's interior, and no idea where Smith had been taken or for what purpose.

Suicide mission.

The thought flitted into her head and she forced it away. Years of working undercover and in dangerous locations had taught her that an operative's most valuable tool wasn't backup or a detailed mission plan or even weaponry, although all those things were important.

The most valuable tool for an operative working undercover was confidence. Ninety percent of the time, people saw what they expected to see. Even if the guards were watching her, as long as she parked the Volga and climbed out like she belonged, the odds were good that none of them would think twice.

Unless they were watching through binoculars. No amount of confidence in the world was going to fool a solider who could see with his own two eyes, up close and personal, that someone other than Olga Trentiova had driven Olga Trentiova's car onto a heavily fortified military facility.

Tracie turned right, toward the administration building, watching in her rearview mirror as the front gate reversed direction and rolled closed behind her. It latched with a loud *clang* that could be heard even through the closed windows and over the old car's engine noise.

She pulled into the parking lot she'd seen the staff members use yesterday, relieved to see it filled with cars but devoid of people. The other women had already entered the administration building, as she'd hoped. After killing the engine and slipping her Beretta back into her shoulder rig, Tracie took a deep breath and exited the car.

She walked through the lot and toward the building, standing tall and exuding confidence.

She hoped.

A few people wandered the grounds, but they were all in the distance and paid no attention to Tracie. The vast majority of workers had already left the housing units and made their way to one of the three warehouse-looking buildings scattered throughout the base that Tracie had begun to think of as subway stations. Based on her previous surveillance, she guessed few if any of those workers would appear again before late afternoon.

If her theory was correct, those three structures—the subway stations—offered access to the underground portions of the facility. That made the structures her intended destination.

She crossed the parking lot and moved in the general direction of the administration building, praying no one chose this moment to exit in the direction of his or her car. It seemed unlikely, since everyone had just arrived to start the day, but who the hell knew?

As she approached the steps leading to the entrance, Tracie turned left and followed a partially shoveled sidewalk across the front of the building. Pathways crisscrossed the facility, offering Tracie access to the structures she wanted to explore, but the price of that access was an unprotected walk over open land in full view of the guard towers.

It was a price that had to be paid. She'd gotten safely onto the base, but merely gaining entrance to the facility would be pointless. It represented nothing more than the first step toward her ultimate goal: saving Ryan Smith.

Tracie passed the end of the administration building and moved toward the closest of the three subway stations. She moved hurriedly, but not so fast she would draw undue attention to herself. She was a worker anxious to escape the bitter cold, nothing more.

So far, so good. No alarm bells rang, no sirens wailed, no soldiers with guns came running to challenge her.

She'd made it slightly more than halfway between the administration building and the closest subway station when a man exited the building through the only visible door. She willed him to turn right and follow an empty pathway but instead he walked straight ahead.

Directly toward her.

It was unfortunate but she'd known it was bound to happen eventually. Tracie swallowed heavily, nerves thrumming, and kept walking. She maintained her previous steady pace and met the man's eyes briefly, offering the polite-but-uninterested half-smile of a woman sharing an elevator with a stranger, or a worker-bee just trying to get through the day.

The man wasn't a soldier, or at least was not wearing a Red Army overcoat. She hoped that meant he would be less likely to challenge her. Tracie had turned her ID around before exiting Olga Trentiova's car in the parking lot, meaning the head shot photo wouldn't be visible to him.

Unless it had flipped back over as she walked. She hadn't really given the possibility any thought until now.

She watched as his gaze flitted from her face to her ID and then back to her face. He didn't react, which meant he hadn't seen that the photo didn't match the face.

He seemed to hesitate, slowing just a bit, even in the brutal temperatures of a Ural Mountain February morning. Then they passed and she breathed a silent sigh of relief. The man continued walking toward the area of the base that Tracie had just left, and for the moment at least, nobody else was around who could be considered a threat.

She glanced up at the door the man had just exited.

It was secured with a cipher lock.

Dammit. Tracie wanted to hit herself in the head like the guy in the V-8 commercials on television. Except, instead of saying "I could have had a V-8," she would say, "I could have preplanned better."

Why hadn't it occurred to her that the damned door would be locked?

What the hell do I do now? She couldn't very well loiter in front of the door, waiting for someone else to exit so she could slip inside. The guards in the ubiquitous towers dotting the facility would notice something like that in about fifteen seconds. Roughly fifteen seconds after *that* she would either find herself face down on the cold ground and leaking blood from multiple bullet holes, or cuffed with her hands behind her back being marched to wherever Ryan Smith was being held.

She continued to walk at the same rapid, measured pace, knowing she had just seconds to come up with some kind of plan or become as noticeable to the Soviets as if she started waving her arms and shouting, "I'm an American spy!"

She reached the door.

Turned three hundred sixty degrees.

Tried to think.

Came up with nothing.

25

February 3, 1988
8:10 a.m.
Ipatiev Military Research Facility

Tracie made the snap decision to try the only ploy she could think of.

"Excuse me!" she shouted at the back of the man who'd passed her moments ago on the icy concrete pathway.

He stopped and turned, eyebrows raised curiously. He glanced in all directions as if unsure whether she was addressing him.

"I'm so sorry," she continued. She raised her hands in the air and trotted toward the man, arranging her expression into the best "helpless female" look she could manage.

"I am sorry to bother you," she repeated when she had gotten close enough that shouting was no longer necessary. She knew at least some of the guards up in the towers must be watching the exchange by now, so she had to make this convincing.

She smiled brightly and shrugged. *Be ditzy.* "I noticed that you just exited the building I need to enter. My coworker gave me the code to unlock the door, but I've already forgotten it. Would you be so kind as to rescue me?"

The man took a step or two in her direction. His forehead was wrinkled in confusion but the instant suspicion she would have expected from a soldier was missing. This guy was something else, maybe a researcher or scientist, but she didn't think he was a man who carried a gun for a living.

Still, she would have to be very careful; there were plenty of guys who carried guns for a living within shouting distance.

Or shooting distance.

"You…don't know the code?"

She scuffed at the frozen ground with the toe of her boot in feigned embarrassment and tried to force tears into her eyes. "No, and I am going to get in so much trouble if I have to go all the way back to the administration building and ask. I just started working here, and one of the other girls sent me over to get something, and she told me the code before I left the office and now I can't remember it and they already think I don't know enough to work here and I'll probably lose my job and—"

"Please, do not cry," the man interrupted. He raised his hands and shook them, palms down, in a clumsy attempt to calm the nearly hysterical young lady in front of him. "I can help you. We will make sure you do not lose your job today, okay?" He started walking back toward the warehouse-looking building as Tracie followed.

She sniffled, hoping she wasn't laying it on too thickly. But no woman could reach her late twenties without becoming acutely aware of how uncomfortable most men—especially strangers—became at the prospect of dealing with a crying woman. Was it sexist? Maybe, but Tracie had always been far too busy running ops to worry about societal norms. And she was not above using sexism or any other tool at her disposal when her life was on the line.

The man turned his head as they walked and glanced at Tracie. The confused expression had returned and he seemed to be slowing his pace. "You…need something…*here?*"

Oh-oh.

She nodded shyly and met his eyes for a half-second, then looked down at the ground.

"What could you possibly need…*here?*"

"Um…I…"

His eyes hardened. "Why do you need to get in here?"

"It's female stuff, alright? I just started my period and I don't have anything with me and one of the girls in the office told me where to find a supply of tampons and oh my God this is so humiliating and…" She started to cry.

The man took a step back. His eyes were wide and his expression couldn't have been any more shocked if Tracie had admitted to being an American spy.

He raised his hands, this time to ensure she didn't start speaking again. "It is okay, really. You do not need to explain further." He hurriedly punched the numbers into the cypher keypad as Tracie watched carefully, still pretending to sob with downcast eyes.

He pulled open a heavily reinforced steel door and held it open for her, the perfect gentleman. She looked up at him through eyes wet with tears and said, "Thank you for understanding. Thank you so much."

"It is nothing," he said without meeting her gaze. He released his hold on the door after she stepped through it and then hurried away as it began to close on its own.

She tried to suppress a smile as the door clanged shut.

* * *

Tracie's first thought was that her assumption as to the purpose of the three subway stations—at least if this one was any indication—had been spot-on.

The structure was nothing more than a heated tin half-moon plunked down on top of a concrete foundation, like a large Quonset hut. As far as Tracie could tell, the doorway through which she'd just entered offered the only access. The interior of the building consisted of a series of elevators and stairways, all offering below ground access, presumably to different portions of the base.

Judging from the number of elevators and stairways inside this unit, the Soviets had constructed a massive facility below the snowy surface of the Urals, especially if the other two subway stations contained an equivalent number of underground portals.

Construction must have taken years, and it had all been kept hidden from United States intelligence services until recently.

Tracie shook her head. How many other secret military bases were tucked away in the hundreds of thousands of square miles of desolation making up so much of the Soviet Union?

It was a frightening thought but one that was irrelevant to her current situation. Right now, Tracie needed to get moving. Anyone could exit a stairway or elevator at any time, and the next person to do so might not be as friendly—or as gullible—as the last man Tracie had encountered.

The question was where should she go? Each elevator and stairway was labeled, but unfortunately the labeling system the Soviets had designed was utterly useless to someone with no working knowledge of the facility: Area A, Area B, Area C, and so forth. The signs meant nothing to her.

Might as well start with A. Once she'd made the decision, Tracie wasted no time. She had no intention of getting trapped inside an elevator, so she strode to the stairway beneath the metal sign with rusting edges marked "Area A," and began descending.

The stairway was dank and the lighting poor, consisting of a single electric bulb placed inside a wire cage and bolted to the side wall every ten feet or so. The bulbs couldn't have been more than twenty or thirty watts each, meaning the descent was conducted in a murky semi-darkness that reminded her of dusk inside a heavily wooded area.

She moved slowly and quietly, not wanting to telegraph her presence to anyone who might be climbing in the opposite direction. The stairway had been constructed in sections, each consisting of a half-dozen steps down to a corrugated metal landing, then a one hundred eighty degree turn and another six steps down to the next landing and another one hundred eighty degree turn.

The design made it impossible to see more than a few feet ahead, so Tracie would need the advantage of surprise should a soldier turn the corner and become suspicious at encountering a civilian in the stairwell. Presumably the majority of the workers used the elevators, but it wouldn't be a military facility without regular armed patrols that undoubtedly included these stairways.

She rounded the second landing, wondering how deep into the side of the mountain the Soviets had dug, and froze at the sound of the metal door clanging open at ground level above. A pair of male voices echoed down the stairwell, sharing a laugh at a joke Tracie hadn't heard.

At least two people had just entered the subway station.

Instinct told her to flee, to charge down the stairs in a desperate attempt to stay ahead of the men should they begin descending to Area A. She took one quick step toward the next landing and then stopped.

The stairs were constructed of the same corrugated metal as the landings, and they were contained inside a square metal shaft. Their method of construction tended to magnify even the faintest of noises, sounds reverberating through the shaft at a volume that reminded Tracie of sitting in the front row at a heavy metal concert. If she started clomping down the stairs now she would almost certainly draw the attention of the men standing above her head, not to mention anyone else who might be within earshot.

So she waited, eyes narrowed in concentration, ears attuned to the slightest whisper of sound, straining to hear whether the heavy boots would begin descending. The men had lots of choices, including any of the elevators, so the odds were in her favor that if she simply stood still and kept quiet that within ten seconds the footsteps would fade away and all would once again be still.

But of course it didn't work out that way.

The men paused for a moment, still chuckling over the joke Tracie hadn't heard, and then the boots began pounding down the stairs, the sound loud and menacing.

Tracie wasn't even surprised. She had just seconds to react and then the two men would round the corner and they would be face-to-face.

Time to execute Plan B.

If only she had one.

26

The way she saw this situation she had just two choices: confront the men when they turned the corner or continue down the stairway and try to stay ahead of them.

Each option offered distinct disadvantages. She had every confidence she could disable two men, even if they were armed and trained Red Army soldiers. She would have the advantage of surprise, which she could use to devastating effect. The men would never expect to be accosted deep inside a highly secure military facility. She could have them on the floor and unconscious almost before they knew what hit them.

But she had no way of knowing how long it would take before someone else used this stairwell and stumbled over the men. If that happened, an alarm would certainly be sounded and then she would be trapped on the base. She would be hunted down and eventually captured. It would be inevitable.

On the other hand, descending the stairs ahead of the men was a risky proposition due to the very fact she was operating blind. She had no clue what might be beyond the next landing, and whatever it was might well represent a greater danger than she currently faced.

All of this went through Tracie's mind in an instant, and she made her decision before the men had passed the second step.

She would continue down the stairs.

There were plenty of disadvantages to being a petite woman, particularly in a business where a premium was often placed on brawn. But Tracie had always managed to rely on intelligence and quick thinking to more than make up for what she lacked in physical strength. And this was one time she was thankful for being small and light.

She raced down the stairs, holding the iron handrail with both hands, using it to take as much pressure off her feet as possible. She stepped lightly on the portions of the stairs that had been bolted to the risers in an effort to minimize noise, and in seconds had rounded the next landing.

Still the stairs continued, winding farther and farther underground. They seemed to go on forever. The men rounded the first landing, boots clattering, arguing loudly about which one had gotten drunker last weekend. They were utterly oblivious, and it occurred to Tracie that she could probably take the stairs three at a time, leaping down to each landing with a loud *thud,* and the men would likely not even notice.

Two more landings and she finally arrived at a door. It was constructed of metal, exactly like the one she'd tricked the researcher—or whatever he was—into opening for her up on the ground floor, except this one had been built with a small window of wire-reinforced impact-resistant glass located at approximately eye level, perhaps three inches wide by nine inches high.

Decision time again. Plunge through the entryway or take on the men still descending the stairs?

She pressed her eyes to the little window, praying now wasn't the time someone would fling open the door from the other side and catch her in the face with the reinforced metal corner.

A long hallway stood on the other side of the window, populated with a series of closed wooden doors running down each side. The hallway was empty, at least for the moment. After a long distance—sixty feet? More?—the corridor terminated at another metal door identical to this one.

The emptiness of the hallway made Tracie's decision an easy one. She eased the door open and slipped through it. There was no other option for the men behind her but to take the identical route, so Tracie knew she had to move quickly.

She had played soccer and run track in high school, and even now, ten years after graduation, could beat almost anyone she knew in a one hundred yard dash. But she could have been an Olympic gold medalist sprinter and she still wouldn't have been able to make it the length of the hallway before the men following her reached the landing.

She stepped to the first door on the right and peered through the small reinforced window, her heart pounding and her hands shaking from the adrenaline racing through her system. The interior looked empty, and although the rooms were labeled only with a letter-number sequence—this was room A-1—it appeared to be nothing more than a simple storage closet.

Tracie doubted there would be many better options and in any event knew she was just about out of time, so she pushed open the door and stepped through.

She reached under the heavy winter parka for her Beretta, snugged up next to her right breast in a shoulder holster, and eased the door closed. The latch caught with a *snick* that sounded like thunder under the circumstances.

The room was illuminated brightly—at least relative to the subterranean dimness of the stairwell—by a series of ceiling-mounted fluorescent bulbs, with no way Tracie could see to dim them. Probably the lights on the entire underground level were controlled by one master switch.

Dammit.

If she could shut off the lights, she could step back from the door and watch the men pass by in the hallway without risking being seen herself. But with the lights on, that plan would be a recipe for disaster.

Instead of moving to the middle of the room, Tracie flattened herself against the wall next to the door on the hinged side. If the men entered, the door would open and Tracie would be shielded behind it. She could then step out from behind it and take them down once they were inside the storeroom.

She eased her head forward until she could see just enough of the hallway to know when the men were passing. A second later the door clanked open out in the hallway and two male figures passed Tracie's hiding place. The men were still arguing good-naturedly, paying little attention to their surroundings.

Tracie decided to push her luck. It was clear the men weren't entering this storage area, but if possible she wanted to see where they *were* going. So she twisted the knob and eased open the door, moving slowly, leaving just enough room to see the length of the hallway with her left eye. These two idiots were so oblivious they would never notice, but there was always the chance someone else would descend the stairs and enter the hallway behind her.

It was worth the risk.

She watched the two men saunter down the corridor. They weren't soldiers, and even though they were still dressed in their heavy winter overcoats Tracie took them to be researchers, or scientists, or academics of some kind, much like the man she'd tricked to gain entrance to the subway station. They appeared unarmed.

They moved slightly more than two-thirds of the way down the hall and then disappeared into a room on the right side.

Tracie leaned out a little farther and counted the doors. She didn't want to discover the hard way that she had been mistaken about where those two men had gone.

This portion of the facility was once again silent and empty.

It seemed there should be more activity given the size of the base and the number of rooms lining the hallway.

How many other corridors like this one had been built in this underground labyrinth?

What might the Soviets be doing down here?

And most importantly, where was Ryan Smith being held and what was being done to him?

So far, more questions were being raised than answered.

27

February 3, 1988
8:30 a.m.
Ipatiev Military Research Facility

Tracie eased the door closed after the two men disappeared into the room down the long hallway.

She was conscious of the time ticking away and the need to keep moving if she were to have any chance whatsoever of rescuing Ryan Smith before she had to escape the facility and make her way to the extraction point. The tunnels crisscrossing the ground below this base were extensive, she could see that already, and there was no way of knowing how many she would have to slog through before locating Smith.

Or if it were even possible.

But she'd been sent to the Ural Mountains on a mission that had nothing to do with rescuing a captured operative: to learn all she could about this newly discovered secret facility. And while her top priority had shifted the moment she saw Ryan exit that cargo truck in chains and under armed guard, she still had a responsibility to accomplish her assignment to the best of her ability.

Which meant she should take a couple of minutes to examine this storeroom before continuing on.

The room was shaped in what appeared to be a near-perfect square. Rows of metal shelving lined the interior, all covered with crates and cartons and boxes. Some were sealed, others had been opened or had their tops removed.

A quick walk-through was all it took for a chill to run down Tracie's spine. There were gas masks of endless shapes and sizes. Tanks that resembled fire extinguishers, some as tall as Tracie and others so small they would fit in the palm of her hand. There were nozzles and hoses and gauges and clear masks without gas filters built in, as well as standard scientific gear, such as beakers and Bunsen burners and cleaning materials.

And there were biohazard suits. Two rows of shelving were dedicated solely to various sizes of full-body coveralls that resembled what an astronaut might wear to conduct a moonwalk. Varying thicknesses suggested differing uses, as well as graduated levels of protection from a variety of substances.

Everything inside this storage area seemed related to one endeavor: the production and testing of toxic chemical materials or hazardous gases.

That in itself was not particularly surprising. U.S. intelligence services had long been aware of Soviet chemical and biological weapons manufacturing programs. Specifics of the programs were nebulous, due to the limited number of operatives working inside the Soviet Union and the sheer vastness of the area throughout which the manufacturing plants were located, but its existence was undisputed.

Tracie was certain that similar programs were being vigorously pursued inside the United States and elsewhere in the world. They were an unfortunate component of modern foreign policy.

But the fact that this research was being conducted deep underground, inside a military base that had only recently come to the attention of the United States, was more problematic than the knowledge the Soviets had opened a new chemical/biological research facility. Was it because this program was dedicated to the most deadly of gases, chemicals and nerve agents, or was there some other reason?

Tracie chewed on her lower lip as she considered the implications. It was clear she wouldn't be able to reach any conclusions based on the inspection of one small storage room, and it wasn't her job to reach those conclusions, anyway. That task would be left to teams of men and women who would analyze reams of data, and high-level intelligence specialists who would interpret that data.

Her job was to continue on.

She snapped a few pictures, then stashed her mini-camera and crept to the door, where she pressed her eye to the tiny window and scanned what she could of the outside hallway. It appeared deserted.

She turned the handle and cracked the door just far enough to check the length of the hallway.

Empty.

Then she pushed the door open a little farther, eased through and began walking down the long corridor toward the exit in the distance. Her concern about being seen by someone inside one of the rooms lining the hallway was minimal, thanks to the size of the windows. Anyone who happened to glance out would see only a small slice of corridor, and if Tracie happened to be walking past at that exact moment, the observer would see nothing more than a split-second flash of movement.

It would be impossible for anyone inside one of the rooms, no matter how sharp-eyed, to recognize the person roaming the tunnels outside as an interloper.

The situation would change in an instant, of course, if one of the doors should open and someone step into the hallway. But Tracie guessed she should be okay for a while in that regard. The workday had only begun ninety minutes ago, and she doubted the Soviet researchers' routines included a liberal break schedule.

She took her time, peering as closely into the rooms as reason-ably possible without stopping and pressing her eyes to the glass. The same situation that made it relatively safe for her to roam the hallway—the tiny windows—was a major drawback in terms of allowing her to examine the rooms on her way by, but most of them appeared to be laboratories or research areas.

A few of the spaces appeared empty, although there was no way to know for sure without entering them, and Tracie didn't dare take that step. But inside most of them men in lab coats or wearing protective gear were hard at work, peering into microscopes or measuring unknown substances in test tubes or heating liquids in glass containers.

No one paid the slightest attention to the hallway, where an increasingly concerned Tracie Tanner slowed at each door and glanced inside.

Before long she had reached the end of the hallway and the reinforced metal door. Without knowing what might be on the other side of the door she had no idea how to proceed, but she supposed there wasn't much choice involved. It wasn't like she had any intention of turning around.

She eased the exit door open as quietly as possible and pushed through.

On the other side, a system of concrete tunnels branched off in three directions. The tunnels were slightly wider than the shafts containing the stairs Tracie had descended earlier, but just as poorly lit and the sound of the metal door closing echoed off in all directions despite the fact she'd tried to be as quiet as possible. Narrow rivulets of water meandered down the tunnel walls in various locations, frozen in place by the bitter Ural winter cold.

Tracie pondered her three options, trying to decide which way to proceed, when the sound of echoing footsteps floated through one of the tunnels.

She stood motionless, listening closely. It was impossible to tell which tunnel contained the person or persons she could hear. The footfalls were everywhere and nowhere, initially little more than a vague rumor but slowly increasing in volume. Someone was definitely approaching.

Tracie remained directly in the center of the small concrete vestibule, determined not to charge randomly down one of the tunnels and potentially straight into a Russian soldier. Each tunnel curved out of sight within twenty feet of her current location, so as long as she chose one of the two empty tunnels to follow, the approaching person would never know she was there.

The heavy clop-clop-clop of footfalls on concrete told her it was definitely a man. That came as little surprise, since with the exception of the half-dozen female administrative staff members, Tracie had seen only a handful of women inside the base. But as the man came closer and the sound gained clarity, she became convinced it was a soldier and not a researcher. The footfalls screamed "combat boots," not winter boots like a scientist would wear.

As was the case with the men descending the stairs behind her a little while ago, Tracie had no doubt she could handle one Russian soldier, particularly given the advantage of surprise. But there was nowhere convenient inside these drab and dirty tunnels to stash a body. The incapacitated soldier would be discovered quickly and once that happened, the nature of Tracie's mission would change dramatically.

It was critical she avoid confrontation as long as possible.

The footsteps continued to get louder, which meant the soldier continued to get closer, and soon Tracie became convinced the man was inside the tunnel to her right.

She hesitated a moment longer to be sure, and then began moving quietly along the tunnel to the left. Silence came from that direction, and the tunnel would place her as far from the approaching soldier as possible, provided he didn't immediately follow. If he was on routine patrol she guessed he would reach the vestibule and turn down the middle tunnel. It would make the most sense from a security perspective.

She moved quickly but quietly, alert for any sign of danger. After the initial curve of almost ninety degrees to the left, Tracie saw that the tunnel straightened and continued for a long distance.

There would be no way to outrun the soldier if he chose her tunnel to patrol, so she stopped just beyond the curved portion and waited, hidden in the shadows. If he rounded the corner she would have no choice but to disable him and worry later about the negative consequences that would follow.

She flexed her fingers and developed a quick strategy to deal with the soldier should it become necessary. Pulling her Beretta was the last option, because a gunshot would sound about as loud as a thunderbolt given the acoustics. She resolved to throat-punch him the moment he rounded the corner. That would put him down, and once he fell she would use the crook of her arm to cut off the air supply through his windpipe.

He would be unconscious within seconds.

Then she would disarm him and continue moving.

She leaned against the cold concrete and listened carefully. The footfalls were loud and well defined, and Tracie thought if she could reach around the curved tunnel wall right now she would likely be able to punch the man in the jaw.

Just seconds to go. The sentry would either appear around the corner or the sound of the footsteps would begin to fade away. Tracie's hands were shaking slightly, not from fear but from adrenaline. She'd been in similar situations before, many times, and she faced them with a confidence born of training combined with experience.

Time slowed as she waited for the soldier to make his decision and unwittingly choose his fate. The footsteps had stopped entirely and for a moment Tracie thought she'd been discovered and that the soldier was now somehow stalking her.

Then the sound of a match scraping against a striker was followed by a flare of light from around the corner and the smell of cigarette smoke. The soldier had chosen this moment to take a smoke break.

Tracie cursed inwardly. She couldn't afford to stand here idle while some twenty-two year old Russian kid sneaked a smoke, but she didn't have much choice, either. If she eased down the tunnel and the kid chose that moment to snuff out his cigarette and continue his patrol in her direction she would be a sitting duck.

So she waited.

One minute passed, and then two became three, and then she heard the scraping of boot on cement that told her the soldier had finished his break.

She tensed up again as the sound of footsteps began anew.

A moment later they began to fade. The soldier had chosen the middle tunnel in which to continue his patrol.

You have no idea how lucky you are. The thought flashed through Tracie's head, and it occurred to her she wasn't sure whether it was directed at the anonymous soldier or herself.

Not that it really mattered.

She took a deep breath and continued moving down the tunnel she'd chosen, silent and undetected, a lonely wraith surrounded by enemies.

28

February 3, 1988
11:05 a.m.
Administration Building
Ipatiev Military Research Facility

"Colonel Kopalev, I am thrilled you have chosen to travel all the way to Bashkir for a personal update on our project," Vladimir Protasov heard himself say. He hoped the lie wasn't as obvious to the KGB man as it sounded to himself.

Kopalev smiled. To Vlad, the look was utterly devoid of warmth. It more closely resembled the expression of a cat toying with a mouse just before breaking its back.

"This trip is long overdue," Kopalev said. "Given the fact that you have yet to offer any tangible return on the KGB's investment of time and money, I felt perhaps a little personal…motivation, shall we say…might be appropriate. As we discussed on the telephone."

"Of course," Vlad answered. The words rang hollow in his ears. It was as if they were being spoken by someone else. A stranger. It was hard to concentrate over the rising sense of panic he'd felt ever since learning Kopalev would be coming to Ipatiev for no other reason than to review Vlad's work.

For a time after beginning this project, Vlad had felt insulated from the expectation of results, Kopalev's near-constant hectoring notwithstanding. Vlad had anticipated a situation similar to what he'd experienced throughout his career in academia: once a year the university administration would request an accounting of Vlad's research, and once a year Vlad would claim progress.

He would back up his claim via a scholarly research paper, often authored by an assistant, and despite the paper being virtually devoid of any evidence of the progress he claimed, everyone would go away happy until the following year, when the process would be repeated.

It was only recently that Vlad had begun to realize doing research for the KGB was far different from doing research for a mostly disinterested university chancellor. Colonel Kopalev expected real results, and Vlad was learning that producing those results was far more difficult than simply claiming them.

For what was likely the first time in his adult life—certainly for the first time since he'd begun this damned project—Vladimir Protasov yearned for the innumerable layers of bureaucracy infused into the Soviet academic world. Those layers had allowed him to develop a sterling reputation and relatively high standard of living without ever actually producing anything of value.

Even worse, the intensity of Kopalev's interest in his project was frightening.

The colonel had recruited Vlad by making it clear that human behavioral modification through electrical brain stimulation was a top KGB priority, and while signing on to such a high-profile project was a good thing in terms of receiving funding, it also came with an unanticipated negative: Colonel Kopalev expected far more dramatic results far more quickly than was reasonable by any scientific measure.

And the colonel was extremely hands-on.

And he was here at Ipatiev.

And Vlad had precious little good news to report.

His surgery on the prized test subject, the American CIA officer delivered to the camp by Kopalev himself, had not gone well. He'd begun work early, practically in the middle of the night, rushing the job in anticipation of Kopalev's pending arrival, desperate for a positive result to show off to the colonel.

But the operation had not gone as anticipated. Vlad hadn't been sleeping well for weeks, and last night's insomnia had been the worst. He doubted he'd dozed for more than an hour, and when he finally arose at four a.m., bleary-eyed and shaky, he downed two cups of strong black tea just to get his blood pumping.

Then he stumbled across the camp, deserted at such an early hour, and down the elevator to the operating room in the center of his research suite.

The operation had begun well before sunrise, and with Vlad sloppy from nerves and lack of sleep the mistakes came almost immediately, one after the other. There was no way of knowing how badly he'd botched things until the subject's anesthesia wore off fully and Vlad could begin assessing the man's condition, but he knew better than to hope for much.

In particular, the depth of the burr hole was a cause for major concern. Vlad had drilled too far, and to top things off he suspected he'd done so at the wrong angle as well. Precision was critical, and even a slight error could cause unexpected—and drastic—negative results, including strokes, seizures, paralysis and occasionally death.

Thus far the subject was alive—or at least he had been when Vlad last checked on him prior to coming aboveground for this meeting—but that was all he knew for certain.

And that would not be nearly enough to satisfy Colonel Kopalev.

The best-case scenario was that the damage Vlad had caused would not be readily apparent at this early stage of the subject's recovery process. Maybe he could hide that damage from the colonel during this visit. Then, once the man returned to Moscow, Vlad would come up with a reasonable explanation for the subject's demise, one that would not arouse the colonel's suspicion.

It would not be easy, but Vlad could only worry about one thing at a time, and his current concern was simply with getting through today alive. Tomorrow's concerns would have to wait.

Vlad looked up at Colonel Kopalev and then across the desk at Major Antonin Stepanov, Ipatiev's Base Commander. He realized with a sinking feeling that he'd been so deep in thought regarding how he might survive the next few hours that he had retreated entirely from the conversation. It was obvious from the looks on the men's faces that one of them had asked him a question, and he had no idea what that question might be.

Or who had asked it.

He cleared his throat. Tried to appear scholarly and guessed he managed only terrified.

"I'm sorry, I missed that. What was the question?"

"I said I did not fly all the way from Moscow to the middle of nowhere to waste my time in an office watching some academician sit with his eyes glazed over thinking deep academic thoughts. I came here to see your work with my own two eyes, and would like to do so at the first opportunity." Kopalev's gaze was unflinching. It was almost as though he could see right into Vlad's head.

That was not a comforting notion.

"Of course," Vlad said. "Let us not waste any more time. We can get started immediately, although I must warn you, my—"

"*You* are warning *me*? Did I hear that correctly?"

Vlad felt the blood drain from his face at Kopalev's comment. All three men had risen from their chairs and Vlad wished desperately he could sit back down for a moment. His legs were rubbery and all that coffee he'd drunk hours earlier threatened to come rushing back up his gullet in an acidy mess.

"Please excuse my poor choice of phrasing," Vlad said through the roaring in his ears. "Of course I am not warning you about anything. I only meant to advise you that our current test subject, the CIA man you arranged to be transferred here, is still recovering from brain surgery. He may not be responsive at this point."

The KGB colonel fixed Vlad with a steady glare but said nothing. After an uncomfortable moment the three men exited the front door of the administration building and began crunching along the sanded concrete pathway toward the tunnels and Vlad's research suite. Vlad now thought he knew how a condemned man felt as he was being secured in front of the firing squad.

They had traveled perhaps twenty feet along the pathway when Kopalev stopped and gazed at Vlad again, this time with a thoughtful expression. "You have already operated on the American?"

"Of course. You said you wanted to see results as quickly as possible."

"But what about your other subjects? Why dive straight into surgery on the American when you can continue working with lesser subjects first, thus gaining as much useful information as possible from them before moving on?"

He doesn't even know my other subjects are all dead. Vlad's breath caught in his throat and for one terrifying moment he was certain he was going to lose consciousness, pass out and drop to the cold ground like a sack of potatoes.

Or a dead test subject.

He almost wished he would. At least then this excruciating deception would be over.

Then he came to his senses. If the KGB colonel discovered progress had been nearly nonexistent over the past year despite Vlad's repeated assurances otherwise, the excruciating deception might be over but the excruciating physical pain Kopalev would inflict on him would likely just be beginning.

"I…" He was aware of both Kopalev and Stepanov looking at him oddly. "I just felt that sufficient progress has been made to begin working with the American, that is all."

There was another long pause as Kopalev regarded Vlad through narrowed eyes. Then he turned and continued walking.

"I guess we shall see about that," he said quietly.

29

Something was wrong.

Ryan wasn't even fully awake and he could tell something was wrong.

He felt cold. Bitterly cold. Teeth-rattlingly cold.

It wasn't a normal kind of cold, like the deep-seated chill he felt when he went skiing and got stuck on the chairlift because someone had fallen getting on and they had to shut the damned thing down for a few minutes.

It wasn't even the kind of cold he'd experienced over the course of the long Russian winter, when the temperatures sometimes plummeted so low at night it was dangerous to leave even a tiny bit of skin exposed for more than a few seconds.

This was a cold that emanated deep inside his body, a cold that was unrelated to the temperature. A cold that seemed somehow infused in his bones. A cold unlike anything he'd ever felt before.

So he knew something was wrong even before he knew where he was or what was happening to him, even as he blinked his eyes in a desperate attempt to stay conscious and avoid sliding back into the darkness lurking just beyond his current semi-conscious state.

He was lying in a bed; he knew that much. He knew also,

somehow, that he was *not* lying in his own bed, the surprisingly comfortable one he'd been provided inside his CIA-assigned Moscow apartment. His safe house. He was not inside his safe house, he could just tell.

He tried to shake his head to wake himself up a little more, tiny little jiggles like he did when he was hung over, but he was surprised to discover he couldn't manage it. Not even a little bit. His head was completely immobilized.

He tried to raise a hand, to get a feel for whatever had been clamped onto his head to restrain him, and he couldn't do that, either. His arm had been immobilized, too.

Understanding returned. The memories flooded back. He'd been captured and was being held—against his will, obviously—at a Soviet research facility located far off the beaten path, even for Russia. The transport truck had taken days to get here, which meant he might not even *be* inside Russia any longer, although there was little doubt he was still captive in a Soviet state.

And if he'd been afraid before, that sensation was easily eclipsed by the terror that descended upon Ryan Smith now. It was mammoth. It was everything he'd ever been afraid of his entire life, all his childhood and grownup fears rolled into one horrifying ball of dread, times one hundred.

One thousand.

Because that crazy Soviet scientist had shaved his head and then drilled a hole in Ryan's skull and inserted electrical wires designed to manipulate Ryan's brain, to force him to say and do things against his will that he would never agree to say or do on his own.

And if that wasn't awful enough, the goddamned scientist had bungled the operation. Protasov had nicked the wrong part of his brain, or drilled through a nerve, or done who the hell knew what, but he'd injured Ryan, and badly, based on the way Ryan felt right now.

He supposed it was technically possible the bone-chilling cold he felt emanating from deep inside was a reaction to the anesthesia the lunatic had used. Ryan's knowledge of surgical procedure was limited to what he'd seen in a handful of movies and television shows, and he knew there was virtually no level of realism to be found in Hollywood.

And his knowledge of *Russian* surgical procedure was even less.

But even as he considered the possibility that he was being affected by whatever drugs the Russian had pumped into him, he discarded it. Because the chill inside his body wasn't the only symptom he was feeling.

Far from it.

His extremities tingled, his fingers and toes buzzing as if he'd grabbed a high-tension wire. His head throbbed and his brain felt foreign to him. It was as though the entire contents of his cranium had been removed and replaced by someone else's, someone dimwitted and slow. His muscles were spasming, random portions of his body clenching and releasing for no apparent reason as his brain sent confused messages out along his nervous system.

Ryan swallowed heavily and for maybe the hundredth time since being taken by the KGB outside that damned Moscow nightclub—had it really been less than a week?—he cursed his stupidity in thinking he could get away with having a night out for a few drinks like a normal man in his twenties.

Because he wasn't a normal man in his twenties. Normal men didn't risk their lives operating undercover inside the boundaries of their home nation's sworn enemy. Normal men didn't leave everything behind, their homes and families and friends, to gather and relay intelligence that could get them killed should they be caught.

And while he hadn't been killed, he *had* been caught, and Ryan was starting to believe he'd have been better off had the KGB hauled him to Lubyanka and filled him full of 9mm slugs on the night they captured him. That fate would have been preferable to this, to being trussed up like a Thanksgiving turkey, lost and alone and now badly injured by a quack researcher.

Ryan tamped down on the fear and forced himself to focus. He was never getting out of here; he knew that now. He supposed he'd known it all along. The Russian's talk of brain tissue manipulation and parading Ryan in front of television cameras to spout propagandist nonsense, as horrible as it sounded, would have at least meant Ryan was alive and well, relatively speaking.

But it was clearly nothing more than the man's own wacky pipe dream. Maybe it was technically possible to control people's minds by stimulating brain tissue with electricity.

Maybe.

Someday.

But Ryan knew that day was far in the future. He knew it based on nothing more than how he felt at this moment. If Dr. Protasov came in right now and started pumping electricity through the hole he'd drilled into the side of Ryan's skull, Ryan didn't know what would happen, but he knew he wouldn't magically start parroting the Soviet line and become the American spokesman for all things Communist.

More likely he would stroke out as his overworked nervous system reacted to the excess stimulation, or he would suffer a heart attack, or his brain would burn out and shut down. He pictured his grey matter fried to a crisp like overcooked bacon, black smoke curling out his ears and billowing from the hole Protasov had drilled into his head.

Even that would be better than this.

Anything would be better than this.

Ryan blinked himself back to his depressing reality. He glanced around at as much of the room as he could see with his head immobilized. He wasn't positive but thought he was inside the same room in which he'd been kept strapped to a hospital bed since his arrival.

In the States a patient who'd just had brain surgery would be moved to a recovery room, where a team of nurses and staff members would monitor his condition closely. Ryan doubted he was being monitored at all, by anyone. He hadn't been attended to by a single nurse since his arrival in this hellhole, just Dr. Protasov and the creepy little bastard who'd done little but scowl at him and mutter under his breath.

He wondered how long he would lie alone and unattended, unable to move. And as bad as it was, that situation was likely better than whatever would follow, when Protasov would begin zapping electricity through a cable and into Ryan's brain, roasting the delicate tissue like meat on a spit.

But the sooner someone came and removed the clamps or the harness or whatever was holding Ryan's head immobile, the sooner he could begin examining his room and everything inside it. Somewhere in this space was an object that could be used as a weapon, perhaps on the wheeled table in the corner, upon which Protasov kept his implements of torture.

Sooner or later Ryan would find that object.

Once he found it he would figure out how to access it.

Then he would kill Dr. Protasov and maybe, if he was really lucky, the creepy little assistant, before turning the weapon on himself.

He was never getting out of here alive; he understood that fully.

He also understood he would have to work quickly. Protasov was doing a tremendous amount of damage to his brain. Soon he would become paralyzed or so debilitated by muscle spasms the Soviets would find him useless and would then execute him. They would kill him without a second thought and dump his corpse into a common grave, just another victim of Protasov's research.

The thought that he would never be found and that his family and friends would never know what had happened to him was almost as chilling as the deep-seated cold permeating Ryan's body.

But he discovered the notion of dying didn't really bother him all that much. If there were any pain at all it would only last for a moment and then he would be gone. He'd always understood that giving his life for his country was a possibility and as frightening as it was to consider, the prospect of continuing on as a human guinea pig or worse, a non-responsive vegetable, was infinitely worse.

So he concentrated on breathing slowly, easily, calmly. He checked out the room as much as possible while biding his time.

While planning.

While trying to ignore the horrible creeping numbness in his fingers and toes and the fact that he was now mostly unable to control the spasms wracking his body.

30

Tracie had hours ago begun to suspect the labyrinthine system of tunnels snaking deep underground below the three "subway stations" dotting the Soviet base were segregated by the type of research being done inside the labs, research areas and meeting rooms associated with each.

It made sense from a security perspective. Not only were the Soviets able to hide their work from the prying eyes of U.S. surveillance aircraft by burrowing into the side of a mountain, by keeping the research areas separate they could also prevent scientists and researchers from becoming overly familiar with the other projects ongoing under the base.

Tracie forced her thoughts back to her more immediate concern: finding Ryan Smith. Her plan was simple. She would investigate the subterranean warrens under the three stations until locating him. Unless the Soviets had executed him already—and what would be the purpose of bringing him all the way here if they were only going to fill him full of Russian lead?—he had to be down there somewhere. Tracie would learn all she could about the work being done under this mysterious military base until stumbling across Smith's holding cell, then she would rescue Ryan and get him the hell out of here.

How she was going to manage all that she wasn't quite sure. A lot would depend upon whether the Soviets had started torturing the captured operative yet, and upon the extent of his injuries if they had. She'd developed the outline of an escape plan last night, one she thought she could implement if Smith were ambulatory, but the fact was that sneaking inside an active Russian military base had been something close to a suicide mission right from the start, and if they were to have any chance of escaping, the plan would have to remain flexible.

Above ground the base was mostly wide-open, barren both of trees and excessive structures. Still, Tracie felt little concern as she moved between subway stations. This area was relatively far removed from the administration building, and the location of the three stations in the middle of the base—more or less—meant the ubiquitous guard towers were reassuringly distant.

It was a false reassurance, to be sure, since the guards were undoubtedly equipped with binoculars and high-powered rifles, but Tracie preferred not to spend too much time thinking about that. Unless she gave them reason to become suspicious of her, to the guards she would look like just another civilian researcher hurrying between the relative warmth of the stations.

Encountering a patrolling Red Army soldier was always a possibility, but a general sense of lax security seemed to permeate the facility. Given the base's extreme isolation and the length of time it had gone undetected by the United States, it would have taken an almost superhuman effort maintain strict security standards. Why would the Soviets be worried about security at a base their enemies didn't even know about?

As Tracie approached Station B she examined it as closely as possible without slowing noticeably or making her activity obvious. As far as she could tell it was an exact duplicate of Building A, right down to the cipher lock on the reinforced metal entry door.

Makes sense, Tracie thought. *These buildings are basically just shells covering the tunnel entrances.*

She moved to the door without stopping and began pressing the entry code the helpful researcher had used to allow her to access Building A to get her "feminine hygiene products." She'd been very careful to watch him and memorize the code as he entered it, and she was banking on the entry codes being the same for all three stations. She guessed they would be.

After pressing the last button she muttered, "Here goes nothing," then pulled on the heavy door.

And smiled in satisfaction as it swung open.

Inside the metal shell, a handful of men were clustered around a snack machine in an alcove located next to the elevators, drinking coffee from paper cups and good-naturedly teasing each other. It was close enough to lunchtime that Tracie guessed they were on a break and had no desire to brave the long walk in bitterly cold temperatures to the dining facility located way out at the front of the camp.

In any event, none of them paid the slightest attention to her. She didn't even think anyone had glanced over at the sound of the entry door opening and then closing, an event that must occur on a semi-regular basis throughout the day, as researchers came and went.

A quick glance around the interior confirmed what she'd suspected: this building—at least the above ground portion—was laid out in exactly the same manner as the first. She was certain that would be the case inside Building C as well.

She moved to the stairs and disappeared through the doors and out of sight of the men taking their break. At this point, Tracie doubted she had much to fear from the civilian researchers by using the elevators, but there was always the possibility she'd get stuck sharing one with a patrolling guard, a scenario that likely would not end well.

Why change a plan that was working?

She hurried down stairs that seemed identical to the ones she'd used inside Building A. The shaft was the same; the iron railings and metal treads were the same. It was obvious the Russians had used the same blueprints to build all three underground facilities.

This time she encountered no one while descending the stairs, and in seconds arrived at another metal door. She peeked through the small wire-reinforced window and on the other side saw a long hallway, again identical to the first hallway she'd seen beneath Building A.

Almost everything looked the same, but with one key exception:

there was no door at the far end of the long hallway. The corridor terminated at a solid concrete-block wall, painted the same drab industrial gray as the rest of the construction.

Odd, Tracie thought. *Whatever's going on down here must be less ambitious. Or more exclusive. Building A had three long tunnels branching off the end of the first hallway, each with their own research areas built off it.*

She also observed that the hallway was empty.

For now.

The time was nearly noon, and Tracie assumed that meant many more people would be joining the half-dozen men she'd seen at the snack machines above-ground or would be walking to the dining hall for lunch.

Activity would increase over the next hour or so. She would have to hurry if she was to remain undetected.

She double-checked the hallway and found it still empty.

Then she took a deep breath and pushed through the door.

31

The purpose of the single tunnel located beneath Station B was not immediately apparent. The setup was similar to what she'd seen in the first tunnel, with a series of doors lining the hallway on both sides. As was the case under the previous building, all doors were closed.

But with the exception of the first door on the right—behind which was clearly an office where a doughy-looking middle-aged man sat with his back to Tracie, writing at a desk—the remainder of the rooms had a distinct hospital feel to them.

Trundle beds on wheels sat in the middle of most of the rooms, next to small bedside tables upon which nothing had been placed. Every room was lit but all appeared empty, not just of furnishings but of patients.

She made a cursory inspection of each room as she passed, at this point more to ensure no soldiers were waiting behind the doors than because she expected to see any of the beds occupied. She'd begun to suspect that whatever the Soviets' plans were for this particular tunnel, they hadn't yet begun to implement them fully. Maybe not at all.

She began to move faster, aware the group of snackers up at ground level might return down to the strange hospital wing at any moment, equally aware that if they took the stairs they would enter the hallway between her and the only exit she'd yet seen. They would effectively seal off her escape route.

She examined two more rooms and again found nothing of interest. She'd now advanced almost halfway down the hallway beneath Station B and the only living thing she'd seen had been the doughy man writing at a desk in the very first room.

Everything changed at the next doorway.

Because behind it, chained to a bed with a bloody white bandage encircling his head, was Ryan Smith.

What the hell have they done to him? The thought flashed through Tracie's head as she stood frozen in the middle of the corridor, her previous concern about being discovered forgotten for the moment. She'd worked with Ryan in Russia just last month and he'd been a competent, if raw, operative.

He'd smuggled her into a closed city at significant risk to himself.

He'd saved her life on a lonely Russian road with a dead-solid-perfect sniper shot from a distance of over forty yards, taking out a KGB operative.

He'd put himself at risk again to smuggle her out of Russia following mission completion.

He had been healthy and intelligent and vital.

Now he looked as though he'd aged several decades. His eyes were glazed as he stared into the distance at something only he could see. He was blinking far more often than normal and as she watched, a series of tremors ran through his body.

Then it happened again.

Ryan didn't seem to notice.

Tracie squinted, focusing on Ryan's bloody head, and blinked in surprise at what looked like an electrical lead poking through the bandage on the left side. The wire hung suspended above his ear and featured a copper lead at the far end. Its placement made Ryan look like an injured alien with a tiny antenna sprouting from one side of his skull.

Tracie's stomach did a slow roll.

Good God, the Soviets had drilled into the man's cranium, and from the looks of things, had done a damned poor job of it.

Had they turned him into a vegetable? There was only one way to tell.

She was at the entrance in one long stride. She turned the handle and entered the room, grateful to see Smith tracking her progress once he noticed the door opening.

His eyes may have been glazed but they widened almost comically at the sight of her. He did his rapid-eye-blinking thing and opened his mouth to speak and then closed it again. Blinked hard several more times, even closing his eyes for a couple of seconds and then reopening them as if unable to quite comprehend that she was actually standing in front of him.

"Fi…Fi…Fi…" He was trying to speak but couldn't form the words and her heart broke for him. She didn't know what he was trying to say, but his abrupt deterioration in the short time since she'd seen him last was jarring.

"Fiona," he finally spit out, and then she broke into a smile. Fiona Quinn was the alias she'd used during her mission inside Kremlyov, Russia, and the name Ryan had known her by. She approached his bed and took his hand and hoped the tears in her eyes weren't too obvious.

"Ryan Smith," she said. "Fancy meeting you here. You come here often?"

"O-o-o-once is plenty," he said.

More blinking and another tremor. "I-is that really you, or am I dr-dreaming?"

"I would classify this place more as a nightmare than a dream, but yes, it's really me."

"H-h-how did you f-find me? And so qui-quickly?"

"I'll tell you the whole story once we get you out of here and someplace safe, I promise. I'll even embellish it to make it as dramatic as possible. But I don't think we have much time. I saw a handful of young guys on my way in here and they'll probably return any minute."

Smith shook his head and for a moment Tracie wasn't sure whether he was disagreeing with her or suffering another mini-seizure. "Young guys? No. N-no young guys."

"I don't understand."

"I've dealt with only t-two men since they ch-ch-chained me

here. Neither of them young. The head man is m-m-mid sixties, thick beard, l-looks like Karl Marx. His assistant is t-ten or fifteen years younger and c-clean shaven."

Tracie thought back to the only other person she'd seen since descending the stairs to the tunnel, the one writing at his desk in an office. Was he the head man or the assistant? His back had been turned to her so she couldn't tell whether he'd been bearded or not.

More importantly, where was the other man, and when would he return?

And where would the men Tracie had seen up top go when they came back to the tunnels?

Smith's words did little to make her feel time was any less of an issue.

He seemed to guess her concern because he said, "We p-probably have some time, F-F-Fiona. They m-mostly leave me to myself down here. I only s-see the assistant once or twice a d-d-day, and the head man m-maybe another one or two times. I don't even th-think they know I'm awake from the surgery yet."

His words made her feel marginally better, but sooner or later someone would enter this room, and it would be far better for all concerned if the two of them were long gone when that happened.

"What the hell are they doing to you, Ryan?" She'd noticed his speech seemed to be slowly improving as he talked, and keeping him occupied would be beneficial as she tried to work up some kind of plan to spirit a seriously injured, impaired man out of a heavily fortified Soviet military base.

"Mind control." No stutter this time. The words came out almost conversational, but still they threw Tracie for a loop.

"Excuse me?"

"Th-the head man's name is Protasov. He's some kind of expert on what the Russians c-call 'psychotronics.' It's a f-fancy term for m-m-mind control using electrical stimulation of the b-brain."

She stared at him in horror. "They're trying to turn you into a zombie."

"S-something like that, yes."

Tracie shook her head. This was even worse than she'd imagined.

She bent and examined the handcuffs chaining Smith to the

bed rail. They were old and featured a simple locking mechanism. She was almost certain she could get Smith out of them even without her lock-picking tools.

She lifted her eyes to his and offered what she hoped was a reassuring smile. Said, "Let's take this conversation somewhere more comfortable, shall we?"

He shook his head again and this time it was clearly no muscle spasm. Rattled his cuffs against the iron bed rail. "Only the head guy has the key. Even the assistant doesn't have one."

Tracie scoffed. "You think a simple handcuff is going to do any more than slow me down for maybe thirty seconds? Come on, Smith, didn't you learn anything when we worked together?"

She was trying to keep it light for the sake of the injured man, but her concern was mounting. She'd been extremely lucky to make it this far without being discovered, but her luck was running out, she could feel it, and now she would have to reverse course across the base when she wasn't even sure the injured man could walk.

First things first. Take a deep breath and get Smith out of these cuffs.

She'd used a series of bobby pins to cover her flame-red hair with a dark kerchief in order to sneak past the gate guards. Now she removed one and leaned over the handcuffs. She placed one end of the pin into the locking mechanism and began feeling delicately for the tumblers.

"No," Smith said, his voice almost a whisper. "Don't bother."

"Ryan, I can't save you if you're chained to a hospital bed."

"Yes, you can."

She shifted her attention from the cuffs to Smith's face. "I'm confused. I can't wheel the damned bed across the base with you in it. How am I going to get you out of here if I don't pick the lock on these cuffs? It's only going to take a minute, I promise you."

"You're not going to get me out of here."

Frustration boiled over. The clock was ticking and Tracie could feel the Russians closing in and she wanted to get them above ground before they were trapped down here by armed sentries standing between the two of them and the only exit.

And Smith was speaking gibberish.

"How am I going to save you with you chained to this bed?" She spread her hands in confusion.

"You're going to save me by killing me."

32

February 3, 1988
12:15 p.m.
Ipatiev Research Facility
Tunnel under Building B

"What?" Tracie gaped at Ryan Smith. There was no question what he'd said but she couldn't quite process the words.

"Y-you heard me. I'll never be able to m-make it out of here, not in my current c-condition."

"Of course you can. I'll help y—"

"No. You d-don't understand. Protasov, he d-did something to me during surgery. He screwed up somehow, Fiona. He screwed up badly."

"It doesn't matter. I don't care what—"

"Listen to me!"

She blinked in surprise and swallowed heavily. His face was a mask of concentration as he continued speaking, the effort to make himself understood grueling and heartbreaking.

"My extremities are g-going numb, Fiona. I'm suffering s-s-seizures and they're getting worse. My vision is blurry and I c-can't concentrate."

They locked eyes, Tracie frozen in horror. Ryan Smith's expression was one of acceptance. Serenity, even.

"I'm dying, Fiona."

Tracie was dimly aware of her face being wet with tears and she couldn't even remember beginning to cry. She shook her head as she searched for words and couldn't find any because there were no words.

But it didn't matter anyway because Smith continued speaking. "I d-don't know how you found me," he said. "And it's a tremendous c-c-comfort knowing I wasn't left here to d-die alone and forgotten. But I *am* dying, Fiona, and I want to g-go out on my own terms, not on the t-t-terms of a lunatic Russian scientist."

"I can't, Ryan. That's the one thing I can't do. Don't ask me to do it."

"You have to. D-do you want to know how I've spent the last two hours?"

She shook her head and had every intention of answering, "Not really." Instead she heard herself say, "How?"

"I've been looking f-for something I can use to k-k-kill myself. Anything. B-but there's nothing within reach, and as m-my motor control deteriorates I b-began to despair, to fear I had n-no way out, that I wouldn't even retain enough control over my b-body to commit s-s-suicide."

He raised his face to hers, his eyes hopeful. "And then I looked up and there you were, m-my very own angel of mercy."

"Ryan…"

"D-don't let me linger, Fiona. Please. I d-don't want to be a vegetable, alone and helpless, th-thousands of miles from home. End it. End me. Just please don't forget me."

"I could never forget you," she heard herself saying. Ryan Smith's pale form shimmered before her through a veil of tears, prone and suffering but nodding encouragingly to her.

The end was in sight for him, but rather than being fearful he was ready.

She shook her head again, even as she was reaching inside her winter coat for the Beretta. She pulled it from her shoulder rig as she was saying, "Ryan, it won't work. People will hear the gunshot and come running."

"Th-these rooms are soundproofed. I heard Protasov t-talking about it with his assistant. The g-g-goal is eventually to stock each room with a m-mind control subject, and they d-d-don't want screams of p-pain coming from one room to p-p-panic subjects in all the other rooms.

"Besides," he added with a smile that made him look almost like the Ryan Smith she'd worked with in Moscow. "I kn-know you well enough to know you have a suppressor under your coat right next to that Beretta."

Tracie pursed her lips and attempted a weak smile of her own. He was right, of course. She *did* have a sound suppressor inside a pocket built into her customized shoulder rig. He must have seen it during the hours they spent riding together inside the cab of the CIA-modified truck in which they'd smuggled Tracie into Kremlyov last month.

She reached under the coat and withdrew it and began threading it onto the end of the barrel. Her hands were shaking so badly it took three tries to lock it into place.

Black images filled her head and for a moment she was back in Moscow, firing through her coat at Slava Marinov, watching the unarmed, elderly man fall to the sidewalk and then strolling away as a shocked crowd began to gather.

The execution had haunted her every night since, and most of the days. She was rarely able to sleep more than a few tortured minutes at a time, suffering horrific nightmares when she did. The dreams were so terrible, so bloody and vivid and jangling, that insomnia had begun to feel like the more palatable alternative.

Now Ryan Smith wanted her to execute him in the same way. He was one of the good guys, a decent young man who hadn't even entered the prime of his life yet, who'd already given more than most people could begin to imagine in service to his country. He would die and she would go on living, and his face—pale and twisted and suffering—would take its place alongside Slava Marinov's in her nightmares.

And how many faces would it take, how many nightmares would she suffer, before she crumpled under the cumulative weight of all she had seen and done? Before she went stark, raving mad and lost herself inside a prison of her own making?

This wasn't what she'd signed up for. She'd joined the CIA to make a difference in the world, to help bring the chance for freedom to oppressed people, to shine the light of democracy and opportunity into the darkest corners of the globe, in places that had known only repression and fear and iron-fisted rule.

She hadn't become an operative to be faced with this kind of agonizing moral dilemma. Where the choice was stark and unimaginable: refuse Ryan Smith's request and condemn him to a slow, solitary death inside what was essentially a Soviet prison, or put her weapon to his skull and pull the trigger, and be forced to live with an innocent man's blood on her hands—literally and figuratively—forever.

She blinked herself back to the present. It was an unimaginable quandary but it was what she faced, and a decision must be made, and the time was still ticking away and they were still exposed and vulnerable inside an underground Soviet military base in the mountains of Bashkir.

"Ryan," she said again without a clue in the world what she might follow it up with.

"You can do this," he whispered, still nodding. Incredibly, he was smiling at her and once again, for just a moment, he looked exactly as he had when they were trading good-natured insults outside Kremlyov. "It's the only way."

"No one can ever know the sacrifice you've made," she whispered as the tears fell harder.

"I'm f-fine with that. You would be, too, if our p-p-positions were reversed and it were you lying in this b-bed and me with the g-g-gun. It's a reality we live with every day, F-Fiona."

He was right. His brain had been compromised by a madman with a drill, and he was slipping away before her eyes, but still he was right.

She made her decision. She realized it had never seriously been in doubt. Ryan Smith was a good man and she could no more leave him to the indignity of his current situation than she could sprout wings and fly him home to the United States, her own inner demons be damned.

By removing her gun from its holster she supposed her subconscious had known what her decision was going to be even before her brain had begun considering the matter.

She placed the Beretta's barrel—now lengthened considerably by the sound suppressor—against Ryan's temple. Her tears stopped as soon as she'd made her decision, replaced by a bleak acceptance, a cold calculation of what it would take to get the job done.

Because that was what the situation had turned into: a job to complete, a mission to accomplish. The self-recrimination, the breakdown Tracie knew to be inevitable, would have to wait.

Ryan continued to smile at her, his eyes never leaving her own.

"Thank you," he whispered without the slightest trace of a stutter.

One of the first things Tracie had learned during her long-ago agency training was how to shoot a gun accurately. She'd learned the trigger was to be squeezed. Not pulled, and certainly not yanked.

Squeezed. Like a lover's caress.

She'd never forgotten that training and every time she'd fired a weapon since, the voice of her instructor had flashed through her head with the reminder to squeeze the trigger like a lover.

Every single time.

That was what she did now. She squeezed the trigger more gently than she'd ever done, and a split-second later Ryan Smith's suffering ended without his eyes ever leaving Tracie's face.

Then they were blank and she was alone.

She hadn't even lowered the gun when the door opened behind her and there was a rustling of clothing and a shuffling of feet on the floor.

And a stunned voice said in Russian, "What is going on here?"

33

February 3, 1988
12:20 p.m.
Ipatiev Military Research Facility

Vladimir Protasov didn't think he'd ever been quite as nervous in his entire life as he found himself at this very moment.

He hadn't had the chance to monitor the American CIA agent's recovery from surgery, thanks to Colonel Kopalev's arrival and Major Stepanov's insistence Vlad greet the colonel personally. Vlad was certain he'd been forced to attend that meeting because Stepanov knew Vlad had been overstating his project's progress on his monthly reports to Lubyanka. The base commander wanted to ensure the KGB's attention was directed squarely toward the guilty party—Professor Vladimir Protasov—and not at Commander Stepanov himself.

And as far as that went, Vlad couldn't really blame the major. It was every man for himself when it came to insulating one's career from the scrutiny of men like Colonel Kopalev.

But since Vlad had not been able to monitor the subject's recovery, he had no way of knowing just how badly he'd screwed the pooch during surgery. The situation was grim, he knew that much after dozens of operations on dozens of other test subjects, but he could not begin to ascertain just *how* grim until the sedatives wore off and the subject regained consciousness.

Unless, of course...

No.

No.

Do not even consider the possibility that the man has not survived, that you will walk into the subject's room in the company of the highest-ranking member of the KGB you will ever meet, only to discover the American CIA agent dead, still chained to his hospital bed.

Vlad swallowed heavily as his extremities turned semi-numb and he realized that once again he'd not been paying the slightest attention to the conversation of the other two men. Major Stepanov had insisted on giving Kopalev a brief tour of the rest of the facility before moving to Vlad's research tunnel, but while the KGB man agreed, the tour had been conducted mostly in a frosty silence, with Kopalev chafing visibly at the delay.

Finally, while observing scientists engaged in the miniaturization of nuclear devices designed to operate as weapons, Kopalev had said, "This is all well and good, and I commend you, Major, on keeping Ipatiev operating smoothly."

Stepanov beamed, his chest puffing out slightly.

"But this is not the reason I left Moscow and traveled all the way to Bashkir," the KGB man continued. "Let us move along. I am a busy man and I would like to see Professor Protasov's work for myself. I look forward to gazing into our American friend's eyes while he rhapsodizes about the glories of the Soviet system."

"Of course, Colonel," Major Stepanov said immediately, and the three men turned and left the nuclear weapons research area behind.

As unhappy as Vlad was to begin moving toward his research suite—it was no exaggeration to say the trip felt like a slog toward his own execution—he still breathed a little easier knowing they were leaving the nuclear lab behind. A lifelong scientist, Vlad was well aware how shoddy the camp's radiation-monitoring equipment really was. And his fellow researchers were doing some extremely risky work deep inside their tunnels.

"Please try to remember," Vlad heard himself saying as the three men crunched along the concrete pathways, "the subject's surgery was completed only a few hours ago. It is often not possible to begin assessing the extent of recovery from such an invasive procedure for days. Only then are we truly able to measure the subject's suggestibility and begin the first steps of the reprogram-ming process."

"It is almost as though you are preparing me for disappoint-ment," Kopalev said coldly. "Is that the case, Professor? Are you attempting to lower my expectations?"

"No, Colonel, of course not. I am merely suggesting there may not be anything of value to see today, in terms of reprogramming. Still, the visit can be a productive one. You will have the oppor-tunity to view the surgical area, receive a briefing regarding the process of reprogramming and the equipment used to accomplish it, and see for yourself how much—"

"What I want to see, Professor," Kopalev interrupted, "is an American CIA operative smiling into a television camera and warning the world of the dangers of the United States of America's imperialist policies. I want to see an American CIA operative taking responsibility for his government's unprovoked aggression in foreign lands. That is what I want to see, Professor."

"But, Colonel, surely you understand these things take time."

"It has already taken 'time,' Professor. You have been working at this facility for well over a year. Over the course of that 'time,' you have sent me glowing reports of your progress every month, while simultaneously demanding more and better test subjects. I would say the time for patience is past and the time for results has arrived."

An uneasy silence descended on the group.

Kopalev added, "Or do you disagree?"

"No, sir. Of course not." Vlad was miserable. He wondered whether his response sounded as ineffectual to the colonel as it did to him. For the thousandth time he cursed his decision to come to this damned research facility in the middle of nowhere.

It occurred to Vlad as they crossed the quadrangle that the crunching of their boots on the frozen ground sounded uncom-fortably like gunshots.

The gunshots that would be fired at his execution.

The execution that would surely follow if they descended into his research lab and found the CIA agent dead in his hospital bed.

Maybe the damage would wind up being relatively minor, blurred vision or something along those lines, something a non-scientist like Kopalev would miss. The colonel was a lifelong military man and intelligence officer, not a trained scientist, so his powers of observation might be less than keen when it came to surgical/medical matters.

By now they had entered the base building, the silence of the walk every bit as chilly as the temperatures outside. Vlad glanced to the colonel's face to find the man staring back at him unblinkingly, and he realized his hopes that the damage he'd done to the CIA agent would go unnoticed were based on nothing more than the rosiest sort of unfounded optimism.

Vlad doubted Kopalev missed much of anything, ever, on any subject.

The silence continued on the elevator ride down to the Psychotronics Suite, Kopalev's intimidating, Vlad's nervous. Major Stepanov just seemed relieved someone besides himself was suffering under the white-hot spotlight of Colonel Kopalev's glare.

They stepped out of the elevator and Vlad briefly considered asking Yuri to join them. He discarded the notion immediately, though. There was no doubt the man was a KGB plant, stationed at the facility to report back to Kopalev. This situation was frightening enough with one KGB man peering over his shoulder, why add a second and make it worse?

Vlad turned left into the hallway and then stopped in front of the door to the CIA man's room. His palms were sweaty and he couldn't seem to stop shaking.

Maybe Kopalev couldn't tell.

He turned the handle and entered first. His plan was to walk far enough into the room to allow the other two men inside, then he would stop and launch into a briefing regarding the project before the colonel could ask any questions. He would attempt to gauge the subject's status as he spoke and would adjust his briefing as necessary, based on what he observed.

It was risky, but what choice did he have?

He took one step into the room and stopped short. Kopalev rammed into him and cursed and Vlad barely noticed in his confusion.

An intruder sat on the edge of February 1's bed holding a silenced weapon to the subject's head. As Vlad watched, the intruder—at first Vlad thought it was a small man but his eyes widened as he realized it was actually a woman—pulled the trigger on her weapon and February 1's head exploded in a spray of blood and brain and pulverized bone.

Vlad blinked, unable to process the scene fully.

He said the first thing that popped into his head: "What is going on here?"

34

February 3, 1988
12:25 p.m.
Ipatiev Military Research Facility
Ryan Smith's room

Tracie never hesitated.

At the sound of the incredulous voice she lifted her gun from Ryan Smith's now-lifeless head and turned to face the threat, assessing the danger.

Three men. The first had stopped unexpectedly in front of the other two and been shoved from behind. He was older, dressed in civilian clothing and sporting a thick salt-and-pepper beard. He seemed frozen in shock and/or fear. He was likely no more than a minimal threat.

The greater threat would come from behind the first man. Stepping past him on one side was the base commander—Tracie recognized him from her surveillance—and rounding the other side was a second man she did not recognize, dressed in the uniform of a Red Army colonel.

Both men were reaching for their holstered weapons.

Tracie reacted in a split second. She swung her weapon toward the base commander and squeezed off a shot that struck him in the upper body and sent him spinning to the floor.

Instantly she turned her weapon toward the second man and barked, "Don't do it."

The Soviet colonel froze with his pistol hovering maybe six inches above his holster.

The first man still hadn't moved.

For a moment time stood still.

Everything had happened so quickly Tracie could feel the last of Ryan's blood showering the back of her gun hand even as she held her weapon on the three intruders.

She glanced to her left and saw that the base commander's weapon had fallen from his hand and skittered to a stop against the wall. It wasn't within his immediate reach but it was close enough where he could still be dangerous, depending on the severity of his gunshot wound.

At the moment he was sprawled on the floor, moaning.

Tracie returned her attention to the Red Army colonel. He'd raised his weapon slightly during the half-second she spent analyzing the situation with the base commander.

He was clearly the most dangerous of the three.

She said, "Drop your weapon and kick it across the floor to me," in Russian.

The man scowled and hesitated.

She aimed at the brass buttons in the middle of his dress overcoat and said quietly, "Do it now or die. Your choice."

Another brief hesitation and then the man did as instructed. The Makarov semiautomatic pistol dropped to the tile with a metallic *clank*. He nudged it with his foot and it spun to a stop in front of Tracie.

"Now, reach back and ease the door closed. Do not slam it. I want you to close it so quietly it wouldn't awaken a newborn baby."

More scowling from the colonel, but again he followed his instructions. The door closed with a nearly silent *snick* of the latch.

Tracie returned her attention to the first man, the older one with the beard. He had to be Vladimir Protasov. He still didn't seem to have moved.

She said, "Did you see what the colonel just did with his weapon?"

He nodded, his eyes glazed and unfocused, aimed more or less in the direction of the now-dead Ryan Smith.

"Good," Tracie said. "I want you to step over your base

commander and kick his gun toward me, exactly as the colonel just did. Can you do that?"

The man she assumed was Protasov nodded and moved to do as Tracie asked. The Red Army colonel hissed something Tracie could not make out and the man flinched but kept going.

A moment later that gun slid to a stop next to the first.

Tracie crouched, keeping her weapon trained on the colonel, and lifted the guns off the floor, one by one. She slipped them into the waistband of her trousers at the small of her back and then rose to her feet.

"Everybody move up against the wall," she said, gesturing with her gun. She wanted to get the three men away from the entry door. She could stand to the side and be more or less out of view through the tiny windows, but she knew if someone should pass by and see three men clustered where they were currently standing, she would likely have a fourth captive to deal with.

And the situation was already dire with three.

The base commander had rolled onto his side, and now he staggered to his feet. Tracie could see that her bullet had struck the man in his upper left arm, and it hung limply at his side. He and the civilian complied, shuffling to the side wall and standing motionless against it.

The colonel didn't move. Instead, he said, "I do not know where you came from or why you just killed an unarmed man, but I am sure you understand you will never make it out of this facility alive."

"Thanks for your perspective," Tracie said coldly. "But if you don't do exactly as your two friends just did and move against that wall, I'm going to put a bullet in your heart and you'll never have the opportunity to see how wrong you were about what you just said."

The man began moving, albeit slowly, presumably to make a point. But at least he was moving.

Tracie continued, "And spare me your false concern about the prisoner lying chained to the bed next to me. You people turned a healthy young man into a near invalid in a matter of days. Before he died, he told me exactly what you were doing to him and it makes me sick. Feigning concern for his welfare now means nothing."

The colonel's eyes darkened and he turned his attention to the civilian. "A near invalid? Is she telling the truth? What did you do to the shiny new subject I provided you, Doctor?"

Protasov swallowed heavily. "I-I don't know what she's talking ab—"

"That's enough," Tracie snapped. She stepped toward the colonel. "You say *you* provided the 'subject' to the doctor? So you're in charge of this shit show you call a project?"

The colonel nodded toward the civilian in disgust. "He is the one who apparently destroyed your now-dead friend's brain in record time."

"That's not what I asked you," Tracie said. "But thank you for clarifying everyone's role in this brutality."

The base commander stumbled forward a half step. Tracie swung her weapon in his direction as he dropped to one knee and said, "I have been shot. I need medical attention."

"I've been in your shoes," she said. "Hurts like hell, doesn't it?"

"I need a doctor."

"There's one standing right next to you," she said with a hint of amusement. "Although, given his track record I can't say I blame you for wanting a second opinion."

"Please," he said. "I am bleeding."

Tracie pursed her lips and considered the situation. The Red Army colonel was not just the most dangerous man in the room, he was also the most important; that much was obvious. The civilian doctor—Protasov—was just another researcher, one of dozens she'd seen during her surveillance and her time on the base, and the commander was the Soviet equivalent of a bureaucratic pencil pusher. If he'd ever fired his weapon in anger it was undoubtedly years ago, maybe decades.

But the colonel was another story.

He was a bigshot.

His status was obvious just from Tracie's brief observance of both the deference the other two men offered him and the way he'd naturally taken charge when confronted with this unexpected situation. He was a man comfortable with giving orders, and someone who fully expected those orders to be obeyed.

And he was almost certainly KGB. The kind of mind control efforts Ryan described before his death would fall under their purview. Therefore, if the colonel scowling at Tracie from halfway across the room was in charge of this abomination, he was a KGB officer. It was as simple as that.

She considered the man's rank, considered the KGB in general and how its structure was remarkably similar to that of the CIA, once you got past the differing political/governmental philosophies. Both organizations featured hierarchies that required virtually blind obedience to orders that often seemed difficult to understand—and even occasionally downright nonsensical—to the operative on the receiving end.

Tracie's own professional history had made her acutely aware of that particular CIA policy. She'd nearly lost her career more than once for questioning it.

Since the KGB operated in a similar manner, maybe there was a way to use that knowledge to her benefit. The death of Ryan Smith—*he didn't just die, you killed him* flashed through her head and then disappeared, but she knew the accusation was accurate, and knew also it would return to haunt her again soon enough—had changed her focus from rescuing a colleague to simply escaping with her life.

She tried to concentrate, to consider the implications of the colonel's presence, but after a moment the base commander repeated, "Please, I require medical attention."

He was still down on one knee. His face was pale and he'd begun shaking as if suffering an extreme chill and Tracie realized he was going into shock.

It was tempting to make him suffer. Ryan Smith had suffered and was now dead because of these bastards, what possible motivation did she have to offer the slightest mercy?

Tracie stared at the men, conscious of the time ticking away.

She had some decisions to make, and she needed to make them soon.

35

She took one step forward and aimed her Beretta between the eyes of the civilian. His face paled and in half a second he looked as ghostly white as the wounded base commander.

"Patch him up," she said.

He blinked. "But this is not my operating room. None of my surgical supplies are here."

"Make do." Her voice was diamond-hard. "And you'd better get moving, because you have exactly three minutes. If that man's arm," she nodded at the base commander with a tilt of the head, "is still bleeding in three minutes, someone's going to die and it's not going to be him. You follow?"

The doctor's eyes widened in alarm, but the threat seemed to spur him into action. He hurried past Tracie, giving her as wide a berth as possible, rushing to the opposite side of the room where he began pulling open a series of drawers.

Tracie backed up against the wall to make herself invisible should anyone pass by in the hallway. She focused most of her attention on the dangerous Red Army colonel while sneaking brief glances at the doctor. He was now rooting frantically through a row of cabinets mounted above a long countertop.

Finally he mumbled, "Ah, here we are," and when he began striding back toward his countrymen he was holding what looked like the Russian equivalent of several Ace Bandages.

"Two minutes," Tracie said.

The doctor blew out a deep breath and began removing the base commander's fur-lined winter coat. The major had already unzipped it and his right arm came out easily, but he'd bled fairly significantly from the bullet wound in his left arm and the material had become wet and sticky.

The commander spit out a curse aimed in Tracie's direction but she ignored it. Finally the coat came off and the doctor began fumbling with the buttons on the man's uniform dress shirt.

"One minute," Tracie said, stepping up the pressure. It hadn't actually been two minutes since she'd issued her ultimatum, but the base commander was part of her escape plan and things felt like they were moving in slow motion. She needed to pick up the pace.

"It's going to take too much time to remove his shirt," she said, her voice a staccato bark. "Remind me what happens if it takes too long?"

"I will die." The man was panting in fear, nearly hyperventilating. Tracie almost began to feel sorry for him, but one look at the bloody, unmoving figure of Ryan Smith still chained to his hospital bed eliminated that momentary weakness.

"Exactly," she said. "So forget about the shirt. Wrap the bandages around the sleeve. The point is to stop the bleeding, not to make his arm look pretty, not that I think you could manage that given what I've seen of your handiwork."

The moment she suggested bandaging the arm over the commander's shirt the doctor began unspooling the roll, starting just below the armpit and wrapping it around and around, as tightly as possible, ignoring the patient's gasps of pain.

Thirty seconds later he'd finished and he spun to face Tracie. Sweat ran in rivulets down his face despite the fact the temperature inside this underground house of horrors couldn't have been more than sixty degrees. He seemed more than a little surprised to still be breathing.

Good, Tracie thought. *My only chance for survival is if no one gets too comfortable.*

The base commander rose to his feet. He was pale and unsteady, but stood without support next to the doctor.

The KGB colonel looked unimpressed as he glanced from the base commander to Tracie. His lips widened in something resembling amusement.

"Congratulations," he said snidely. "You've succeeded in wasting a significant chunk of what little time you have left. You are now even closer to being captured or killed. You should just surrender and spare yourself a sudden, violent death."

Tracie pushed off the wall. She raised her Beretta as she walked slowly forward, stopping only when the silenced muzzle was pressed firmly against the colonel's forehead. The wounded base commander and the terrified doctor parted at her approach, neither inclined to interfere.

"One of us is close to a violent death, all right," Tracie said through gritted teeth. "But it's not me."

The colonel had been holding his hands down at his sides, and one twitched ever so slightly. His fury at being threatened by a woman, and an American woman at that, was obvious.

Tracie smiled coldly. "I know what you're thinking."

"Is that so?"

"Yes. You're thinking, 'She's made a grave tactical error by putting herself within arm's reach of me.'"

The man's eyes gave away nothing.

"You're thinking, 'She is weak and slow, while I am strong and fast.'"

He blinked.

"You're thinking, 'I can slap her gun aside with one hand and punch her with the other and knock her out. I can end this right now.'"

His eyes narrowed and he said nothing.

"But you only *think* that, you don't *know* it. Not for sure. And if you're wrong, if maybe you're not *quite* as fast as you think you are, this ends with your brains splattered all over the wall behind you."

She shoved his forehead hard with the barrel and stepped back two paces. "And now it's too late."

She flashed another smile at the man. "I know how humiliating it must be to be taken prisoner inside your own facility. Well, your humiliation is just beginning, my friend, because you are going to escort me out of here. My escape will be entirely your doing."

He snorted. "That will never happen. I would never help you escape."

"Oh, it will, and there's nothing you can do about it. If you were going to risk everything to stop me, you would have done so ten seconds ago. Your ass belongs to me now. I know it, and more importantly, you know it."

He opened his mouth to respond and she cut him off. "Shut up. You have nothing to say that I want to hear."

She turned and faced the base commander. He seemed to have regained a bit of color, although he was sweating heavily, clearly in shock.

"You," she said, and pointed to a telephone hanging on the wall. "Go over there and call the guard shack and guard towers. Notify them that the colonel just received an emergency call from Lubyanka. Tell them he must leave immediately and that they are to have the gates open and ready for his car to exit."

"Lubyanka?" the colonel said. "You have no idea what you are talking about. How would Lubyanka call me?"

Tracie ignored him and continued. "You will tell the guards that the colonel will be accompanied by yourself and by a civilian and that *no* delay is acceptable. Tell them that anyone who even thinks about interfering with the colonel as he exits this facility will spend the rest of his life in the stockade. Do you understand everything I just said to you?"

"But it is impossible," the commander said. "It cannot be done. Those telephones are connected only to the other offices inside this suite. They cannot call anywhere else."

"Well, that's unfortunate for you then."

"I do not understand."

"If you can't make that call, then you're no good to me. And if you're no good to me, then you're just in the way. And if you're just in the way, I have no reason not to eliminate you and cut down on the number of people I have to keep track of."

Tracie had moved away from the three men after threatening

the colonel, but now she approached again, halving the distance between herself and her prisoners.

She raised her weapon suddenly, holding it eye-level in a two-handed shooter's grip, and said, "Goodbye, Major."

"Alright!" he shrieked. "Alright, I will make the call, do not shoot!"

The KGB colonel shook his head in disgust and clucked his disapproval and Tracie grinned. "Just remembered the phones have more capabilities than you thought?"

The commander looked at her dully and she said, "That was a close call. Guess it's your lucky day, isn't it?"

The man trudged across the floor, the KGB colonel tracking him with a smoldering gaze. He reached the telephone in seconds and then stood staring at Tracie.

"Don't forget I can hear everything you say," she told him. "If so much as one word comes out of your mouth that I don't like, you get a new hole in the head and I move on to Plan B, do you understand?"

He nodded in resignation.

"Good. Don't forget it. Now make the call."

36

By the time the base commander finished his call, Tracie thought she could have lit a match on the KGB colonel's eyeballs. They were flinty and cold and he stared down the commander with all the loathing he offered Tracie.

She didn't care. The major had done as she asked and as far as she could tell had volunteered nothing during the call that might have raised the suspicions of his men.

Aside from making such an unusual request in the first place, of course.

The base commander replaced the phone on the cradle and Tracie knew speed would now be essential. The more time the guards and the commander's underlings had to consider the strange order and the fact it had not been made in person, the more likely it was that someone would become suspicious.

Would they become suspicious enough to disobey the order? She didn't know. She also didn't want to find out.

"Move back next to your two friends," she said, flicking her weapon in the direction of the KGB man and the doctor.

The commander looked like he would rather drink gasoline, but reluctantly did as instructed. Tracie hoped the KGB colonel wouldn't kill him before she could finish using him to effect her escape.

He hadn't even finished crossing the room when she pointed from the doctor to Ryan Smith's body. "You. Unlock this man's handcuffs."

Protasov stood frozen in confusion. "But, he is…dead."

"Thanks for the expert medical opinion, Doctor."

"But if he is dead, then why—"

"You have the key to the cuffs, do you not?"

"Well, yes. Of course I do."

"Then walk over to the bed and unlock the cuffs like I told you once already."

He glanced at the KGB man as if for support, or perhaps an explanation as to what the crazy woman across the room thought she was doing, but the colonel returned the look blankly.

So he did it. He trudged past her to the bed, trying to avoid stepping in Smith's blood as he got close but unable to manage it. He pulled a large key ring from the pocket of his trousers and selected the proper key. There were a lot of choices on the ring but he found the handcuff key quickly, as if he'd used it a lot. Undoubtedly he had.

He wasted no time slipping the key into the locking mechanism of the handcuff encircling the bed rail. He clearly wanted nothing more than to fulfill Tracie's bizarre request and get away from the dead man sprawled on the bed with his skull blown apart.

Before he could turn the key, though, Tracie said, "No, not that one. Unlock the other one."

"What?"

"I want you to leave that cuff attached to the iron bed rail and unlock the one around the dead man's wrist."

"But…why?"

"*Do it.*"

His head snapped back as if he'd been slapped and his eyes widened in alarm, but he did as instructed. He had to lift Ryan's hand to insert the key and as soon as the cuff snapped open the hand flopped nervelessly onto the bloody bed.

The doctor breathed deeply and turned to rejoin the other two captives and Tracie said, "You're not finished yet."

"What now?" He closed his eyes briefly as if aware he was not going to like the answer.

"Now get up on the hospital bed."

The man's forehead wrinkled. "I...I'm sorry, what did you say?"

"You heard me. Get up on the bed. Now."

A trace of a smile flitted across the KGB colonel's face, just for a moment, and then the hard fury returned, but the doctor still didn't seem to understand or perhaps couldn't quite believe what he was being asked to do.

"I...but there is...a..."

Tracie decided to help him out. Move things along. "A bloody corpse on the bed?"

He nodded and turned his confused gaze from the Ryan Smith to Tracie. "Yes. Exactly. A bloody corpse is on the bed."

"That bloody corpse is on the bed because of you. Get up there with him. This is the last time I'm going to ask."

Her voice was flat, thick with implied violence, and the doctor didn't hesitate. He lifted one leg and climbed onto the bed, slipping in the blood as he did so. Then he lifted the other, using his hip to shove Ryan Smith's body against the iron rail.

Then he leaned over and puked onto the floor.

Tracie said, "Cuff your wrist to the bed."

She expected another argument, or at least another claim that he didn't understand what he was being told to do, but he surprised her. Any fight left inside him had evaporated, replaced by a look of nauseous resignation. He used his left hand to slip the open cuff over his right wrist and then slapped it closed with a metallic whir.

"Tighter," she said.

He pushed a little harder and managed one more click.

"Show me you're secured."

The doctor lifted his arm away from the bed rail and the cuffs clanked against the iron. Tracie watched them pull taut against his hand, stretching the skin, and she nodded, satisfied he could not escape.

She shifted slightly and once again faced the two Russian officers. "Now it's time for us to—"

Without warning the door swung open and a man entered.

He'd begun speaking before he walked into the room, saying, "Doctor, I think we…"

His voice trailed away and he froze for no more than a quarter-second, taking in the scene: his boss chained to a bed next to the bloody corpse of a man with part of his head blown off, a woman holding a gun on the base commander and the VIP guest.

Then he reacted. He reached behind his back and in the blink of an eye his hand reappeared holding a pistol. The swiftness of his reaction was impressive and somewhere in the back of her mind, Tracie thought, *Another KGB officer.* He spun toward Tracie, dropping to one knee and raising the weapon in two hands.

But Tracie's gun was already out, already aimed in the general direction of the door. She'd been hyper-aware that the room's entrance was her point of greatest weakness and had told herself to remain vigilant, to be prepared for this exact occurrence: an unexpected entry by another potential threat.

So even though the intruder was quick, Tracie was quicker. She swiveled her wrist and fired. She had anticipated the man dropping into a shooter's position and her slug caught him square in the chest, driving him to the floor where the back of his skull struck the tiles with the *crack* of a lightning bolt.

He scrabbled with his heels on the floor in a desperate attempt to escape and she fired again.

Again the shot hit the man center-mass.

This time his legs stopped pumping.

Tracie squeezed off a third shot and the man went limp.

And the room fell still.

After a moment Tracie became aware of a whimpering coming from Ryan Smith's hospital bed. Doctor Protasov was trying to remain quiet but couldn't quite manage it. The two Red Army officers said nothing but the base commander had gone suddenly pale again. The KGB man seemed unaffected.

Tracie pointed at the base commander and spoke quietly, working to keep the adrenaline from causing her voice to shake. "Kick that man's weapon over to me."

He complied at once, shuffling past the KGB colonel and sending the gun skittering toward Tracie with a swing of his boot. She ignored it for the time being.

"Now, check your comrade for a pulse."

The commander grimaced but dropped to a squat, careful to avoid soiling his uniform trousers in the blood that had begun pooling on the floor around the intruder's chest. He placed the first two fingers of his left hand lightly on the man's neck, just under his ear, as his injured right arm dangled at his side. He held his fingers in place for several seconds before shaking his head.

"This man is dead."

"Check his wrist for a pulse."

The colonel sighed, but did as instructed. A moment later he shook his head a second time.

"Still dead," he said.

"If I find out you're lying to me, you'll be joining him on the floor in a pool of your own blood, do you understand?"

"I am not lying. You shot him three times in the chest from close range. He is dead."

"*Answer my question.* Do you understand what will happen to you if I find out you're lying about this man being dead?"

"Da. I understand."

"That's better. Now get up and rejoin your buddy. We're going to take a little road trip. Won't that be fun?"

37

February 3, 1988
12:45 p.m.
Ipatiev Military Research Facility
Ryan Smith's room

The KGB colonel spoke up as the base commander rose to his feet and moved next to him. "You must know you will never escape this facility."

Tracie smiled. "That's the best you can come up with? You've already shoveled that pile of crap at me, and I'm not paying any more attention to it now than I did the first time you tried it."

"Fine with me. It is your funeral."

"We'll see about that soon enough, I guess. Now, if you want to avoid *your* funeral, here's what's going to happen. The three of us will leave this room and walk to the elevator. If anyone is in the hallway you will ignore them unless directly addressed by someone."

"And if we are directly addressed?"

"Then you will deal with the person as briefly and in as general terms as possible."

The KGB colonel scoffed. "And you do not think that will raise suspicions?"

"Not even a little bit. This is a military facility, yes, but it's largely staffed with civilian personnel. And not just any civilians, but researchers and scientists. The type of people who will be intimidated by the presence of the military in general, and officers in particular. I think the people on this base for the most part will go to great lengths to ignore you in the hope that they will go unnoticed in return."

The colonel did not answer and Tracie continued. "We will take the elevator up to ground level and will then move across the quadrangle to the front parking lot, near the administration building. We will maintain a brisk pace. After all, you've been called away on an emergency, isn't that right, Colonel?"

No answer.

"We will move directly to your car, where we will climb in and exit the front gate, which will be standing open for us. Does anyone have any questions?"

Silence.

Tracie looked both men in the eye, KGB colonel and then the base commander, and said, "I want to emphasize something to both of you. If things go south, you two will be the first to die. What happens after that will be irrelevant to you because you WILL be dead. Do I make myself clear?"

"Crystal clear," the KGB colonel said. "And may I remind you if that happens, you will die also." He still appeared calm and collected, in stark contrast to the base commander, who was plainly terrified. This KGB man was one tough customer.

"Thanks for the reminder," Tracie said, "and now I have one for you. My weapon will be in my coat pocket. My finger will be on the trigger at all times. Not on the trigger guard, on the trigger. I strongly suggest you do not do something stupid simply because my weapon is no longer visible. Now, help the major with his overcoat and let's get moving."

As she finished speaking, Tracie reached back and clubbed Doctor Protasov in the side of the head with the butt of her Beretta. Smith had said the rooms were soundproofed, but she wasn't taking that statement on blind faith. A conscious Protasov would undoubtedly start screaming within seconds of Tracie leaving the room, and if it turned out Smith was wrong about the room's acoustical properties, she wouldn't make it within five hundred feet of the front gate.

Protasov moaned softly and his head fell to the side as blood leaked out of a gash in his skull. He was still semiconscious, but was stunned and would take at least a few minutes to regain enough of his senses to comprehend his situation and then to attempt to do something about it.

Hopefully that would be long enough.

She'd never taken her eyes off the Soviet officers, even as she was pistol-whipping Protasov. The KGB colonel had reluctantly lifted the major's overcoat from the floor and helped him into it while Tracie was dealing with Protasov.

Now she flicked her gun in the direction of the door. She hated leaving Ryan Smith's body, but getting it off the base would be impossible and burial was not an option. She knew she would never forgive herself for what she'd done to him, so the guilt of leaving him now would simply comprise one more addition to the ever-growing mountain of regrets she would somehow have to live with.

One by one the hostages stepped over the prone body of the man Tracie had shot to death. She was pretty sure it was the same man she'd seen writing at a desk in the office when she first entered the tunnel.

Not that it mattered now.

While the two Russians moved toward the door, Tracie quickly unscrewed the sound suppressor from her Beretta. The silenced weapon was far too long to fit into her coat pocket—squeezing it in there was going to be a challenge even without the suppressor—and the moment they left this room it would be rendered meaningless, anyway: if she had to shoot one or both of the officers, it would be because they were trying to signal their situation to other Russians with guns.

Tracie would at that point be emptying what was left of her magazine before being cut down herself.

The base commander reached the door first. He pulled it open and stepped into the hallway. The KGB colonel lagged behind, exactly as Tracie had known he would. He was trying to give the commander an opportunity to pass a message should someone be standing or passing by in the hallway.

Tracie shoved the colonel hard in the back and slipped the gun into her pocket as she followed him through the door. A quick look in both directions confirmed the hallway was empty.

She pulled the door closed. There was no way to lock it but Smith had said he'd been ignored by everyone inside the facility except the doctor and his assistant, the man she'd just killed. She would have to hope her luck held and nobody decided within the next few minutes they needed to retrieve something from inside that room.

The KGB man's disappointment at encountering an empty hallway was plain, and even in the face of almost debilitating pressure Tracie suppressed a smile. The odd-looking group moved awkwardly along the hallway to the elevator, where the base commander pressed the call button.

The disparity between the two hostages was striking and might have been humorous were the situation not so dire. The base commander wanted nothing more than to do exactly as he was told, get Tracie off the base as quickly and quietly as possible, and by doing so maybe survive. The KGB man was delaying and cooperating as little as he could get away with, obviously hoping for the situation to turn in his favor.

The elevator had just a single floor to descend so it took only a moment to arrive. The men entered first and Tracie forced them to the side of the elevator car. Once inside, she stepped behind them as the doors creaked closed.

Less than a minute later they had arrived above ground. Tracie took the opportunity to remind the men of their fate should they act suspiciously or in any way arouse her ire. The base commander swallowed heavily and the KGB man pursed his lips in annoyance, but neither answered.

When the door opened, all three stepped into the vestibule and Tracie was relieved to find it empty. The half-dozen researchers she'd seen on her way inside had long-since returned to work, their breaks over. She realized she'd probably passed by a room or rooms containing some of them on the way to the elevator.

They moved to the entryway and trudged out into the bitter cold. The day had begun overcast and grey, but during the time Tracie spent underground the clouds had lowered, and that was cause for concern. Tracie's pickup from Bashkir was scheduled for this afternoon, and as competent as the flight crew had proven to be during her ride from Turkey a few days ago, she knew there was no way they would be able to land the big bird on a frozen lake if the ceiling dropped so low they could not safely descend into the mountainous terrain.

There would be no navigational aids to follow, so the crew would be flying blind if the weather got much worse than it was right now.

They would be forced to abort the mission for their own safety. Return to Turkey and try again tomorrow.

Tracie would be stranded, undoubtedly with the entire Soviet Army hunting her.

For the first time, the near-hopelessness of her situation struck her, and panic threatened to overcome reason. What had started out as one of the simplest missions she'd ever been assigned—conceal herself on the side of a mountain and observe a military base from a safe distance for a few days—had gone straight downhill with the appearance of the truck carrying Ryan Smith.

Now, not only had she been unsuccessful in extracting Ryan, she'd killed him herself and in all likelihood would wind up facing the same fate he'd suffered. If she were to be captured and survive, there could be little question she would become the next test subject for the loony Doctor Protasov.

And he wouldn't be inclined to treat her gently.

She realized she'd begun to breathe shallowly and rapidly, the panic building, and she forced herself to lock the fear away. *Get your act together. Worry about one thing at a time. If you let your attention wander, you'll never make it off this base and your fears will become a self-fulfilling prophecy.*

They made it halfway between the subway station covering Protasov's tunnel of horrors and the identical station Tracie had first explored upon her arrival on the base. That was the good news.

The bad news was that a man was rapidly approaching on the snow-covered concrete path, and it was not a researcher. It was a Red Army soldier.

A patrolling guard.

And all at once the significance of the bullet wound to the major's right arm occurred to her.

The approaching soldier would salute his commanding officer as they passed.

He would be expecting a return salute.

He would not receive one.

Tracie tightened her grip on the Beretta and tried to remain calm as the soldier approached.

38

February 3, 1988
12:55 p.m.
Ipatiev Military Research Facility
Central quadrangle

The guard slowed and saluted.

The base commander's right hand flinched as he tried to return the salute, but he was successful in moving it no more than a few inches and then he gasped in pain.

The soldier's forehead wrinkled in confusion and he stopped moving. He was blocking the narrow pathway, there wasn't enough room for the three of them to clear him without shoving him into the snow, and Tracie could smell trouble.

She knew she could fire through her coat and put him down before he could draw his sidearm or lower the automatic rifle slung over his shoulder, but what would be the point? Almost before the man's body hit the ground the sentries in the guard towers, most of whom were undoubtedly tracking the progress of their CO and his guests visually after the unusual telephone instructions they'd received, would have drawn their own high-powered rifles and returned fire.

Tracie would die.

Her finger twitched on the Beretta's trigger as she tried to maintain a bland outward expression.

The soldier said, "Are you…is everything alright, Sir?"

The base commander coughed and then he stammered something unintelligible, and Tracie knew she was seconds away from capture or worse.

And then the KGB colonel returned the sentry's salute. It was the last thing she would have expected, given the man's previous hostility and lack of cooperation, but he snapped off a salute of which any military man in any branch of any country's service would have been proud.

Obviously he'd taken Tracie's warning to heart regarding who would fall first once the shooting started.

The soldier looked from his commanding officer to the KGB colonel and back again, and then glanced at Tracie for good measure. He'd become instantly suspicious at the lack of a return salute from the major and this turn of events didn't seem to have done much to lessen his concern.

Finally the base commander found his voice. "Will there be anything else, soldier?"

"Uh…no sir. No."

"Did you get the message about the colonel being called away from the base on an emergency?"

The sentry had begun eying Tracie more closely after his first bewildered look between the pair of Soviet officers, but now his attention was fully engaged by his commanding officer. "Uh, yes sir, I did."

"Then is there some reason you are blocking our path when you know it is essential our guest leave as quickly as possible?"

"No, sir. I am sorry, sir." The kid stepped back and to the side like he was being pushed by an invisible bulldozer, his previous suspicion of Tracie forgotten in his concern for his own wellbeing.

The two officers brushed past him imperiously and Tracie trailed behind, knowing she had to follow them but well aware how odd it must look for an unknown civilian woman to be trailing behind two high-ranking Soviet officers.

With her right hand jammed into her coat pocket.

She stared straight ahead as she passed the kid and felt his eyes boring into her back as they continued toward the administration building. She wanted to glance back to see whether he'd continued his patrol but knew doing so would be a mistake.

She hadn't been cut in half by a hail of bullets—yet—so she supposed she should consider it a win.

They circled past the first subway station without further interruption and the administration complex loomed straight ahead. Above ground pedestrian traffic was minimal, presumably because the noontime lunch break had been less than an hour ago. Most researchers had probably eaten at that time and were now back at work in their labs.

Tracie began to think maybe this spur of the moment escape plan would actually work.

Moments later they were skirting the front of the administration building. The small group was retracing the route Tracie had taken upon her arrival inside the facility a few hours ago virtually step for step, but in the opposite direction.

The skies continued to darken and it seemed inevitable the snow would start falling at any moment, and her previous concern about getting stranded with no way out of Bashkir returned. Simply making it off the base would do little to ensure her survival. The village of Mezhgorye was isolated and remote, and it would be an easy matter for the Soviets to seal off the town's few access roads and begin an exhaustive search.

If that happened, she would be trapped and would eventually be found. So she needed not just to escape the gates of the base, but the confines of the village as well. If she could be on the road to her extraction point by the time the carnage inside Protasov's lab was discovered, she felt confident she could elude the Red Army long enough to get on that plane.

Assuming the plane could land.

She tried to estimate the cloud height and guessed the ceiling was still sufficient to allow the crew to descend through the clouds and make a safe approach to the frozen lake. But if the weather continued to deteriorate, that would not be the case.

And she would be stuck alone overnight in the brutal subzero temperatures of the Ural Mountains in February.

The panic started to rise again, and again she forced herself to focus on the here and now. They passed the front steps of the administration building and had almost arrived at the parking lot. The car sitting in the base commander's designated space closest the building was a Volga limousine, nearly new, and Tracie knew the commander had given up his prime slot for the day so the KGB colonel could park as close as possible to the admin building.

The KGB man angled toward the driver's side door and reached to pull it open. Before he could, Tracie stopped him.

"No. Wait right here and allow the base commander to get into the front passenger seat first." Managing the two men's entry into the vehicle would be tricky. If it wasn't handled properly, one of the men could take advantage of an opportunity to race away from the car and begin screaming for help, bringing the weight of the Soviet military crashing down on Tracie in seconds.

Based on what she'd seen, the KGB man would be far more likely to try something like that than the base commander, so Tracie stood just behind him and waited as the other officer pulled open his door with his uninjured left arm and slid into the vehicle reluctantly but without undue delay.

She knew the incident might look odd to anyone paying attention but didn't care. Her feeling was that this represented the least risk out of her available options. It was a split-second decision and she would live—or perhaps die—with the result.

Once the base commander had sat, Tracie said, "Go," to the KGB colonel. The man opened his own door. The moment he'd pulled on the handle, Tracie opened her own rear door and entered the car at the same time as the Russian.

"Start the car and move."

The moment the colonel began backing out of the parking space the first of the two security gates began swinging open, exactly as the base commander had ordered. The colonel shifted into first gear, and within seconds the car crossed the lot and turned toward the access road.

Seconds after that they were rolling through the open first gate.

This was where everything could fall apart. If sufficient suspicion had been raised, or if the commander had somehow managed to alert the sentries to the fact something was wrong, the gate guards could simply close the first gate without opening the second, and the Volga would be trapped between the two.

Tracie risked a glance behind her and saw the first gate swinging slowly closed. The second had yet to open.

She resolved to go down fighting. She would kill the base commander first and then swing the gun over to the KGB colonel's head, taking him out immediately after. Once both men were dead she would leap into the driver's seat, shove the colonel's body onto the floor, and then jam the accelerator to the firewall and ram the exterior gate with as much speed as she could muster.

Hopefully she would break through it and race down the access road.

Failing that she would take out as many Soviets as she could before they cut her down. She would not allow herself to be taken alive, to become another lab rat upon which Doctor Protasov could conduct his grisly mind control experiments.

She pulled the Beretta out of her coat pocket and began raising it, keeping it hidden below the passenger window and out of sight of the guards, but training it through the back of the seat on the spine of the base commander, and her jaw dropped in surprise as the second gate began to open.

It was moving slowly, much more slowly than Tracie would have preferred, but damned if it wasn't opening! The Volga would have to slow to a crawl to compensate for the leisurely rate at which the damned thing was swinging open, but she didn't think they would have to stop completely.

They rolled past the guard shack and Tracie stared straight ahead. The KGB colonel returned the salute she had known he would receive in the manner befitting a high-ranking officer: casually and with barely a glance in the direction of the guard.

The next few seconds were excruciating, as the Volga continued to brake, the gate widening slowly. Then there was sufficient room and the colonel guided the vehicle through the opening.

And they began to accelerate, and Tracie realized she'd been holding her breath and she blew out a relieved sigh.

She still wasn't home free.

The Soviets could send armed vehicles after them at any moment.

The skies continued to darken and the weather could very well prevent her pickup by the C-130 crew.

But it was a start. She was still breathing and was leaving the base behind.

Tracie stared through the windshield as the road to the village grew larger and larger up ahead.

39

February 3, 1988
1:05 p.m.
Mezhgorye, Bashkir

"Well, what now?" The Volga slowed as it approached the main road, and the KGB man glanced expectantly into the rear view mirror.

"Turn right," Tracie said.

There was no oncoming traffic, and the limousine accelerated onto the roadway and turned toward the village.

"I was not asking which direction to turn," the colonel said drily.

"Then you should learn to speak more clearly."

He ignored the remark and said, "I meant in a more general sense. We did as you asked, and you are now outside the gates of the facility."

"What are you looking for, gratitude? You weren't trying to help me, you were trying to save your own ass."

"Obviously."

"If it's so obvious, why did you bring it up?"

"Because gratitude is not what I was referring to. I meant now that you have successfully escaped the base, presumably this is where you kill us and dump our bodies on the side of the road to slow down pursuit once the men you murdered inside the facility are discovered."

The base commander stiffened at the colonel's words. He clearly didn't like the direction the conversation was taking, and didn't appreciate the fact his fellow officer was the one taking it there.

"I have no intention of killing you and dumping your bodies, on the side of the road or anywhere else, unless you force me to by making a move I don't like."

"Is that so?"

"That's right," Tracie said. "If I wanted to kill you and dump your bodies, I would have two options: do it inside this car and push your corpses out the door, or force you both out of the vehicle and shoot you on the side of the road."

The base commander cleared his throat and coughed into his good hand. He seemed to have turned a shade paler, a development Tracie would not have believed possible.

"Thank you for clarifying," the KGB man said. Even while discussing his potential death he seemed entirely unaffected.

"You're welcome," Tracie answered. "My point is that neither of those options is worth the risk. If I shoot you both inside the car, there will be blood everywhere. The second man I shoot will put up a fight since he'll have nothing to lose, which will make the mess even worse. Driving around in a limousine with blood-spattered windows would invite much more attention than I prefer."

"It is nice to know you've given the matter serious thought."

"Damn right I have."

"Then, please, do not leave me hanging. Fill me in on why you don't wish to simply force us onto the side of the road and shoot us there."

The base commander huffed and pursed his lips angrily. He opened his mouth to speak and then snapped his jaws closed before saying anything. His fury at the KGB officer for continuing to discuss methods of their execution was obvious, but so far not sufficient to overcome his respect for the man's rank.

Or perhaps his fear of the man's recklessness.

Tracie understood perfectly what the colonel was doing. He was probing, gathering information, poking and prodding in search of a way out, some bit of information he could use against Tracie to turn the tide of events in his favor.

And at the very least, if she was busy talking to them she wasn't busy killing them.

So she understood his motivation, but was perfectly happy to play his game. For now.

"Okay," she said. "Since you're so curious, I'll tell you. But first, turn left here."

The colonel complied and then Tracie continued. "It's midday. Even in a town the size of Mezhgorye there is far too much traffic coming and going for me to know with any kind of certainty that I'll be able to make you stop the car, force both of you outside, and then step out and put bullets in both of your heads, all without anyone coming along and witnessing the event. Again, the potential exists for more attention in that scenario than I wish to deal with."

This time the colonel had nothing to say. Tracie told him to turn again and he did so without speaking.

"And there's another advantage to the situation as it currently stands."

"What might that be?" The KGB man's voice had turned sour, brittle.

"I believe I'll be able to leave this town behind and be two hundred kilometers north in the mountains, even on these subpar Soviet roads, before anyone back at that base discovers anything is wrong."

She turned to the base commander and said softly, "Your security was really lax, Major, but I suppose you've already reached the same conclusion, haven't you?"

The man's jaw muscles tensed angrily beneath his skin but he said nothing, and then Tracie turned her attention back to the driver.

"Anyway," she said. "I *think* I can be two hundred kilometers north of here before anyone begins looking for me, but just in case I'm wrong, and someone back at that slipshod outfit disguised as a military base happens to stumble onto the scene back in Doctor Protasov's lab, I feel I'm much better off with two high-ranking birds in the hand. I can trade you boys for my freedom."

"You think so?"

She shrugged. "If you're not valuable enough for your friends to agree to a trade, I at least get the satisfaction of executing you in front of them before I'm killed myself."

It was all a lie.

While there was a certain amount of truth to her explanation regarding the risk involved in killing both Soviet officers, she knew she could manage it relatively easily if she chose to. She could take both of them out before either man knew what hit him, and could do so in a relatively clean and risk-free manner.

But Tracie knew that even in a facility as poorly secured as the one she'd just escaped, the bodies of the dead men would be found sooner rather than later. Someone would glance through the tiny window as they were walking past in the hallway, or would enter to ask the doctor a question, and the slaughter inside the room would be discovered.

When that happened, all available resources would be mobilized and an intense search would begin for the person who had infiltrated the base and killed two men before escaping with a pair of Soviet officers as hostages.

The Red Army would coordinate with local law enforcement, or more likely would simply steamroll local authorities. They would conduct a thorough search of a very small town, blanketing the area with police and military personnel and in all likelihood go door-to-door.

Tracie's window for escape would slam shut.

But her entire taunting conversation had been conducted with the KGB colonel for one purpose: to plant the seed that her escape route would be to the north, over the Ural Mountains. She'd mentioned it twice in an effort to emphasize her intended direction, but had tried to do so in an offhand manner. She wanted to leave the impression that the information had slipped out mistakenly, so the intelligence officer—who was as sharp as anyone Tracie had encountered on the Soviet side of the fence in her nearly eight-year career—would consider the information reliable.

That was her real reason for leaving the men alive.

Killing them would seal her fate, likely eliminating any possibility of escape.

Allowing them to live might just give her a chance.

40

It was clear the KGB colonel sensed a trap when Tracie told him to turn into the apartment complex parking lot. He asked for clarification twice, and then tensed up more than she'd seen ay any point since taking him hostage.

His forehead wrinkled in confusion as he glanced at her in the rear view. "Stopping for a visit with old friends before we continue on? Perhaps we are going to share a cup of tea with other enemies of the Soviet State?"

Tracie ignored him. She considered mentioning her fictional northern escape route one more time but decided against it. If she placed too much emphasis on the direction, the KGB man would recognize it as a trick. Her smokescreen would either work or it would not, there was nothing she could do about it now. She would simply have to wait and see.

"Park here," she said, indicating an open spot a few spaces away from where she'd left her four-wheel-drive Lada this morning.

The colonel gazed at Tracie through the mirror one more time, eyes mere slits in his angular face, and then eased the Volga to a stop with the grille face-in to a massive snow bank.

"Good boy," Tracie said, and the colonel grunted in anger.

"Here's what's going to happen," she continued. "You're both going to exit the car. You're going to move to the building on our left. We will all walk through the front door and down the hallway to the middle apartment. We will then enter the apartment and close the door quietly behind us. Are there any questions?"

No one spoke and Tracie said, "I made it clear that I prefer you both alive, but if either of you raises your voice, or tries to sound an alarm, or in any way causes me the slightest concern, I will kill you without hesitation and continue on alone. My plans are extremely flexible. Understood?"

Again nobody spoke.

"Get moving," she said.

The car emptied out, Tracie lagging behind as she had done before, ready to turn her weapon on either man until they'd both stepped into the cold. Then she slid the Beretta back into her coat pocket and joined the pair in the parking lot. She glanced in all directions for potential threats but the place seemed deserted.

The walk to the apartment entrance took less than thirty seconds, and in another thirty they'd moved the length of the hallway and stood outside Olga Trentiova's apartment door.

Tracie's luck held. No one exited any of the other apartments.

She risked removing the gun from her pocket and aimed it in the direction of the pair of officers as she fumbled in her pants pocket for the apartment key. She located it and tossed it to the KGB man.

"Open the door and go inside," she said quietly.

The colonel complied and as he was inserting the key into the lock Tracie closed the distance between the men until she was standing directly behind them. She seriously doubted she had anything to worry about from the base commander, but getting within arm's reach of the KGB officer wasn't ideal. It was a risk she had to take, though, because if she lagged back too far it would only invite the hostages to rush inside and then slam and lock the door, sealing Tracie out.

The two men and one woman crowded into the apartment and then Tracie kicked the door closed. She moved immediately to the side, regaining the space she'd had to sacrifice to enter.

There was no door between the apartment's living room

and kitchen, just an arched entryway, and Tracie could see Olga Trentiova bound and gagged at her dinner table, exactly as Tracie had left her. She sat in a puddle of her own urine and her eyes were red and swollen from crying, and despite the fact she must have been terrified at Tracie's return—not to mention confused as to why she'd come back with a pair of army officers in tow—she stared daggers at her over the dishtowel gag and behind all the duct tape crisscrossing her face.

The hostages stopped in the middle of the room and looked from Trentiova to Tracie and then back again. Their movements couldn't have been more perfectly choreographed had Bob Fosse been directing the action.

Unsurprisingly, the KGB man was the one to speak. "Obviously you were here earlier."

"Obviously," Tracie agreed.

"You make friends wherever you go, don't you?"

"Shut up."

"Just making an observation."

"I said shut up." Tracie nodded in the direction of the trussed-up secretary. "You two will be joining Miss Trentiova now. I want each of you to pull a chair out, one on either side of her. Then you will turn your chairs around and sit. You will not move. You will wait quietly for me to secure you. Is that understood?"

The KGB man ignored her and said, "I thought you wanted to keep us with you in case you needed a bargaining chip."

The base commander's frustration at the KGB man's words was palpable. He seemed to welcome the idea of being left behind, even if it came at the cost of being gagged and tied to a chair for some indeterminate length of time.

Tracie smiled. "I told you already, my plans remain flexible. Haven't you ever heard it's a woman's prerogative to change her mind?"

He didn't answer and Tracie said, "Do as instructed, Colonel, please. You won't like what happens if I have to ask you again."

The base commander had already begun moving to the kitchen table and selecting his chair. The KGB officer joined him, his forehead scrunched in suspicion. Tracie could see the colonel considering the possible ramifications of this sudden change in their captor's plans, and she realized if she were to stand any chance of the colonel—and thus the Soviets in general—accepting her story of a northern escape route, she would have to offer some sort of explanation.

She had left her backpack containing the duct tape inside Olga Trentiova's apartment when she left this morning, and now she backed into the living room and picked it up off the floor while keeping her prisoners covered with her weapon. She pulled out the tape and began securing the more dangerous man—the KGB colonel—first.

In a conversational tone she said, "Since I've got a little busy work to do here, I'll indulge your question, Colonel. The answer is quite simple. I changed my mind because it seems obvious I'll have no problem leaving Mezhgorye far behind before anyone inside your facility even becomes aware anything is amiss."

Before the colonel could answer, the base commander surprised Tracie by saying indignantly, "I think you are selling my men short."

"You can think whatever you want," Tracie said amiably, "but the fact of the matter is I should never have been able to get onto the base in the first place, and once there I certainly shouldn't have managed to kidnap the two highest-ranking officers within a thousand miles in any direction."

The major opened his mouth to interrupt, but Tracie talked over him. "And once I did *that*, it should have been impossible to escape right out from under the noses of dozens of men armed with automatic weapons. So you'll have to excuse me if I don't put too much weight on your opinion."

She wound the tape around the KGB man's wrists first and then repeated the process with his ankles. It was not an easy chore to accomplish while keeping her weapon trained on the colonel and far enough out of his reach that he wouldn't be tempted to grab for it or push it aside and hit her. She kept her voice light but breathed much easier once she'd successfully restrained the more dangerous of the two men.

As she worked, she continued to speak. "As I said, it seems clear I'll be long gone before anyone at the base realizes anything is wrong. That being the case I can move much faster alone. By the time the alarm is sounded I'll be so far away you'll have no chance of running me down. This area is so remote there are a million places for me to disappear. A billion."

"I disagree," the KGB man said. His eyes glittered dangerously and his voice was acid. "I look forward to the day we meet again. And when that day comes, you will regret ever stepping foot inside Bashkir. By the time I've finished with you, you will be begging to die. You will wish you could change places with your dead CIA friend."

Tracie finished securing the base commander and then glanced up at the KGB man with a sweet smile. "Thank you for the reminder. I almost forgot to gag you."

She stood and walked to the kitchen drawer from which she'd retrieved the towel she used to gag Olga Trentiova this morning. Removed two more and in seconds had silenced both men, only one of whom had been speaking.

"That's better," she said. She smiled again at the KGB colonel. "There's nothing quite so sweet as blessed silence, don't you agree?"

He glared at her and she winked. "'Til we meet again, comrade."

She tossed her tape into the backpack and zipped it closed. Shrugged it over one shoulder and returned her weapon to its shoulder holster.

Then she turned and walked out the apartment door, locking it securely behind her.

41

February 3, 1988
2:20 p.m.
Somewhere south of Mezhgorye, Bashkir

The road south out of Bashkir was mostly deserted. Whether because of the impending storm or the extreme isolation of the village, Tracie encountered almost no other traffic once she'd passed a couple of miles beyond the town's border.

After leaving the Soviet officers lashed to their chairs in Olga Trentiova's apartment, she'd thrown her backpack into the front seat of the Lada SUV and driven at a reasonable speed toward her exfiltration point. She half expected to hear screaming sirens, to see flashing red and blue lights, to encounter roadblocks and angry-looking soldiers with automatic weapons, the entire town locked down like a prison as the Red Army searched grimly for the intruder who'd slipped into their midst and then escaped holding their two highest-ranking officers hostage.

But the streets were quiet, the traffic light. Snow had begun falling lazily, dropping onto the frozen pavement and blowing away in eddies as the Lada motored past, the flakes as grainy as sand thanks to the brutally cold temperatures.

As she drove, Tracie couldn't help replaying the last few minutes of Ryan Smith's life on a continuous loop inside her head. She hated the way things had ended, hated especially her inability to save the man after finding him alive.

The irony was beyond bitter; it was downright cruel. To have the good fortune to be surveilling the base just as the Soviets were delivering their CIA prize to Protasov's lab—a million-to-one shot, approximately the odds of a three-legged horse winning the Kentucky Derby—only to then locate Smith mere hours too late to rescue him, chafed on Tracie in a way nothing else had ever done. It was almost a physical pain, as if her soul had been flayed open with a dull knife and then salt poured inside the wound.

Could karma possibly be so heartbreakingly cruel?

She chuckled bitterly at the thought, alone inside the Russian-made SUV. Of course karma—or God's will, or fate, or whatever you wanted to call it—could be so damned cruel. If one point had been hammered home to her over seven-plus years of CIA field work, that would have to be it.

There was no fairness to life.

The good guys didn't always win.

Tracie shook her head bleakly as the Ural Mountain scenery rolled past, its magnificent beauty blunted by the sheer monotony of the trees and the snow. Ryan's face would haunt her nightmares forever: the intensity in his earnest eyes as he begged her to end his torment, and then the spark of life disappearing from those same eyes when she granted his wish.

She realized she'd started tearing up, a dangerous development for someone driving down poorly maintained mountain roads in the early stages of a winter storm while attempting to escape a country where she would face untold suffering if captured.

She forced her mind off the recent past—it wasn't easy—and back where it belonged: navigating the slippery, winding road.

She thought she was getting close to the extraction point.

She'd known she would have trouble locating the narrow wooded trail leading to the frozen lake. The area was secluded and desolate and the trees crowding every stretch of the road looked exactly the same as the trees crowding every other stretch of road. There were no signs or kilometer markers, no houses or stores or lodges or any other evidence of human habitation.

Just mile after mile of lonely Bashkiran roadway.

To combat the possibility of driving right past the trail without realizing she'd missed it, Tracie had taken careful note of the mileage on the Lada's odometer when she'd driven out of the forest after being dropped off four days ago by the C-130. She'd then noted the mileage reading upon entry into Mezhgorye, giving her a fairly accurate gauge as to when to begin looking for the marker she'd left at the trail's entrance.

According to the vehicle's odometer, that marker should be coming up soon, a bright red scarf she'd tied to a tree branch a few feet off the side of the road. She eased off the accelerator, peering through the falling snow, when she rounded a corner and almost barreled through a wooden sawhorse placed in the middle of the road.

Idling next to the sawhorse was a UAZ-469, the Soviet equivalent of a small Jeep.

Roadblock, Tracie thought. *Dammit. I should have known this was too easy.*

She hit her brakes hard and slid to a stop a few feet in front of the barrier. Fortunately she'd been moving slowly to begin with or she would have rammed the damned thing. In their desire to make the roadblock a surprise to drivers they'd chosen a risky location, placing the barrier much too close to the sharp curve.

Tracie snapped out of her funk and into operational mode, focusing her attention on the idling vehicle across the roadway. Given the bitter cold, the soldiers would almost certainly be sitting inside the UAZ to stay warm. And there would be two of them. The Soviets would not risk using just one man to secure this isolated motorway if they'd finally discovered the carnage inside their secret facility.

She'd removed her Beretta from its shoulder holster upon leaving Mezhgorye, anticipating exactly this type of occurrence. It lay on the passenger seat, held in place by the weight of her backpack. Now she reached over and, without taking her eyes off the Russian military vehicle, slid the weapon across the seat and under her right thigh.

The passenger door of the UAZ-469 opened and a young soldier stepped into the cold. He moved slowly, clearly reluctant to leave the warmth of the vehicle behind. Tracie imagined the two occupants doing a quick coin flip to see which of them would get to avoid stepping into the cold.

The soldier approached the Lada with his weapon holstered at his side. He motioned for Tracie to roll down her window.

After she had complied, he bent and in Russian said, "I am sorry for the inconvenience, but…"

His voice trailed away as his eyes widened in surprise. He'd obviously been told he was looking for a young woman, possibly accompanied by the two officers she'd kidnapped but more likely traveling alone.

He started to step back from the door and reach for his gun but before he could manage either action Tracie raised her Beretta quickly, reaching through the open window and placing it against his forehead. The positioning of the soldier's body would prevent his partner from seeing her weapon, but there was no way to know whether he'd noticed the man's panicked reaction.

If he was paying attention, he probably had.

It was too late to worry about that now.

"Don't move and you might survive," she said softly, and he nodded once in an abbreviated motion.

"Now," she continued. "Let go of your weapon and leave it holstered. Place both hands on the window frame where I can see them."

When he had complied, she said, "I want you to leave your right hand on the door. Half-turn to face your partner and wave him out of the truck."

"But we were told to be sure only one of us approaches any vehicles we stop. The other is to maintain a safe distance."

"Is the person who gave you those instructions currently holding a gun to your head?"

He swallowed heavily and instead of answering, did as instructed. He swiveled at the hip and began gesturing toward the UAZ. A moment later the driver's door opened and another soldier stepped out of the vehicle, this one every bit as young looking as the first. He took a few tentative steps toward Tracie's Lada but then stopped, his hand resting on the butt of his holstered weapon.

"What is it?" he shouted across the pavement. "You know our instructions, we are to remain separated during any traffic stops." The wind had begun picking up in advance of the storm, and his voice sounded weak and reedy, knocked down by the freshening breeze.

"Get him over here," Tracie whispered through clenched teeth.

"Just come here, Sergei, please," the kid shouted, waving again with his free hand.

The soldier moved forward another couple of steps but Tracie knew her hastily devised plan—to disarm both men and leave them trussed up inside their vehicle—was never going to work. It had never stood a chance of working.

The second soldier was drawing his weapon.

And she acted on instinct and training. She squeezed the trigger once and the gun roared and first man's head exploded as he dropped like a felled tree onto the road next to the Lada.

His body hadn't even hit the pavement when she swiveled her wrist and fired again. She'd been holding the gun awkwardly in her attempt to keep it hidden from view of the second soldier and hadn't had a chance to aim properly, and the slug flew off into the wilderness.

The startled soldier dived to the road and rolled, but he was in no-man's land, fully exposed with nowhere to hide and the cover of his vehicle behind him, useless. He rolled onto his back and came up firing, but his shots sprayed the area, none of them coming close to striking Tracie or even the Lada.

Tracie, on the other hand, knew she had the luxury of time once she saw the kid hit the ground. She took advantage of that time, aiming carefully before squeezing off her next round.

When she fired, the shot took the kid squarely in the chest and left him motionless. His gun had dropped to the road but it still lay within reach, and Tracie kept her full attention on the second soldier as she climbed out of the Lada.

The first man's head had been pulverized by the 9mm slug fired from such close proximity and she knew the odds of him still being alive—much less posing a threat—were virtually nil. The same could not be said of the second soldier. Although he still lay unmoving in the road, he could still be alive.

Therefore, he still represented a threat.

He could be playing possum, could reach for his weapon and squeeze off a shot as she approached. It was unlikely but possible.

Tracie wasn't going to give him the chance to do anything of the kind. She left her door open and the vehicle idling. Kept her weapon trained on the second soldier as she knelt and removed the first man's gun from his holster and tossed it into the front seat of the Lada.

Then she reached down and felt for a pulse on the first soldier. The kinetic energy of the slug had blown the man's hat off and his skull was a jagged, pulpy mess. Blood soaked his neck and chest and the roadway immediately surrounding his body, melting the light dusting of snow and staining the area a dull maroon.

She'd known there would be no pulse and there wasn't.

Next she stood and crossed the roadway to where the second soldier lay. He still didn't appear to have moved. She kicked his gun toward the Lada and then repeated the exercise she'd just undertaken with the first soldier, kneeling and searching for a pulse.

Again she found none. From the bullet's entry point it appeared it had penetrated his heart. She'd managed a kill shot from thirty feet under tremendous stress and through a howling wind.

It was an impressive feat.

She felt nothing.

42

Tracie glanced at her watch and cursed softly. She'd nearly been out of time for her rendezvous with the C-130 even before encountering this roadblock. A firefight was the last thing she needed to deal with.

But leaving two Russian soldiers dead in the middle of the road was no kind of option, even considering the minimal amount of vehicular traffic Tracie had seen. There was no way around it; the men would have to be moved.

She hooked her arms under the second soldier's armpits at the elbow and dragged the man back to the UAZ-469. He'd left his door partly open and she dragged/shoved/tossed him as far as she could into the vehicle. He was heavy and she was light and even after marshaling all her strength his legs hung limply out the door, boots almost but not quite touching the pavement.

She hurried around to the other side of the vehicle and opened that door, then bent inside and dragged him fully into the truck. She was sweating from exertion and shaking from adrenaline, the familiar sensation of post-combat jitters flooding her body.

She ignored it and returned to the Lada. Bent and grabbed the first soldier under the armpits and began dragging him across the road as she had done with his partner. A significant amount of blood dripped onto Tracie from the grotesque head injury, and she choked back the vomit that threatened to explode onto herself and the dead Russian kid and the wet, snowy road.

By the time she'd dragged him to the UAZ she was gasping for breath. This soldier was even bigger and heavier than the first, and her strength was flagging, and the best toss she could manage only got him halfway into the vehicle. The soldier's corpse fell onto his partner's body with a wet thud, and Tracie bent, hands on her knees, as she attempted to catch her breath.

After a moment she circled the truck and dragged the second soldier the rest of the way inside. She was forced to crawl into the cab and onto the first man's body to get a decent grip and enough leverage to finish the job. The corpse already felt limp and elastic and inhuman, despite the fact he'd only been dead for minutes.

At last both men were fully inside their vehicle. Tracie back-tracked out of the UAZ, covered in blood, and this time there was no avoiding the reaction her body insisted on. She bent and puked into the dirty snow on the side of the road.

She moaned in misery and swiped the back of her hand across her mouth to remove the stringy greenish-yellow leftover saliva, gulping great breaths of supercooled mountain air. Then she returned to the middle of the road and grabbed the sawhorse the soldiers had been using as a barricade. She dragged it behind the UAZ and placed it as far out of sight of any passing motorists as possible.

One final trip into the road. Tracie retrieved the hat that had fallen off the first soldier's head when she shot him and tossed it into the UAZ on top of the dead men. She locked both doors and then slammed them closed. On her return trip to the Lada she picked the second soldier's gun up off the road and brought it with her into the vehicle, tossing it onto the passenger seat next to her backpack and the first soldier's gun.

It felt like thirty minutes had passed since Tracie first came upon the roadblock but a glance at her watch told her it had been less than five. No other vehicles had passed in that time.

She took one last long look at the scene and shrugged. She'd done the best she could to hide the evidence of the deadly confrontation given the extreme time pressure under which she was operating. It was much more important to get to that damned frozen lake before the C-130 took to the skies for Turkey than it was to fool any passersby about what had happened here.

And Tracie's rush-job cleanup wouldn't fool many people for very long.

If all went well the rest of the way, she would be in the sky before the Soviets could react to the deaths of two more of their soldiers, even if someone came along and found the corpses the moment she pulled away.

But the point of concealing the bodies was to buy at least a little time. Once the dead men were discovered, her ruse regarding a northern escape route would be blown, assuming it had ever been believed in the first place. The C-130 was perfectly suited to a mountain exfiltration atop a frozen lake, but not so well suited to outrunning a Russian MiG fighter jet. Tracie wasn't sure where the nearest Soviet air base was located, but wanted to give the C-130 crew a fighting chance to be as far from here as possible before the Soviets scrambled any chase aircraft.

And that was if all went well.

If all *didn't* go well, if she arrived at the frozen lake only to discover she was late, and her exfiltration crew had already come and gone because they were unable to wait any longer for her, she would face almost certain death anyway. It might be from the incoming storm and the bitterly cold temperatures and the fact she would be stranded with no friendly faces for thousands of miles in any direction, or it might be or from the reprisals of the Red Army.

Neither fate struck her as desirable.

She blew on her hands, which had become red and raw. She hadn't been wearing gloves during the confrontation at the roadblock and hadn't taken the time to pull them on during her cleanup efforts, so her fingers were now almost completely numb.

She hit the gas and continued down the lonely road, clapping her hands and rubbing them together in an effort to stimulate circulation, and before she'd gone another half-mile, found herself at the marker she'd left behind four days earlier.

The trail looked narrow and lonely but she didn't hesitate. She wheeled the Lada off the road and plunged into the wilderness, bouncing along the ruts, driving as fast as she dared. She tried to guess how long it would take the falling snow to cover her tire tracks and concluded it really didn't matter.

The key to her survival was the C-130.

If the plane was still there, she might live.

If not, she likely stood no chance.

* * *

Branches hung low across the trail. They were weighted down with snow and formed one more obstacle in what was becoming the most frustrating and disheartening mission Tracie had ever attempted. She dodged them when she could and rammed them when she had to, certain that at any moment the Lada would become stuck in the trail and she would be forced to continue on foot.

But to her surprise, the Russian-made SUV continued to grind over the rough, slick terrain. Sooner than expected, she spotted an opening in the trees that could only be the frozen lake. The next minute or so would determine her fate. Either the C-130 would be waiting, or she would face a potentially agonizing death.

Heart pounding, she shoved down on the accelerator, forcing more speed out of the truck than was wise. The vehicle slipped and slid, bouncing and jolting, threatening at any moment to impact a tree or slip off the trail and into a snowdrift.

Tracie didn't care.

She had to know.

The Lada burst through the opening in the trees and raced down the rocky embankment, and Tracie's heart leapt. The big four-engine prop plane was there, looking incongruous on its skis but as welcome a sight as she'd ever seen.

But there was a problem.

Of course there was.

The confrontation with the Soviet soldiers had taken too much time, and the C-130 crew had obviously decided they'd waited as long as they could. The plane was sixty feet away and facing in the other direction. The crew had taxied toward the embankment and then turned toward the middle of the lake to make as much room as possible for their imminent departure.

From their present position and at their present angle, they would not be able to see Tracie in the little SUV.

And the engines were even now beginning to spool up. In seconds the plane would lurch forward and then it would lift into the sky and disappear.

And Tracie would be left behind, despite being so close to the aircraft it almost seemed she could reach out and touch it.

She didn't hesitate. She slammed the accelerator to the floor, while the Lada was still on the dirt/rocks/snow of the embankment. The four wheels spun crazily and the rugged tires kicked the dirt and the rocks and the snow up from under the vehicle, and after a moment the tires gained traction and the vehicle shot onto the frozen surface of the lake in a spray of powdery snow that splashed thirty feet in all directions.

The C-130 began moving as the Lada approached, inching forward at first but quickly gaining speed, the powerful propellers blasting the loose snow away, turning the moderate snowfall into a raging blizzard behind the aircraft. Tracie kept her foot to the floor and angled the truck toward the plane.

Steering was almost nonexistent now that she'd left the embankment behind, but so far it looked like her course was taking her toward—and in front of—the plane. It was what she needed if she stood any chance of getting the truck to a point where she would become visible inside the flight deck, to let the crew know she was here.

The lake was relatively small, and they would have to spot her soon, or else the big C-130 would reach the point of no return: there wouldn't be enough room remaining to stop the aircraft before it simply slid off the lake and into the trees at the far end. Once they reached that point, the crew would have no choice but to lift off even if they saw her.

The Lada's engine screamed, but soon the sound was drowned out by the heavy thrumming of the C-130's four massive props as the plane and the truck approached on a near-collision course. The plane's speed was increasing rapidly, and while Tracie's snap judgment had been that she could outrun the aircraft to the middle of the lake, she now began to question her assessment.

Part of her feared that not only would she be unable to get in front of the plane, the little Lada and the massive C-130 would collide before the crew could react.

Everyone would die.

But it was too late to stop.

Too late to change direction.

She was committed.

She kept going.

43

The SUV's tires were spinning madly and losing their already-minimal traction when the vehicle skidded across the C-130's path.

Tracie held her breath and tried to milk every last bit of speed she could out of the Lada, knowing anything less would guarantee a collision. The plane's engines roared, throaty and angry, sounding like they were about to cut through the sheet metal and rip Tracie to shreds.

She risked a glance into the rear view mirror and gasped. The gigantic fuselage was all she could see, and it was barreling ever closer.

And then she was clear of the airplane's path. It rocketed past, missing the rear of the vehicle by no more than ten feet.

And it was slowing!

The crew had obviously seen her—how could they not?—and instead of climbing into the sky they were desperately trying to stop the aircraft before they ran out of room. The pilot engaged the reverse thrust and the props churned the thin mountain air relentlessly, dragging the aircraft to a stop in an absurdly short distance.

The snow that had been blown behind the aircraft now choked the air in front of it and for a moment the C-130 disappeared entirely, lost in a screen of white. Seconds later it reappeared, taxiing out of the blowing snow as if nothing out of the ordinary had occurred.

It moved across the lake and eased to a stop in the exact location Tracie had seen it when she blasted out of the forest, engines now idling quietly. She shifted into reverse and backtracked across the lake, not wanting to take the time to try to steer the truck in a circle on the icy surface. She reached the embankment and kept going, moving backward until the truck had pulled fully clear of the ice and would present no potential obstacle to the departing aircraft.

The crew had lowered the cargo door by the time she stepped out of the Lada. She slung her backpack over one shoulder and began shuffling as quickly as possible across the ice. As she reached the aircraft, she looked up to see Lieutenant Schlichter standing in the entryway.

He was shaking his head as he watched her approach, but a smile lit up his face and he said, "What's the matter? Four days alone in the heart of the Soviet Union didn't give you enough excitement, so you decided to play chicken with an airplane big enough to pulverize you?"

Her heart was still racing from the near-collision and she could feel her arms and legs quivering, but she grinned. "Never a doubt. I had it all the way."

"We actually lost sight of you as you passed in front of us, that's how close we came to squashing you like a very pretty bug."

She waggled her eyebrows. "'Almost' doesn't count except in horseshoes and nuclear war, remember?"

His eyes widened when he caught sight of the blood staining her clothing, but he said nothing. He was still shaking his head as she passed by and moved deeper into the airplane.

*   *   *

The lake had appeared impossibly small to Tracie during the landing four days ago. But now, surrounded by centuries-old trees that lookcd hundreds of feet tall, the task of getting airborne seemed all but impossible. She'd seen the crew manage it after they dropped her off, but from this vantage point—inside the flight deck, looking out at the thick forest surrounding the lake—she wouldn't have bet any money they could do it again.

The rest of the crew greeted her upon her arrival, but the reunion was a brief one, the air thick with tension. Tracie thought it might be thanks to their annoyance at the stunt she'd just pulled, and maybe that was part of it. But then she recalled Schlichter's statement that the amount of fuel carried inside the C-130's auxiliary tanks was barely sufficient to allow for a return trip to Incirlik.

If they expected to make it home without falling out of the sky, they could afford no more than a minimal delay in Bashkir. Between the time they spent idling on the surface of the lake while awaiting her arrival and the fuel they'd been forced to burn in the aborted takeoff, undoubtedly the issue was uppermost in the minds of the crewmembers.

Tracie wasted no time strapping herself in, and before the buckle on the safety harness had even snapped closed, the powerful engines were once again spooling up for departure. As it had when she was approaching in the Lada, the C-130 began moving slowly, but within seconds was rocketing across the lake on its skis, moving ever faster toward the trees—and certain death, it seemed to Tracie—on the far side of the lake.

Her knuckles were white when the plane finally lifted into the air, the end of the lake looming through the windscreen. Major Corrigan eased the nose of the plane toward the sky and the trees slid out of sight. She imagined the tops of the firs polishing the aluminum along the C-130's belly as the engines roared, fully committed to an aggressive climb rate.

It took a long time before Corrigan eased off on the steep-angled max climb. Bashkir was located deep inside the Ural Mountain range, and Tracie imagined rocky peaks on all sides, dangerous instruments of death waiting to gash holes in the fuselage or chop the wings right off the plane. Visibility was virtually nonexistent, as an increasingly heavy amount of snow continued to fall.

Tracie turned to Lieutenant Schlichter, who had taken a seat next to her as he'd done for most of the earlier trip. "How...?"

Her voice trailed off as she realized she wasn't sure how to ask her question.

She didn't have to. Schlichter seemed to know what she was thinking. "How did we climb through the mountains without being able to see fifty feet in front of the plane?"

"Well...yes. I'm incredibly grateful to all of you for coming through, but given the weather conditions, how did we not end up at the bottom of a smoking hole in the side of a mountain?"

"Beats me," he said, shrugging and shaking his head. "Sheer luck, I guess."

Tracie felt her eyebrows rise incredulously and Schlichter laughed. "Just kidding. I'm sorry, I couldn't help myself."

"Fair enough. I deserve a little payback after the trouble I've caused you guys. But..."

The grin left his face and he turned serious. "I assume you noticed after our aborted takeoff that we returned to the exact same spot on the lake to make the second departure attempt?"

"I did notice that, yes."

"It wasn't by accident. We did so because we plotted the exact departure path we would take in the event of these kinds of weather conditions, including climb rate and minute course corrections necessary for obstruction clearance, before we ever left Incirlik. It was all based on surveillance photos taken over the course of many SR-71 flybys, as well as our own experience operating on the lake four days ago."

She swallowed heavily. "I'm kind of glad I didn't know that before we left. You put a lot of faith in that intel."

He nodded. "That's true, but it's not like we haven't practiced this exact maneuver hundreds of times in mountainous terrain during clear weather. We would never have attempted it in these conditions unless we knew we could pull it off one hundred times out of one hundred."

Tracie must have looked unconvinced, because he smiled and said, "I'm sure you've flown overseas many times in your line of work, right?"

"Sure."

"And some of those flights must have been conducted in weather much worse than what we're climbing through right now."

"Of course, but those flights were conducted with the benefit of navigational aids designed to plot a precise climb or descent path around all potential hazards."

"Exactly," Schlichter agreed. "And that's no different from what we just did. Instead of electronic navigational aids, ours were a little more old-fashioned, a little more labor-intensive maybe, but the fact that we're sitting here having this discussion proves they were every bit as effective."

Tracie shook her head and laughed. "You guys are amazing."

"Well, thank you, but what you saw is nothing more or less than the product of hundreds of hours—"

"Thousands," Major Corrigan interrupted. Tracie hadn't even thought he was listening, that he was too busy flying the airplane in the lousy weather to pay attention to anything else.

"Right," Schilchter said. "Thousands of hours of practice and training."

"Two more questions, and then I'll stop bothering you," Tracie said.

"You're not a bother, believe me," he said. "But go ahead, hit me. If I don't know the answer I'll make one up and we'll see if you can tell the difference. It'll be a fun way to pass the time."

Tracie smiled crookedly, unsure whether he was kidding or not. "Okay, Question One: Are we going to have enough fuel to make it all the way to Incirlik, or will my stunt with the Lada cause us to drop into the Black Sea?"

Schlichter and Major Corrigan exchanged a quick glance, and Tracie said, "I guess that's my answer. I'm so sorry."

"We'll be okay," Schlichter said. "We might have to amend our routing to something a little more direct than we had planned, but barring any other unusual occurrences, we'll make it back. And you don't owe us any apology. We know you can't talk about what you were doing over here, but we sure as hell understand you weren't taking a guided tour of the countryside. We knew sticking to a schedule would be difficult and we anticipated the possibility you might not be exactly on time."

"Thank you, but I don't understand. What does all that mean?"

"It means we didn't have to transport the Lada over here like we did the first time, so the difference in weight means we'll eat less fuel this time. It also means we had room to install a second aux fuel tank and partially fill it. Like I said, we'll be okay."

Tracie felt an invisible weight lifting off her shoulders. Risking her own life was one thing; she was accustomed to doing that on a regular basis. But as sick as she felt inside after executing Ryan Smith, it would have been even worse had this talented and professional flight crew lost their lives because of her actions.

She realized Schlichter was staring at her with a look of amusement on his face and she said, "What?"

"You told me you had two questions. Math wasn't my best subject in school, but I'm almost positive that was only one."

"I was trying to determine whether you were bullshitting me on the first one before I asked the second," she said with a laugh. "But I've decided I'll take your word for it, plus I saw the second tank on my way to the flight deck."

Now it was Schlichter's turn to laugh.

Tracie said, "How do you know where to fly while we're in the clouds? I understand you mapped out a specific flight path to get off the lake, but you couldn't possibly have done the same thing with the entire route back to Turkey."

"Yes and no," Schlichter said.

"What does that mean?"

"It means that we know more or less the general course we need to fly that will give us the best chance to exit Soviet airspace without any unwanted MiG encounters while also pointing us in the general direction of Incirlik."

"But..."

"But we also have a nav system most people don't know about."

"I don't follow."

"It's classified, but I suppose I could share a few details with the young woman who just accomplished some kind of secret mission deep inside the Soviet Union."

'Accomplished' might be a bit of an overstatement, Tracie thought, but she kept her mouth shut and after a moment Schlichter continued. "Have you ever heard of the Global Positioning System?" he asked.

"I've heard of it," she said, thinking back to an operation a few months ago that had brought her into contact with Dr. Edison

Kiley, the elderly researcher who'd developed electronic circuitry for the early stages of the U.S. military's GPS project.

She decided to keep that information to herself and continued, "I can't claim any particular expertise on the subject, though."

"It's available for military and select law enforcement use only," he said. "It's based on satellite triangulation."

"Okay…"

"As long as enough of the satellites orbiting the globe are operational, GPS allows us to plot our location to within ten feet anywhere on earth. Or in this case," he added, "anywhere above the earth."

She shook her head again. "Unbelievable."

"So how did I do?" he asked with a smile.

"I'm sorry?"

"Were my answers satisfactory?"

"Like I said before, you guys are amazing."

"And I didn't even have to make anything up."

44

February 5, 1988
7:30 a.m.
McLean, Virginia

"So let me get this straight," Aaron Stallings said. "You were unable to investigate the third Soviet research area located under Ipatiev thanks to your rescue attempt of the operative known to you as Ryan Smith, is that correct?"

"Yes sir, that's correct."

"And you were unable to successfully effect Smith's escape."

"That's also correct."

"So the mission was an abject failure, then, wouldn't you agree?"

Tracie had come straight to Stallings' home office from Andrews Air Force Base after her flight from Turkey. She was tired and frazzled and had known exactly how this debrief was going to go: Stallings would be his usual aggressive, blustery self, and she would respond to his insults with a sharp tongue of her own, approaching—and perhaps crossing the line into—insubordination.

She'd been determined from her very first interaction with the CIA director last year not to allow him to bully or intimidate her, as he seemed to do to everyone else in his professional life. She had known that standing up to Stallings was not without its risks, and in the intervening months had lost her job, gained it back—sort of—and been tossed out of the man's office more times than she could count.

But to her surprise, he seemed to respect the fact that she refused to knuckle under to his constant criticism and steady barrage of insults. A wise emperor knew enough to keep at least one person around unafraid to tell him he wasn't wearing any clothes, and he'd apparently decided that for him, Tracie was that person.

So she was utterly unsurprised at the tone of the conversation. Today, though, she simply didn't have the energy for their typical verbal thrust and parry. She couldn't stop thinking about Ryan Smith, and about the sickness she'd felt deep inside when she'd pressed her weapon to his head and squeezed the trigger. An ugly black cancer had wormed into her soul in that horrible moment, and she knew it would continue to metastasize until eventually it consumed her.

And it would be no more than she deserved.

"Did you not hear me, Tanner?"

She realized she'd been staring down at the plush carpeting between her feet, and now she raised her eyes to meet Stallings' hard gaze. "I heard you. Yes, I would agree with your assessment that the mission was an abject failure. I further stipulate it was entirely my fault. I'll save you the trouble of having to spell it out. I already understand that fully."

There was no point even attempting to argue the fact she was to blame. She'd spent the last thirty minutes describing the disastrous mission in humiliating detail. The director was now every bit as aware as Tracie of her missteps and failings in Bashkir.

Stallings pushed back from his desk. His ample belly seemed to expand to fill the available space until finally the desk chair had wheeled far enough away that a sliver of a gap appeared between his dress shirt and the desk. Then he pushed his glasses down his nose and stared at Tracie over the frames.

He thrummed his fingers on the paperwork he'd been studying upon her arrival.

The intensity of his gaze was unnerving, even to Tracie, who had thought she'd seen everything her boss had to offer, intimidation-wise. Her reflexive reaction was to return his stare with a steely one of her own, to give away nothing, but it wasn't easy.

For what felt like a very long time, nobody spoke.

Finally Stallings did, and what he said caught Tracie completely off guard. "I wasn't always old and fat, you know."

She blinked in surprise. "Excuse me?"

He removed his glasses and tossed them on the desk, then ran a hand through his thinning gray hair. "Over the decades, I've grown old at Langley. But I didn't always sit behind a desk pushing papers around and manning a telephone. Once upon a time I was a young man, an operative just like you, putting my life on the line in the field."

"I...I'd heard that sir." Tracie felt off-stride. Discombobulated. She hadn't expected the conversation to veer off in this direction and had no idea where Stallings was going with his remarks. The uncertainty made her uncomfortable, much more so than getting yelled at.

More silence and another contemplative stare from the CIA director.

"I'm telling you this," he finally continued, "because I want you to know I understand what it's like to be in a position where you have to make snap judgments, where you have to do things in the heat of a mission that might seem abhorrent in any other context. It's been more than forty years, but I've been in your shoes, Tanner, and I still remember the feeling."

"Sir, I—"

"You did what you had to do when you decided to override the original mission objective in an attempt to rescue Smith, and you did what you had to do a second time given Smith's condition and the situation you encountered under that military base. I don't blame you or judge you for either choice you made. Quite the contrary, in fact. I think in both cases you took exactly the appropriate actions."

Stallings paused again and the room fell deathly silent. From somewhere far away came the chiming of a grandfather clock.

"Sometimes things go sideways and missions fail, Tanner. It sucks, but that's just the way it is in this business. It's a constant. It might be the *only* constant."

She nodded. "But I don't know how I could ever face Ryan Smith's family."

"First of all, you'll never have to, because you will never know who or where they are. But in the hypothetical situation where you did encounter his grieving parents, you could hold your head high.

You saved their doomed son from enduring further torture by a government willing to go to any lengths to learn what he knew of his country's secrets."

"But—"

"I'm not finished yet. By taking the action you did, you also allowed a good man to die with dignity, under his own terms, rather than those imposed on him by the very people he dedicated his life to opposing."

Tracie wondered where the dignity was in being shot in the head by a silenced Beretta and realized she'd again been staring at the floor. When she lifted her eyes, she discovered the director's were locked onto hers.

"I'm telling you this," he said, "for a reason, and not because I like to hear myself talk. I've been where you're sitting. Faced a similar scenario. Not exactly the same, mind you, but close enough. I resolved the situation in a similar manner and then began to doubt myself, to question every move I made. You know what happens when an operative acts hesitantly in the field, Tanner?"

"You put yourself at risk."

"Damn right. By second-guessing your actions you take what is already a dangerous, often nearly impossible job and make it even riskier. There is nothing wrong with a healthy dose of introspection, Tanner, but not while you're on an assignment. When you're alone and thousands of miles from home, decisive action is imperative. You took the kind of decisive action you deemed necessary at the time. You were right to do so and now that it's over and done, you need to move on. Am I making myself clear?"

"Yes, sir." The response was almost automatic. Tracie spit it out despite the fact she wasn't sure she could ever "move on." She appreciated Aaron Stallings' highly uncharacteristic attempt to raise her spirits, but wanted nothing more at the moment than to wrap up this debrief and get the hell out of Stallings' office.

The director stared at her a moment longer and then sighed. "You're not listening to a thing I'm saying, are you?"

"I am, sir. It's just going to take some time, I guess." *And about a million nightmares.*

Stallings nodded.

Leaned forward and slipped his glasses back on.

Said, "I wish I could tell you to take few weeks off."

"Sir, I don't want or need—"

He raised a hand to stop her. "I said I *wished* I could give you a vacation, not that you were getting one. Think about what I've said this morning and get your head straight over the next few days, but don't stray too far from your phone. I'm guessing you'll be hearing from me sooner rather than later because there are some things going on in the world we may need your skillset to deal with."

She rose from the chair and flashed a tired smile. "There are always some things going on in the world."

"That there are, Tanner, that there are."

The walk from his office to her car took forever, and the drive home took even longer. She entered her apartment and fell into bed fully clothed.

The nightmares began almost immediately.

Tracie Tanner will return soon in her seventh action-packed thriller. To be the first to learn about new releases, and for the opportunity to win free ebooks, signed copies of print books, and other swag, take a moment to sign up for Allan Leverone's email newsletter at AllanLeverone.com.

Reader reviews are hugely important to authors looking to set their work apart from the competition. If you have a moment to spare, please consider taking a moment to leave a brief, honest review of *The Bashkir Extraction* at your point of purchase, at Goodreads, or at your favorite review site, and thank you.

About the author

Allan Leverone is the *New York Times* and *USA Today* bestselling author of nearly twenty novels, as well as a 2012 Derringer Award winner for excellence in short mystery fiction and a 2011 Pushcart Prize nominee. He lives in Londonderry, New Hampshire with his wife Sue, and has three grown children and two beautiful grandchildren. He loves to hear from readers and other authors; connect on Facebook, Twitter @AllanLeverone, and at AllanLeverone.com.

Also by Allan Leverone

Thrillers

Parallax View: A Tracie Tanner Thriller
All Enemies: A Tracie Tanner Thriller
The Omega Connection: A Tracie Tanner Thriller
The Hitler Deception: A Tracie Tanner Thriller
The Kremlyov Infection: A Tracie Tanner Thriller
The Lonely Mile
Final Vector
The Organization: A Jack Sheridan Pulp Thriller
Trigger Warning: A Jack Sheridan Pulp Thriller

Dark Fiction

Mr. Midnight
After Midnight
The Lupin Project
Paskagankee
Revenant
Wellspring
Grimoire
Covenant
Linger: Mark of the Beast (Co-written with Edward Fallon)

Novellas

The Becoming
Flight 12: A Kristin Cunningham Thriller

Story Collections

Postcards from the Apocalypse
Letters from the Asylum
Uncle Brick and the Four Novelettes
The Tracie Tanner Collection: Three Complete Thriller Novels